COOL SIDE
OF THE PILLOW

What Reviewers Say About
Gill McKnight's Work

"A departure from the run-of-the-mill lesbian romance, *Goldenseal* is enjoyable for its uniqueness as well as for its plot. This is a story that will engage and characters you will find yourself growing fond of."—*Lambda Literary*

"Gill McKnight has given her readers a delightful romp in *Green Eyed Monster.* The twists and turns of the plot leave the reader turning the pages to see who is the real victim and who is the villain. Along with the roller coaster ride, comes plenty of hot sex to add to the tension. Spending an afternoon with *Green-eyed Monster* is great fun."—*Just About Write*

"Angst, conflict, sex and humor. [Falling Star] has all of this and more packed into a tightly written and believable romance. McKnight has penned a sweet and tender romance, balancing the intimacy and sexual tension just right. The conflict is well drawn, and she adds a great dose of humor to make this novel a light and easy read."—*Curve*

In *Green Eyed Monster*…"McKnight succeeds in tantalizing with explosive sex and a bit of bondage; tormenting with sexual frustration and intense longing; tickling your fancy and funny bone; and touching a place where good and evil battle it out. … the plot twists, winning dialogue laced with sarcasm, wit, and charm certainly add to the fun. I recommend this satisfying read for entertainment, fantasy, and sex that stimulate the brain like caffeine."—*Lambda Literary*

Visit us at www.boldstrokesbooks.com

By the Author

Falling Star

Green Eyed Monster

Erosistible

Cool Side of the Pillow

The Garoul series

Goldenseal

Ambereye

Indigo Moon

COOL SIDE
OF THE PILLOW

by

Gill McKnight

2011

ISBN 10: 1-60282-633-1
ISBN 13: 978-1-60282-633-5

This Trade Paperback Original Is Published By
Bold Strokes Books, Inc.
P.O. Box 249
Valley Falls, NY 12185

First Edition: August 2011

Credits
Editor: Cindy Cresap
Production Design: Susan Ramundo
Cover Design By Bold Strokes Books Graphics

Dedication

For Matthew in the middle.

CHAPTER ONE

Clara Dearheart tossed the disposable gloves and mask into the hazardous waste bin. The tubing and dishes were already in the sink for scalding, and disinfectant would soon be added to the basins containing blood and body fluids before they were tipped down the drain.

They were nearly through.

Clara had spent all morning embalming Mrs. Lepucki while the radio blared out heavy rock. She always let her cousin Ronnie choose the music when he assisted her. She liked the emotional distance his hard-edged, testosterone-fuelled sounds gave the task at hand. It wasn't her first choice in music, but she found it numbed her just enough while she prepared the body of the woman who had taught her sixth grade.

The vascular system along with the abdominal and thoracic cavities had already been aspirated and refilled with a formaldehyde mix. An antiseptic body wash completed the most dehumanizing part of the process. Clara moved on to the final and, for her, most important part—restoring Halina Lepucki's dignity and preparing her to face her family and community for the last time. She wanted the Lepuckis' final memory of their mother to be peaceful after months of painful decline.

"I'm going to make coffee." Ronnie tidied away the stainless steel trays.

Clara grunted, barely acknowledging him as he banged and thumped around the prep room. They worked well as a team. Ronnie's blunt pragmatism complimented her brooding silences. If it weren't for his bustle and blunder, Clara could quite happily turn to dust inside the Dearheart Funeral Home, steadfastly ignoring the outside world and all its agitations. She enjoyed his company and, nepotism aside, was pleased he'd wanted to come work for her. The funeral home was a family firm, and the Dearhearts liked to keep it that way.

"Do you need help with anything else?" Ronnie asked over the clatter.

It was their usual procedure for Clara to be alone to dress the body. She guarded this chore jealously, happy to do it herself rather than bring in someone from outside. As a mortician, it wasn't part of her job description, but as the current director of Dearhearts Funeral Service, she allotted the task to herself alone.

"No. Go take your break." She didn't look up. All her concentration was on Halina Lepucki and a delicate fragrance of violets and rose water. It filled the room as she washed the frail body and thinning hair. She had especially selected this scented soap remembering Mrs. Lepucki liked violets. Clara closed her eyes and was pulled back to sixth grade. Mrs. Lepucki was leaning over her shoulder explaining something in a textbook, and all young Clara could concentrate on was her floral perfume. The bouquet of a thousand distilled summers would always remind her of Halina Lepucki.

Dressing the body was always awkward, but Clara had it down to a fine art. She was proud that she never once had to cut a seam. She smoothed foundation cream carefully across arched cheekbones and an aquiline nose, appreciating the fine bone structure under her fingertips. Next, she selected rouge and lipstick and applied it sparingly. She gently rubbed more makeup onto fragile hands, massaging it into fingers knotted with arthritis. Finally, she picked up a hairdryer and comb and fluffed the thin, silver hair, coiffing it into its usual elegant style.

She surveyed her work. Mrs. Lepucki had always been a handsome woman; however, three vicious strokes had broken her elderly body, etching her face with deep lines of suffering. Clara had worked hard to salvage that former refinement. It was important to her. She lifted a small envelope from the work cart and tipped a newly polished wedding band into her palm. The ring slid onto Mrs. Lepucki's third finger on her left hand, Clara stood back. She was done.

The scent of violets grew stronger.

"We buried Leonard with his wedding ring, too." The lilting voice came from over her shoulder, just as it had in sixth grade. Clara glanced behind her and smiled a welcome.

"I wanted Irena to have it, but she insisted her father wear it to his grave." Mrs. Lepucki came to stand beside Clara. She looked down at the body on the porcelain table before them. "You did a lovely job, Clara. The peach lipstick is a nice touch. Funny, it's not a color I'd ever have thought of for myself."

"Thanks, Mrs. Lepucki." Clara touched the simple wedding band. "I think Irena was right. It's nice that you both have your rings with you." She turned to face the graceful woman shimmering before her in a pearlescent glow. Countless hues of color danced off her in a gentle, prismatic pulse. Clara was suffused with a profound contentment; the beautiful violet scent wafted around her soft as silk. She could feel it drift across her skin almost lifting her up onto her tiptoes with delight until she tingled all over. She always felt blessed in the presence of the recently deceased.

"How is Irena?" Mrs. Lepucki asked after her daughter. A little anxiety crept into her voice, and the colors pulsing off her dipped and fluttered.

"Tearful," Clara answered honestly. This was a standard question and an understandable one. "But relieved you're not in pain anymore. It's hard for her, but she'll get there. She chose your clothes, by the way."

"She remembered my favorite blouse."

"You've got a good family, Mrs. Lepucki," Clara said. "Tell Mr. Lepucki I said hello." She carefully drew the conversation away from the living world to the place Mrs. Lepucki had to go.

"Of course I will. Any other messages?"

Clara hesitated. Her throat went dry.

"What about Frances, dear?" Mrs. Lepucki prompted gently.

"Tell her…Tell her I miss her."

"Clara. I need cigarettes. I'll be back in five." Ronnie's yell startled her. A door slammed farther down the hall. Clara blinked and stood staring at air. Mrs. Lepucki had gone. She looked at the body lying before her and carefully reached over to fix a stray curl back into place.

"Godspeed, Mrs. Lepucki," she whispered.

❖

It was after five p.m. when Clara and Ronnie finally called it a day.

"You going down to Petty's for a practice session later?" Ronnie called, mounting his Kawasaki. Clara stood on the top step by the funeral parlor doors and shook her head. The gray drizzle had finally stopped and the steps were slippery under her shoes.

"I'll give it a miss," she called back. "I'm heading over to Aunt Esme's."

She wasn't in the mood for an evening of pool and beer. Esme had invited her over for dinner. That easily outweighed the rowdiness of Petty's Bar on a Friday night.

"Well, you better play sharp as tacks next Saturday. We drew Culpepper's Deli and they finished third last year. So no slacking, okay?" He flipped his visor and took off with a roar, kicking up wet grit.

Clara watched him go with a shake of her head, bemused by his jitters. He was all hyped up about the annual Trader's Pool Competition. Dearhearts was a good enough team, so she guessed he'd bet money on them winning. Probably too much money.

She glanced down at the discreet brass door plaque and gave it a surreptitious swipe with her cuff.

Edwin Dearheart & Sons. Funeral Directors. Established 1808.

Clara was the ninth generation of Dearhearts to run Preston's oldest, and only, funeral home. She buffed the brass out of pure habit until it shone against the bruised mahogany of the door. The Dearheart funeral home was an austere narrow building, three stories high. It had been built with small red bricks and the best timber of the day and sat on a wide, oak lined avenue, the oldest building on one of the oldest streets in Preston.

Over two hundred years ago, the Dearhearts had started their undertaking business in this very building, though another story had been added at the turn of the last century for extra living space.

Clara had grown up in the top floor apartment. It had been her childhood home. Her parents had lived there up until six years ago when they retired to Florida to be near Clara's brother and his family. Ronnie rented it now.

Clara still loved the character of the old building, but it had not been her home since her early twenties. As soon as she could afford a shack on the curved shingle beach with its big Atlantic rollers, she had moved out. She lived down on the beach now, the last in a row of small holiday shacks at the far end of Three Mile bay.

Clara set the alarm, locked up, and crunched across the parking lot to her much-adored Ford Bronco '87. This was her kind of ride, rescued and restored in all its retro glory. The sleek black limos and stately hearses tucked away in the garages out back were not for her. That was Ronnie's area. He loved those big, black, shiny monsters.

Gulls dipped and cried overhead, and the late afternoon sky was graying out to the color of their wings. She felt tired and heavy now that the day was done, as if she'd sponged up all of its drabness through her pores until she was bloated with weariness.

Clara pulled the Bronco out onto East Avenue. Last chance sunshine seeped from behind the cloudbank and peeped through the new buds on the oak tree branches, weaving faint patterns on the damp asphalt. Clara signaled left and headed for the outskirts of town and the garden center she and Esme favored. She would bring Esme a gift—some seeds or perhaps an herb pot for her back step. Clara loved browsing through the plant aisles in the artificial world of the greenhouses. Plants lived vibrant, uncomplicated lives. They rooted, grew, blossomed, slept through winter, and began the cycle all over again come spring. Complex or compound, each plant was a minor miracle to her. They pulsed with simple, wholesome energies, radiating a contentment in just being. *Why can't I have contentment in just being?*

Clara shook off her maudlin thoughts. It took effort, but she made herself do it. She deliberately scoured her mind for a replacement thought that would make her happy. Perhaps she should surprise Esme with an exotic specimen like a pineapple or banana plant. Clara grinned at the idea but ruled it out. Much as she liked to indulge Esme, her aunt was a traditionalist when it came to gardening. She turned on the radio and filled up the cab with manufactured emotions and bouncy, feel good tunes. Slowly, she began to shrug off the deflated feeling she always carried after someone had passed over. It had taken her many years to realize this was merely the residue of spiritual energy. The serenity she felt in the presence of the dead ebbing away to leave a brutal emptiness.

Clara was truly pleased for Halina Lepucki. Glad she was so eager to move on when many spirits weren't. Still, it left a hard space to fill, but Clara had tricks to help her cope. She concentrated hard on the quality things in her life, like the evening ahead of her, for instance. Esme had invited her to dinner, and afterward Clara would help prune her roses. They would talk about Esme's garden plans for the summer ahead and no doubt argue over architectural foliage or color versus pattern. Clara smiled, and the tension in her neck and shoulders began to ease. She would go straight to the garden center and select a gift for Esme. She would not stop off at home, not even to change out of her work clothes and into her scruffy sweats. Clara didn't like going directly home. She had no tricks to fill the emptiness there.

❖

"Arlene McCall's niece is a lesbian," Esme Dearheart said casually, snipping back the winterkill on a *Robusta rugosa*.

Clara glanced over. Esme was immersed in her task and did not look up. They both stood thigh deep in Esme's rose bed stooped over hybrids and teas, floribundas and Chinas, enjoying a mild Friday evening after the early afternoon rainfall.

"So?" Clara used the same casual tone right back. "You interested?"

A puff of exasperation floated across the rose bed, and Clara's lips twitched. She cut a dead cane from the *Rosa Alba* near the back of the border and waited.

"You're such a wiseacre. I meant *you* might be interested," Esme said.

"Well, it'll take more than the word lesbian to have me knocking on Arlene McCall's door with a box of candy and a dozen Sexy Rexys. Come on, Aunt E, pimp her properly. Make me want her."

"I am *not* pimping. I'm just saying." Esme sniffed primly.

Clara grinned and watched Esme move off to inspect her Sexy Rexy roses. Sometimes she was so suggestible.

"Good, because the poor girl would starve if you were her daddy."

"You're even pricklier than these roses." Esme huffed.

"Yes, roses grow thorns for a reason," Clara murmured. She moved on to the Albertine ramblers. They were thick with vicious prickles and she had to be careful around them, even wearing garden gloves. "The girl hasn't even arrived and already you're meddling. Does Arlene know what you're up to?"

"I am *not* meddling. I was merely commenting. If she's minding Arlene's house for the summer she could get lonely for company her own age. It might be nice for you to drop by and say hello. What's wrong with that? Arlene thinks it's a good idea."

"Arlene would. You're her best friend. She thinks all your ideas rock. Like telling her to disappear to Australia for three months."

"You agreed she needed a break." Esme tried to sound hurt. It didn't work on Clara's practiced ears. "She nursed her mother for the last seven years. It's only right she gets a proper vacation now. And she's so looking forward to seeing her grandchildren."

"I never said Arlene didn't deserve a vacation. I know Temperance's passing was tough on her."

Temperance McCall's passing at the age of ninety-seven had provided Preston with the biggest funeral it had ever seen. But her death had left a void for her daughter-in-law Arlene, who had been her primary caretaker. Family and friends had rallied to make sure Arlene got the vacation she richly deserved, a trip to Australia, all expenses paid, while some niece or other house-sat until her return.

"So which niece is the lezzie?" Clara studied the crossed branches on the rose climber and, selecting the misdirected one, snipped it away. *If only life could be like that. One snip and we're back on track.* Esme was trying to pull her into something. She could feel the tug all the way down to her shoelaces.

"Arlene has several dozen," she continued. "At Temperance's funeral there were hundreds of nieces and nephews. You know how these big Irish families are."

"It's Bebe. Bebe Franklin." Esme's answer was a little too enthusiastic. "You might remember her; she's the strawberry blond."

Clara shook her head. "It was a big funeral. Too many McCalls and affiliates to remember," she said. "And they're nearly all ginger."

"Strawberry blond," Esme corrected her. "Bebe used to spend her summers in Preston when she was little. She used to play with you and the rest of the neighborhood kids." Esme tried to prompt her.

"Ah. I remember her now," Clara said. "Dumpy wee thing. Her nickname was Brick because she had this mop of ginger hair."

"Brick?"

"Red and square-shaped. Always tripping over. Clumsy kid."

Esme harrumphed at the ungracious description. "Nonsense. Anyway, she's grown into a lovely young woman. And she's a *strawberry blond.*"

Clara already knew what a lovely young woman Bebe Franklin was. She'd heard of Bebe's unquestionable loveliness often this past year. Bebe was a favorite with Esme. Every time Esme and Arlene went up to the city, it was Bebe who met them at the train station. And Bebe who took them shopping, or arranged for dinner and the theater. It was Bebe who hung out with them and made the visit fun. Weeks later, Esme would still be brimming with all the wonderful things she'd seen and done, and Bebe Franklin in all her strawberry blond splendor, was at the center of every story.

"She works in television, you know," Esme told her for the zillionth time.

"I know. You tell me every time that goddamn awful program comes on."

"It's not that bad. Temperance loved *Valley of Our Fathers*. She never missed an episode."

"Of course she was a fan. Her granddaughter wrote the trash. Anyway, Temperance was addicted to daytime brain rot. As long as it had high heels and low morals, she was glued."

"Temperance *adored* Bebe. She was her favorite granddaughter." Esme ignored Clara's daytime soap critique. She had to. *Valley of Our Fathers* was an atrocious show filled with inane, one-dimensional characters and ridiculous storylines, and they both knew it. Clara knew Esme abhorred it as much as she did; though every so often she tuned in…but only to view the episodes Bebe actually wrote. Arlene always told Esme when those were airing so she'd be sure to catch them.

"You really should drop by and say hello," Esme persisted.

"She's not even here yet."

"She can't be long in arriving. Arlene leaves next week."

"She might be married." Clara tugged on a stray weed.

"Married? Bebe? But she's a lesbian."

"To another woman, Aunt E. Brick might be cemented in a relationship. Ever thought of that?"

"I already asked Arlene, and she says Bebe's singl—"

"Ah ha. Meddler!"

"I am not. It came up in conversation, that's all. For goodness sake, all I'm asking is for you to be neighborly."

"But I'm not her neighbor. You are."

"All right then." Esme peeled off her gardening gloves, snapping the elasticized wrists in displeasure. "*I'll* call and show some manners for the both of us."

"Good. Say 'Hiya, Brick' for me." Another dissatisfied humph floated over the flowerbed toward her.

"Cool side of the pillow, that's you." Esme sounded peevish. Then, with a slight plea in her voice, "At least come along with me to Arlene's for coffee someday soon. She'd love to see you before she leaves."

"Will Bebe be there?"

"No, she's coming later in the week. I told you, I'm not meddling."

Clara relented on her teasing. Esme was such a determined old bird when she got an idea stuck in her head, but Clara was equally adamant: there would be no interfering with her love life, such as it was…or wasn't. She *was* the cool side of the pillow, and she liked it like that. A cool pillow soothed the fevered head.

"I'll think about popping over before Arlene goes, okay?" she said.

They worked on in silence for several minutes until Clara said quietly, "I saw Halina Lepucki today."

Esme looked over sharply. "Did you…Did she…?" Esme didn't share the Dearheart gift, if it could be called that. She couldn't see the dead. "I was very fond of Halina. She was a good friend," she said.

Esme had taught science at the local high school, while Halina had taught at Preston Elementary. They had met through their teachers' union and had eventually retired at the same time. "Was she okay?"

Clara nodded. "She looked lovely. So light and happy. She shimmered like a pearl, Auntie E."

"Like a pearl," Esme repeated, her eyes shining. "Yes. Halina deserved happiness. I wish her the best of journeys."

"Well, she's on it." Clara was glad she'd shared. They gathered up the cuttings in silence.

"Let's call it a day." Esme broke their reverie. "How does supper sound? Will you stay over tonight?"

Clara smiled and nodded. She was pleasantly tired now and it would be nice to sleep over at Esme's. She often did. She looked around the garden, content at a job well done.

"Rain's coming," she said. She could taste it on the air, carried in on the salty wind. She followed Esme across the lawn and down a gravel garden path to the primrose yellow back door. They left their tools and muddy boots outside to be tidied away later. She looked up at the sky; it was muddied with evening clouds. The chill of a late March wind seeped through her work jacket and settled on stiff shoulders. Spring had arrived, well, at least the birds and buds believed it had, even if her aching bones didn't.

With a happy but tired sigh, she entered the toasty warmth of Esme's kitchen, glad this door was always open to her. Esme and her home, with all its love and goodness, lay at the core of Clara's life. It would be an unbearable existence without her.

CHAPTER TWO

Despite the air-conditioning, Bebe's hands were clammy and her face slick with perspiration. She took another gulp from her juice box and felt Carter's eyes on her every movement. The producer smelled blood in the water and was circling his wounded team looking for an opening. Someone was going to be the meat on his menu this afternoon. He'd make sure of it.

Bebe hunched down further in her seat. She hated staff meetings. These days they were more like Russian roulette than a brainstorming session for their failing show. It was tiresome wondering when the loaded chamber would point her way, and she knew it would one day.

"Okay, let's get this show on the road." Carter looked over the top of his designer glasses at the faint ripple of laughter at his bad pun. He had called a disaster recovery meeting to address the poor ratings *Valley of Our Fathers* had received three months in a row. In TV soap land, that was a death rattle.

Forget on the road; tow the damned thing to the junk yard. Bebe had her own opinion. One she wasn't sharing. It was important for all their careers to get the trends reversed. *Valley* was a mediocre daytime soap at the best of times. Recently, it had bellied up big time and the studio axe was days away.

"Jayrah, bring us up to speed, darling," Carter purred at his favorite writer.

Across the table, Suzzee Wang, one of the leading actors, winked at Bebe. Normally, the cast escaped meetings like this, but Carter had wanted the leads to attend this one in particular. Everyone's next paycheck depended on it, and Bebe had worked with him long enough to know it was important to Carter that everyone had a say—so he could override and ridicule it.

Jayrah very succinctly brought them up to date, skillfully avoiding the greater catastrophes that had plunged *Valley* into the small intestine of public apathy. Everyone could feel Carter's tension build with each passing minute. There was no hiding the mess his decisions had made, not that he was ever going to admit it. Instead, other heads would roll.

Quickly, as if sensing his darkening mood, Jayrah rolled easily into her own pitch for recovery. As usual, it was full-on drama: car chases, angsty hospital bed scenes, and extramarital affairs galore. Suzzee Wang's Berry Ripe character carried a lot of the story arc. Bebe noticed the actress shift uneasily in her chair. There were sullen faces among her colleagues. Suzzee was the flavor of the month, and had been for most months of the year. Much of Jayrah's work hung heavily on Berry Ripe, a character she had consistently pushed to the fore through her scripts.

Carter brightened at some of Jayrah's suggestions, and Bebe felt her shoulders sag. Her own story arcs were too subtle and understated compared to Jayrah's burn-and-die approach. An even bigger part of her misery was the growing realization that this was not the direction she wanted to go with her writing career. Car explosions and drive-by shootings were overrated. She could see the violent imagery already simmering in Carter's head. He was such a boy with a toy where this show was concerned. Bebe knew she was in the wrong place at the wrong time, like one of Jayrah's extras, but it was a job, her only job at the moment, and she needed it for leverage into someplace better. She was forever hopeful that *Valley* would eventually open a secret door to some other creative universe.

Carter indicated it was her turn by tapping his pencil on the table and glaring pointedly at her. Bebe took a deep breath and laid out her idea to expose Berry Ripe to blackmail and then move forward with the conjoined twins thread that had been stagnating in the background for the last few weeks. Out of the corner of her eye, she saw Suzzee smile. Bebe's hopes lifted. If Suzzee liked her spin, perhaps Carter would. He didn't. He cut her off with a curt rebuff before she'd even finished and moved on to Danny, the next writer in the firing line.

"I really liked your ideas," Suzzee said later. "It's better than Berry lying comatose in the hospital for four weeks like Jayrah wants."

She'd asked Bebe to grab lunch with her before the final summing up later that afternoon.

Bebe shrugged, unconcerned she had bombed out. She had expected to. Carter probably had a course already mapped out for Suzzee and her Berry Ripe character involving zombies and weapons of mass destruction. And who knew? It might just work.

"Carter will never go for anything low-key and emotional. I was stupid to even try," she said.

She lifted her heavy curtain of hair to cool the nape of her neck. The coffee shop was far too hot and crowded. They were squeezed into a corner near the restrooms and people kept nudging Bebe's shoulder as they passed to and fro. She found it impossible to relax and enjoy her sandwich.

"That's what I liked about your angle," Suzzee said, her face petulant. "Jayrah dumps me right in the middle of all the ridiculousness. You give me margins to actually act in." She lounged cross-legged and comfortable in her chair well away from the restroom traffic.

"I thought you wanted to be in the thick of it? Don't all actors?" Bebe ducked as an oversized handbag came straight for her head. Her coffee sloshed into the saucer and burned her thumb.

Suzzee was a friend as well as a leading *Valley* actor, and she constantly beseeched both Jayrah and Bebe to slip more scenes her way. Well, at least she had at the start. Jayrah had willingly complied, but Bebe had been reticent. There was more to her job than showcasing Suzzee's career. In fact, now that Bebe thought about it, Suzzee had been a lot less pushy recently. Was she finally happy with her B-list status? Somehow, Bebe doubted it.

"Look, Beebs, this is strictly off the record, okay? But I have a chance at a cop show in L.A. They want a steely-eyed Asian DA. I want that part so bad I'd skin my own mother. I've been thinking about the West coast for a while now." She sipped her latte and fixed Bebe with a conspiratorial look. "To be honest, I've wanted off this handcart to hell for ages. My contract is up in two months and I want out."

"Wow, Suz. That's great timing. If you're up for renewal you can easily leave and take the new job, no harm done."

"It's a bit awkward. I'm sleeping with my agent, and *Valley* is as good as this guy gets. I need to dump him. I've got a shot at a much hotter guy in L.A., but I have to be free of my old commitments first. I want to dump *Valley* and my agent all in one go."

It sounded brutal, but it was the way of the world—Suzzee's world.

"I hope it works out for you," Bebe said.

"You could help."

"Me? How?"

"By coming up with a brilliant storyline that lets Berry die, and line it up perfectly for my contract ending. That way Carter will have nothing to be pissed about. Well, nothing he can do anything about. Dead Berry, dead contract, that's fair enough."

"Why can't Jayrah do it for you? She's bound to get the idea accepted. She can have you torpedoed while snorkeling or something. You've got to admit I'm pretty hit-or-miss these days. We both know I'm on the slippery slope."

Suzzee wrinkled her nose. "Jayrah and Pebble don't know I plan to quit yet. Jayrah would be...upset if I left. She wants me in for the long haul."

Jayrah and Pebble were also Bebe's friends. Jayrah, Suzzee, and Bebe had all joined *Valley* within a few weeks of each other and clung together in a tight little knot of insecurity. They'd formed a friendship of sorts, though Bebe suspected it was built on individual needs rather than a real commitment to each other. Then again, in a big city and backstabbing job, these friendships were a sort of preventative medicine that stopped the rot of loneliness and isolation from setting in.

Jayrah and Pebble had been dating off and on for nearly two years. Pebble had been with *Valley* since forever. She worked in wardrobe and heard all the gossip first. Her big, sorrowful brown eyes had been mooning at Bebe a lot recently. It didn't take a genius to figure out Bebe was shuffling toward the exit.

"Why not?" she said, puzzled. "Jayrah's your friend. She'd want you to get the L.A. job—oh." Suddenly Bebe got it. Suzzee's laser stare helped her join the dots with crystalline precision. Suzzee and Jayrah were having an affair. Bebe's guts shriveled like overheated plastic. *Poor Pebble.* She could feel her cheeks scorch. A blob of mayo dripped from her sandwich onto her skirt.

"How long?" Bebe dabbed frantically at the stain. Her voice sounded small. No wonder Jayrah pushed Berry Ripe's storylines so determinedly. She was sleeping with the actress who played her.

Suzzee shrugged. "It's not important. If it makes you feel any better, it started long before Pebble and Jayrah got together."

How could that make her feel any better? Her friends had been having a secret affair all the time she'd known them. It hurt *her*, never mind what Pebble would make of it. If she ever found out, that was. Bebe hated secrets like these. Why did Suzzee have to tell her? Now Bebe was contaminated, as if Suzzee had just sneezed her snotty little secret all over her.

"Don't judge." Suzzee pointed sternly.

"I'm not judging." Bebe blinked. She kept dabbing at the mayo stain. Why was she always being emotionally sucker punched? Why had she not noticed anything? She was meant to be sensitive to the human condition. She was a writer, for God's sake. But Bebe liked happy endings, and she desperately wanted her friends to have them, not this run ragged angst. She sighed and tossed her napkin aside. The stain on her skirt had spread into a large smudge. "I'm just welling up a little."

"Don't well up either. There's no point. We're all adults, and anyhow, Jayrah and Pebble have an understanding." Suzzee was impatient with her now.

Yes, they have. A so-called open relationship. So why is this conversation a secret? Bebe nodded mutely, ashamed of her judgment, her cowardice, and her ridiculousness at not really knowing her friends, at not knowing anything.

"So will you try? Please, Beebs." Suzzee was back on her original topic. "I promise to tell Pebble and Jayrah I'm leaving nearer the time. Just not right now. All the pieces aren't in place yet."

"I'll think about it. As far as Carter is concerned, there's little I can do right these days. I may be gone before you are."

"That doesn't matter. Just plant the idea in everyone's head before you go. Show them that Berry can die. Say that it might be best for the ratings to have one of the lead actors exit in a big, dramatic death scene. That it will give the show a shot in the arm. You know…crap like that. Put the idea out there before you get dumped."

And the truth came out. Suzzee was asking her to sow the seeds for her own exit. Bebe was doomed anyway, so it didn't matter that this would push her over the edge as far as Carter was concerned. And afterward, someone else, probably Jayrah, would get to run with the trailblazing idea. Suzzee would maneuver it that way, making it Jayrah's compensation for the end of their affair. Then Suzzee could move on, free of her lesbian fling and her unwanted agent to start afresh in L.A., while Bebe choked on her dust.

Suzzee was way ahead of Bebe in this game. So was Jayrah. They were voracious, so sure of their goals and their career trajectories. Bebe couldn't think, never mind act as aggressively as they did. *Valley* wasn't the place for her. She simply didn't belong. She outlined the grease mark on her best work skirt with a finger. She was just a big, cumbersome herbivore in the land of Tyrannosaurus rex.

❖

"Bebe, have you got a minute?"

"I'm on my way to the airport, Carter. Will it take long?" Bebe had hoped to slip away during the meeting's closing minutes, but Carter had grabbed her at the door.

"Oh, I forgot, you've got a family funeral." He managed to make it sound like her next career move. "An aunt or something."

"That was four months ago. My grandmother passed away just before Christmas."

He didn't even look abashed. "So you're going away…why?"

"I'm house-sitting for several weeks. We agreed I could work remotely, remember?" She panicked. Was he going to pull the plug on her plans?

"But you'll be in contact by conference call for next week's meeting?" he said. Relief washed through her. She had at least another week of employment.

"Yes, and I'm prepared to jump on a plane the second you need me," she rushed to explain. She really didn't want to do that, but he would make her if he sensed any reluctance on her part, so she tried to sound as enthusiastic as possible about it. He nodded impatiently, not picking up on her dodge; his mind was on something else.

"It's make-or-break time, Bebe. I'm willing to consider your blackmail idea, but your next offering better cut it or you're out. I need something I can use," he stated bluntly.

Bebe already knew this. Everyone at the table knew it. The people pushing out past them pretending not to listen knew it. Some had it hanging over their heads more than others. Carter had his favorites and his not-so-favorites. But to be singled out like this was mortifying. Bebe nodded automatically, a tight smile glued on her lips.

"Sure. I'll have something to run by you for next week. Now, if you'll excuse me, I have a cab waiting. I better go grab it." It was a lie. She was running for the airport shuttle, she refused to shell out good money on a cab. These days every penny counted if she wanted to finance her future as an unemployed writer. Her studio apartment was leased for the summer, but the contract meant she had to leave sooner rather than later. Fortunately, Aunt Arlene was cool with that. It was a relief to get out of the city and away from all the poison.

"Next week then, Carter." Bebe tried to sound smooth, like the unfazed professional she was…in some parallel dimension. She turned to the door with as much poise as she could muster through her haze of public humiliation. It took several seconds of fruitless handle rattling before she realized she needed to pull not push.

❖

"Bast-tard."

"Darling, that's not very nice," Arlene McCall scolded her African Grey Parrot then turned back to pouring coffee. "He only does it for attention."

"Bastard," Darling squawked again and settled on his perch with a contented gleam in his eye.

"Way to go, Darling." Clara fed him a sliver of her apple. "You've been listening to the garbage men again, haven't you? You're a clever boy, the way you pick out only the best words." She had graciously given in and accompanied Esme for morning coffee. Now she sat idly listening to the gossip fest that kept these two old busybodies on top of their game.

"So when is Bebe arriving?" Esme asked Arlene, abruptly steering their conversation away from the goings-on of the people of Preston.

Her answer came with a mighty sigh. "Soon, Lord help me."

Clara raised her eyebrows. "You don't seem to have a lot of faith in her considering she's house-sitting for you."

"Desmond has warned me over and over not to leave her in charge of the house. He'd rather sit through a hurricane than have Bebe house-sit again. Not after the Dresden crinoline incident. I don't know what shattered more, Desmond's nerves or the figurine."

Clara rolled her eyes at the thought of Arlene's prissy brother crying over broken porcelain. So Bebe the Brick was still a full-on klutz? It wasn't much of a surprise.

"Surely he was insured?" Esme asked.

"You can't insure snobbery, Esme. For Desmond, it's not about the money. Lord knows he's rolling in it. He gets his buzz having things others don't. And for that to work, they have to be in one piece."

"Accident prone or not, you still need a parrot sitter. Just lock up the crystal and hide the key." To Clara it was tediously obvious. She went back to feeding Darling tidbits of apple.

"I already have." Arlene joined her at the bird perch and stroked Darling with her forefinger until he fell into an ecstatic, swaying dance. Ordinarily, Arlene would have locked up her house and left for the airport, except she had inherited Temperance's pet parrot. Now any break away involved finding a sitter for the emotionally disturbed bird. That's why Bebe had been drafted.

"I'll miss you the most, you handsome fellow," Arlene crooned.

Clara suppressed a snort. Darling was a handful at the best of times.

"It's wonderful that you're going at all," Esme said. "But I will miss you. Just lock away all your breakables like Clara said. And remember, I'm only around the corner if Bebe needs help with anything."

Arlene had been widowed for almost fifteen years. She still lived in her family home and had been Esme's neighbor and closest friend for all that time.

"I'll leave several notes to that effect," Arlene said. "And I'll be sure to drum it into her before I go. But it would be wonderful if you could maybe drop by from time to time, just to make sure she's all right?"

"If Bebe doesn't mind. I don't want her thinking she's being spied on."

"Oh, she won't. But please. For Darling's sake?" Arlene said. "He's been pulling at his neck feathers."

"Of course I will. Maybe Clara will call around, too."

"Oh?" Arlene's eyebrows rose nearly as high as Clara's.

Esme smiled and shrugged nonchalantly. "Why not? You might as well say hello, Clara."

"Perhaps. But right now I have to say good-bye." Clara rose hastily to her feet. "I need to get back to work." She went to collect her coat from the hall closet.

"Esme, do I smell matchmaking?" Arlene's discreet question floated out after her through the partially open door. Clara's ears burned.

"Oh no. Not me." Esme tried to sound genuinely aghast but failed miserably. "Though, Lord knows if anyone needs a push in that direction it's Clara."

I knew it! Meddlesome old crow. Don't you dare get Arlene involved. Clara scowled as she shrugged on her jacket.

Esme carried on unaware she was being overheard. "Anyway, I prefer to think of it as theoretical physics rather than matchmaking. Throw two diverse elements together and see what happens."

Clara listened in disbelief as Esme tried to joke away her blatant tampering. *Well, I prefer to think of it more as theoretical buttinsky. Throw my toe and your butt together and see what happens.* Clara ground her teeth. Her toes itched to deliver, and then her nose twitched. The headiness of musk roses suffused the air, as if every blossom on the heavily floral wallpaper had exploded its scent into the hallway. Clara's senses reeled under the onslaught.

"You'd break your toe on that bony backside of hers," a creaky voice spoke directly into her ear. Clara jumped.

"Temperance! What are you doing here?" She dragged in great lungfuls of majestic musk roses and mimosa mixed with vanilla, trying to mellow out the blast before it overwhelmed her system entirely.

"I miss Darling." Temperance McCall shimmered before her in a smoky pink cloud that undulated with every vibration of her voice.

"It's not polite to eavesdrop on your grieving family," Clara scolded her in hushed tones, one ear still fixed on the conversation in the living room.

"Pfft. Believe me, it's the best bit about dying. And you're the one who's eavesdropping, not me." The air around Temperance rippled as she spoke. The pink plumes of cloud finally settled into a smattering of static dust that seemed to adhere to her every movement.

"Only because Esme's meddling," Clara said.

"When did she not meddle? She's always interfering. That woman couldn't let Jell-O set. Now, how's my Darling doing? I know he's missing me dreadfully."

"He's as rude and unmanageable as ever."

"I can't believe that daughter of mine is going to abandon him the minute my toes point upward," Temperance continued complaining. "Australia indeed."

Clara quietly closed the door on the living room conversation, shaking her head. She'd heard enough.

"And don't you shake your head at me. Your wretched love life is of no interest to anybody with half a brain, but Darling is, and I'm worried for him."

"Well, don't be." Clara yanked open the front door, still disgusted at Esme's conniving. "Bebe is going to look after him while Arlene's away."

She trudged through a downpour to her truck and hoisted herself in.

"Bebe?" Temperance was already waiting, lighting up the passenger seat with little pink sparkles. Silver and pink stars swirled in the air around her. "Lovely girl, but she'll kill him. You'll have to keep an eye on her."

"Esme's keeping an eye on her. Esme's keeping an eye on everything. As usual," Clara muttered as they drove along Hope Street. "It's all under control."

"Ha! It's far from under control if Bebe's anywhere near it. I'll have to do it myself if you won't help."

"Don't you dare. You shouldn't be hanging around here at all."

"Darling's in shock. He's in mourning. You can't prepare a parrot for respiratory failure in the elderly. He needs love and attention. Now more than ever."

"And he's getting it in spades. You can't come back here and haunt your parrot. You'll upset him, and he's been a handful as it is since you…left."

Temperance snorted. "I wouldn't upset my best boy. I'll just tune in from time to time to make sure Bebe looks after him properly. And only until Arlene returns from her self-centered frolic to Brisbane. Then I'll go for good."

"Temperance, you can't—"

"Turn left onto Aspen! Here."

"What?"

"Quick. It's an emergency." Temperance was adamant. Perfume poured off her in thick waves until Clara's sinuses felt like they would explode. Her eyes began to water. The pressure was intense.

"What? What kind of emergency? You're dead. The dead don't have emergencies, they have eternal rest—"

"Dry up and turn left. I'll rest when I'm good and ready."

"I don't want to go left. That'll take me down to Main Street and I'm heading to work."

"Left!"

Clara swung left onto Aspen. "Jeez. You're as ornery as ever. Death did not sweeten you up one little bit."

But she was talking to herself. Temperance had gone.

Clara rolled her truck down Aspen in the opposite direction of where she wanted to go, bemoaning the fact that she was surrounded by crazy old ladies from this life and the next. Between Temperance's highhanded orders and Esme's sneaky meddling, she felt flustered and annoyed, and more determined than ever that Bebe Franklin would not be on her calling card this summer. Darling would have to be swinging upside down from his perch before she set foot over Arlene McCall's doorstep.

"What the…" Clara slowed her truck to a standstill. Aspen was blocked. A Subaru had rear-ended a taxicab. The vehicles were skewed across both lanes, and their drivers were having a stand up argument in the middle of the road.

In typical Preston fashion, a small knot of bystanders gathered. Clara sat back and watched from the comfort of her truck, as idly interested as the rest of the spectators. She supposed she could mount the sidewalk and drive on by, but she was in no real hurry. Small town life was her bread and butter. It quietly amused her to watch the small theater of everyday life played out before her. As Preston's only mortician, she had her part to play, too.

The cab's female passenger stood to the side looking distressed and abandoned. Clara examined the stranger dispassionately. She was attractive enough if you liked meat on the bones. Her raincoat was clinched tightly at her waist, the hem flapping awkwardly around her knees. An ugly waterproof hat was jammed onto her head, and wet tendrils of hair hung around her shoulders. Why was she standing out in the rain like a lunatic?

The woman plunged her hand into her pocket and then pressed a tissue to her nose. *Jeez, lady. Wait inside the car. You'll get pneumonia standing in the street with the rest of the rubberneckers.* Clara wondered at the stupidity of the woman, then inhaled…and inhaled again, deeper. She couldn't be sure, but she could have sworn she smelled Night-scented stock. Surely she was wrong? She began looking for its source and sniffed the air freshener. No, that wasn't it. She sniffed her coat sleeve and shirt collar. Maybe it was her detergent? No, not that either. The smell grew stronger then receded. It thrummed in the air, ebbing and flowing, pulsing around her, warm and satisfying. Cocooned in the truck cab with the wind whistling outside and the rain pelting off the windshield, she felt as if she were sitting inside a heartbeat.

Clara held the scent and waited, but no spirit appeared. She associated these delightful perfumes with the deceased; each ghost had its own unique scent that became as recognizable as a calling card to her. This Night-scented stock combination was new to her. She drew it in and sampled it, breaking it down to its component pieces. It was a hot and edgy scent, unraveling into higher layers of clove and heliotrope with spicy undertones of musk and tonka bean. It was rich and delightfully addictive. Clara greedily sucked it in until the scent thinned and finally wafted away leaving her sitting in her cooling cab, the chill wind sneaking through the ill-fitting doors. She shivered, annoyed at the loss, and irritated she hadn't fixed her broken heater. Cold and bored, she turned her attention back to the spectacle on the street.

Once again, the taxi passenger caught Clara's attention. The wind had blown her hat back on her head and her hair whipped around her beet red face like wet cord. It was a pretty, heart-shaped face, what Clara could make of it through the bundle of tissues the woman had pressed to her nose.

The slanting rain slowly dispersed the gawkers, despite the wail of approaching police sirens. The best bit of any small town drama was the arrival of the emergency services. Clara guessed the wind was too bitter even for the most hardened snoopers. Soon, only the obdurate drivers and the shivering passenger were left standing in the street.

Clara watched the quarreling men, wondering which one was more likely to throw the first punch. It was getting to that stage. Maybe it was a good thing the police were on their way. She glanced over at the woman and sat up straighter. The tissues pressed to her nose were blood soaked, and she was awkwardly riffling through her pockets for more. Clara left her truck and strode over, uncaring that she was getting wet through.

"You okay?" She pulled out a clean handkerchief. "Here. What happened? Did you bang your face?" She looked hard at that face—what she could see of it from behind a bloody tissue.

"Thank you." The voice was muffled. The old tissue was crammed in a pocket and Clara's fresh handkerchief quickly applied. The woman promptly turned scarlet and blinked at Clara through rain-specked glasses. Her eye color was an unusual violet blue. She blinked again, and Clara realized she had been staring. *I bet those eyes get her anything she wants.* She took a step back, slightly unfocussed. Night-scented stock swirled around her, the scent damper and somehow sweeter for it.

"It's been a stressful day. I get nosebleeds when I'm upset." The woman was talking to Clara, mumbling from behind her hanky. Clara shook the nonsense out of her head and concentrated on the woman's words.

"Go sit in the car and try to stay dry," she said, wishing she had more tissues. The woman was shivering and the nosebleed looked nasty.

"I wish I could." The woman blushed even more and nodded at her coat hem. It was trapped in the cab door. "When the driver went off to rant, he locked the doors. My coat is caught and I can't open the door to free it. I'm sort of stuck here until he comes back."

"Oh, for God's sake," Clara snapped. It was preposterous the driver had left her. The woman was hurt and freezing. What a jerk.

"It's not like I haven't tried to tell him." The woman sounded overly defensive and more than a little frazzled. She was embarrassed, and Clara felt bad for snapping, but the driver needed a hard kick up the butt to leave his passenger there like that. She turned to where the men stood arguing.

"Hey!" she called. "Need help here, buddy."

The men continued to bawl into each other's faces, ignoring her.

"See," the woman said. "He's in such a rage he can't even hear straight."

"You! Keys! Now!"

That got his attention. At least he stopped growling long enough to look over. Clara pointed to the bloody tissue. "What? You don't give a damn about your passenger? You will when she sues your ass off the road."

He was over in milliseconds apologizing and opening the doors. He fussed over the woman asking if she was okay. A patrol car pulled up, and local officers Doyle and Garcia clambered out to set about moving vehicles off the road and taking details.

Doyle ambled over.

"Hi, Clara. Did you see anything?" He nodded at the cars.

"Not a thing. I arrived just after it happened. This lady is the taxi passenger. She has a bad nosebleed."

"Are you okay, ma'am?" Doyle puffed his chest like a Barbary ape, eager for the chance to play the gallant. Clara headed back to her truck and left him to it. She had no wish to compete over a damsel in distress. She needed to be on her way. She had work to do. The road was now clear and if she took a left she could cut across to Dearhearts. As her truck crawled past Doyle, she overheard the conversation with the passenger.

"...Bebe Franklin, officer. I'm staying with a relative for a few weeks, but my suitcase is stuck in the trunk of the cab and the other car rammed the lock shut..."

So that's the new improved Brick? Clara felt as if she'd been hit by one.

She took a long, hard look as her truck rolled by. The ugly heightened color had gone, the nosebleed had all but stopped, and Bebe Franklin's face had come out from behind the tissue to reveal a creamy complexion and a rosebud pink mouth. The grown-up Brick looked as sweet as homespun sugar.

A wisp of Night-scented stock blew into the cab. It became stronger and then vanished altogether. *That scent is hers?* Clara frowned. What did it mean? She braked gently until she was barely moving. The scene unfolding before her was ridiculous. Bebe stared up at Officer Doyle from behind her glasses, her eyes wide and intense with worry. Her face was damp, and wispy tendrils of hair clung to her cheeks and forehead. She seemed fragile as a china doll, yet she crackled with vibrancy. Clara imagined Doyle's knees puddling out from under him. He fancied himself a local lothario. Sure enough, he whipped off his cap despite the rain, tucked it under his arm, and beamed a cocky, overly confident smile that elicited nothing more than a long, nervous stare from Bebe.

Clara giggled, picking up speed as she drove on down Aspen. She shook her head. Had Temperance brought her out of her way for an initial contact with her granddaughter? Why? What was the point? They'd barely spoken, and it was Doyle who was in the throes of rescuing her.

Between her nosebleed, her coat caught in the car door, and now her suitcase jammed in the trunk, Bebe the Brick seemed as lucky as ever. Maybe Temperance was right to worry for Darling's safety. But if she thought Clara was going to play guardian angel for her granddaughter, or more likely, her parrot, then she had another think coming. Clara's thoughts turned sober. She had enough on her plate without being manipulated from beyond the grave.

She put the mini melodrama behind her. She wasn't going to let Esme or Temperance bind her up in their shenanigans. Clara was wrapped in enough chains as it was, and they rattled all the way down to hell.

CHAPTER THREE

I'm coming. I'm coming—Oh, sweet Jesus!" Bebe Franklin's shin crashed against the edge of the coffee table. She yelped in pain and limped toward the front door.

"Oh, sweet Jesus." Darling flapped in startled agitation.

"Shush. Stupid bird." Bebe flung the door open and gazed with delight at her visitor.

"I'm coming," he echoed after her.

"Esme. Esme Dearheart. Am I glad to see you." Bebe stood back, allowing Esme to enter.

"Good afternoon, Bebe." Esme swamped her in a hug. "Surely you knew I'd call over and say hello sooner rather than later?"

"I had a suspicion you might. You've no idea how often your name came up in my debriefing." They clung together tightly. "You're looking fantastic, Esme." Bebe stood back.

"Thank you. And I can say the same for you. Preston's sea air certainly suits you." Esme smiled. "You're looking a lot more relaxed since I last saw you. I take it Arlene warned you I might drop by."

"Your phone number is taped to every electrical appliance in the house. You'd think you were the local fix-it shop. Come in and have some tea. It's wonderful to see you again."

"What happened? You're bleeding?" Esme pointed at Bebe's leg.

Bebe glanced at the thin trickle of blood running down her shin. "Damn. I hit it on the table when I was running for the door." She sat on the pale gray couch to inspect the cut.

"Not on the chenille, dear." Esme gently took her elbow and led her away. "Let's go to the kitchen. There's a first aid box in the bottom drawer."

❖

"I'm so excited to be here." Bebe examined her Band-Aid. "It's so nice to be out of the city. I can't believe it's been nearly a week." They sat on the back deck in the early April sunshine, sipping hot peach tea and catching up with each other's news.

"Preston's beautiful at this time of year, especially Aunt Arlene's garden," Bebe said. Springtime was definitely underway in the large garden. White and blue crocus tips peeped through the lawn. New greenery was filling out the winter worn shrubs, and the magnolia and rhododendrons were pushing out shy new buds.

"Arlene won't be back in time for the Preston flower festival. It seems such a pity," Esme said.

"Will you be entering? Your garden is lovely, too."

Esme shook her head. "Clara and I usually give the show a miss. Too much trouble, and Clara hasn't the same time since she took over from her father." She looked around her. "When the strawberries start new leaves, call Mr. T. He'll need to dig in the straw mulch. Ask him to fertilize the lawns, too."

"Mr. T?"

"Teodor, he's the man who does the heavy gardening. Arlene will have left his number out for you."

"Okay, I'll do that. Call Mr. T. Mulch the strawberries. Fertilize the lawn." Bebe ticked off her new inventory.

"Why don't I call back tomorrow and we'll make a list of all the things Mr. T can get on with? How does that sound?" Esme said. "Though I'm sure Arlene has spoken to him before she left."

"Oh, yes, please. I know how much Aunt Arlene loves her garden. I want it to look magnificent for her return." Bebe was relieved at the offer.

"Will you be working while you're here? I've been watching the show," Esme asked. "I saw your last episode, where Buff caught Shahandrah in the shower with whatshisface...the one with the scar, just before the bar mitzvah."

Bebe guessed Arlene had tipped off Esme that things were going badly for her at *Valley of Our Fathers*. She gave a mirthless hoot of laughter.

"It was rubbish, and we both know it." She wrinkled her nose. "Pays the bills." She might as well be honest. "Who knows, maybe with all this peace and quiet I can turn things around?" But even to her ears the words rang hollow.

"I really miss Grandma Temperance." She changed the subject. "It's not the same here without her. I'm glad Aunt Arlene took a vacation. It must be hard for her adjusting..." She tailed off. She missed the ladies of the house.

"I know, dear." Esme patted Bebe's hand. "But Darling's here to keep you company, and I'm just around the corner."

"A penis. A penis." Darling snapped out of his light doze at the mention of his name and flew into a squawking flurry. Esme's eyebrows shot up in surprise and Bebe stared at the bird as if he were possessed.

"Happiness, you stupid bird," Bebe scolded him. "HA— ppiness. Say the HA." She turned to Esme, flustered. "I'm teaching him an affirmation a day to calm him down."

Esme's eyebrows continued skyward.

"Aunt Arlene hadn't been gone five minutes when he called me a bastard and started pulling at his feathers," Bebe said. "I know he's missing Grandma Temperance, and the affirmations help calm me, so I thought—" She stopped, feeling stupid.

"An affirmation a day is a lovely thing to teach him. But he is an old rascal. It's almost as if he senses what will cause the most upheaval. He takes after his dearly departed owner in that way." Esme gently tapped him on the beak. "Be good for Bebe, Darling."

"Bebe, Bebe, Bebe, Bebe," he crowed and took off to a favorite spot on top of the kitchen door.

Bebe watched with alarm. "Do I need to get him down from there?"

"He'll come when he's good and ready. You can lure him into his cage with treats if you need to. I'm sure Arlene showed you where she keeps them."

Bebe nodded.

"But he's fine wandering around the house. He never goes outside. It makes him panic. We think he's agoraphobic," Esme said.

"Poor Darling." Though she had genuine sympathy for his plight, Bebe felt apprehensive around the beady-eyed bird. There was something about him that made her certain he had her measure, every last ounce of it. "I'm glad you dropped in, Esme. Please feel free to pop over anytime. In fact, come for lunch next Monday?"

"Now that's an offer I can't refuse. Is there anything else you need help with before I go?"

"Yes." Bebe leapt to her feet. "One more BIG thing. In the basement."

❖

"Arlene's old boiler is acting up again. For the life of me, I don't know why she doesn't just get a new one." Esme fussed about the kitchen piling roasted chicken and potatoes onto enormous dinner plates. "Peas and carrots?"

"Are they homegrown or store bought?" Clara asked.

"Homegrown. I defrosted them this morning." She set a heaped dinner plate before Clara. "Maybe you could drop by and look at it?"

Clara began to eat, watching Esme salting her food with a look of angelic innocence. She chewed carefully and swallowed as Esme fussed over her plate.

"Bebe needs a boiler man, not a mortician," she said. "Unless she tries to fix it herself," she added as an afterthought.

"Clara! Lord forbid," Esme exclaimed.

"Well, stop pushing, old woman. And stop over-salting your food. The doctor told you to go light on the salt."

Esme sniffed, set down the saltshaker, and took a dainty sip of her Merlot.

"The boiler worked okay for Arlene all this time." Clara's attention was back on her dinner. "It's probably got ten more years in it yet."

"Don't know how you can say that without looking. What?" Esme managed to look genuinely offended at Clara's stare.

Outside, the rain rattled on the windows. In the background, the radio softly played show tunes. They sat at the kitchen table and shared their day.

"Bebe invited me to lunch next week."

"That's nice," Clara answered disinterestedly.

"She's a great cook. Want to see if I can wrangle you an invite?"

"Nope."

"All right, all right. I was just asking." Suddenly, Esme sat upright bursting with news. "I've just remembered. Bebe's been teaching Darling affirmations."

"You're joking. How's that going?"

"You'd be surprised. Bebe was."

Soon they were howling with laughter at Darling's idea of happiness.

"You really should call by." Esme wiped tears from her eyes. "Things are bad if she's resorted to talking to Darling."

"She's only been here a week. She'll need more staying power than that if she's to survive Darling." Clara took the empty plates to the sink. "Anyway, I'm far too busy for visiting."

She ran hot water and added detergent. Suds filled the basin.

"Did I tell you that Ronnie has entered us in the Town Traders pool competition?" She deftly changed topics and began washing dishes.

Esme was as slippery as the suds, but Clara could sidestep her easily enough. Bebe Franklin could teach Darling to whistle Dixie for all Clara cared. She was not going to visit her.

❖

"Hello, Marcus," Clara said.

Marcus squinted up from the wreaths strewn over the fresh mound of earth. She had caught him hunkered down reading the cards. His lips moved slowly around each syllable.

"Hi, Clara. This was a big one. Did you do it?" He waved his hand at the new grave piled high with flower wreaths. Petals shivered in the breeze, pastel and pretty against the smooth green lawns. In the distance, a lawnmower hummed.

"No. It came in from Bangor direction. It's an old family plot. I think he was a great-nephew or something."

Marcus stood up to his full six foot four, a shower of silver sparks shot off him, hopping and fizzing around his feet like flashes of solder. He gave Clara a big, pink-cheeked grin. Clouds of fresh mint blew across her face, and she could see the moisture on his eyelashes. She grinned back. He was embarrassed at being caught tearing up at reading other people's last farewells. Marcus was a big softy.

"Not local then. I knew I didn't recognize the name," he said.

Clara shook her head. "Not a local boy at all."

"Do you know what happened to him?"

"Heard it was a motorcycle crash."

"Same as me." They stood looking at the headstone. It was a huge, striking affair in charcoal granite. The boy's name had been added in bold gold lettering, contrasting brightly with the weathered names of his ancestors.

"You were younger." Clara pointed to the crisply etched dates.

"Only by eighteen months. He was twenty."

"Why are you still here, Marcus?" Clara asked softly. "It's been a while."

"How long?"

"Fourteen years."

Marcus shrugged off the time. "I promised my mother I'd look after her."

"You're waiting for her, then?"

"Yeah, I suppose. Plus I like seeing what's going on. I'm in no hurry." He looked at the lunch box tucked under her arm. "You going to have lunch with Frances?"

"You've seen her?" she asked hopefully.

"No." He gave her a sorrowful look. "Sorry."

Clara nodded. "It's okay." She walked away, leaving the cheerful mint smell and silver sparkles behind. "I'll catch you later."

"You too, Clara. Bye."

On the other side of the cemetery, Clara lay on the fresh cut grass. It tickled her nose and made her smile. It was one of her most favorite smells in the whole world, a simple but universally happy smell. Lots of people loved it. Clara wondered why that was. Was it some primeval trigger for harvest time, or merely a childhood memory of lazy summers? Idly, she pondered, flat on her back, gazing up through the treetops to the blue cloudless sky. Her hands were clasped behind her head, a newspaper splayed across her stomach, and her lunchbox sat unopened beside her.

All cemeteries should have cloudless blue skies. If she ruled the world, it would be engineered that way. She frowned as the thought of Bebe Franklin's eyes danced into her mind. They were a deeper, almost violet blue, like the horizon where the sky met the sea. A warm breeze ruffled her hair. She could swear that Night-scented stock hung on it, but perhaps it was more a memory than the scent itself? The sweet clove undertones teased her thoughts in a different direction. She hummed tunelessly.

Or maybe a warm, scented breeze is my most favorite thing? Better even than fresh cut grass. She turned her head to silently question the gravestone of Frances Jane Plummer. *What about you, Frances? What's your favorite?*

It surprised her that she genuinely didn't know the answer. It felt like something important and integral that she should know, and she'd somehow failed by not knowing. But it was too late to ask now. Another lost fragment from their past. It seemed the longer she lived, the more pieces of her life with Frances kept turning up missing.

CHAPTER FOUR

B ebe proudly led her friends down Preston's main shopping
street to her favorite lobster house for an evening dinner
par excellence.

"This place is just so cute it's to die for," Jayrah drawled.
"Please, somebody kill me."

Suzzee and Pebble burst into laughter.

"Much as we adore your cooking, Beebs, I'm glad you're
taking us out to show off the bright lights." As usual, Pebble tried
to take the sting out of Jayrah's words, and as usual, it was a tad too
late and slightly off the mark.

Bebe looked around uncertainly, trying to see the town
through Jayrah's cynical eyes. She didn't get it. Preston *was* cute.
Okay, touristy cute, but then that was what it was all about. Every
pastel painted storefront was either an art gallery, a coffee house,
or a tasteful gift shop of some description. They skirted narrow,
cobblestoned streets that would be lined with flower displays in the
high season. As a child, Bebe had the best summer vacations here.
Tonight, dainty lights strung across the narrow pedestrian walkways
and dressed up the whole commercial center beautifully.

Preston was an old fishing port, set on one of a series of small
islands in Penobscot bay. For centuries, its sardine fleet had been its
only prosperity, and a road had been built along the old causeway to
truck the daily catch to the canneries farther up the estuary. When
the sardine industry fell away, the causeway road had brought in

the replacement industry of tourism. The town had a population of about twelve hundred, and that easily quadrupled for the summer months. It was quaint. Picture postcard quaint, but deliberately so. Preston grimly hung on to its early eighteenth century visage. It took hard work and careful planning to hold back time like that. Bebe was surprised her friends didn't appreciate it more. They all spent a lot of time in front of the mirror trying to do the same.

This was her third week of house-sitting, and Jayrah and her girlfriend Pebble had visited, as promised. What had thrown Bebe was the unexpected addition of Suzzee to the weekend party. Bebe felt edgy around all three friends now that she was privy to Suzzee and Jayrah's little secret. Had they come clean to Pebble yet? Had Suzzee told her friends about leaving *Valley*? Or about asking Bebe to write her demise? There were far too many secrets, and Bebe was uncomfortable. She had a habit of getting things catastrophically wrong where secrets were concerned.

Please don't let this be a weekend of denouements. Please let them reveal the horrible truth to each other back in the city and not here. Oh...and please, please don't let me be the one to blab! Bebe didn't have a god, so she peered up at the coral sunset and prayed to a big pink-tinged cloud. A fluffy, benevolent-looking one.

It surprised Bebe that her friends had managed to peel away from city life at all. She could only assume the tension at *Valley* was nearing the breaking point and the trip out here was a cheap and necessary distraction. Bebe was glad to see them for her own reasons. It was beginning to get lonely with only Darling and an occasional visit from Esme for company. Granted, it meant she could get on with her work. She had three episodes of *Valley* to flesh out for Carter, but found she was struggling. Her personal disenchantment with the show was making it harder to wade through Carter's creative sludge. She still hadn't come up with a showstopper of an idea to save her ass. The blackmail line Carter wanted her to expand upon was awkward to weave into all the other action threads. And Suzzee's private wish to kill off her Berry Ripe character was still a non-starter. She hoped Suzzee wouldn't press her too hard on that this weekend.

Bebe's stomach fizzed with nervousness. She peeked across at Pebble and Suzzee who seemed as equally unaffected by the small town's charms as Jayrah. They passed a shop window and Bebe took a moment to look objectively at herself and her friends in the reflection. She saw a posse of dressed up city girls out for some weekend fun. All had hard, nervous smiles and tight, anxious movements. The only real connection they shared was that they lived the same dream and worked in the same nightmare.

Maybe it was a good thing they had gotten together to let off steam. They were all under intense pressure thanks to Carter. The soap magazines were full of gossip that *Valley* would go belly up this year. Everyone was twitchy. Everyone needed a break, which made Bebe wonder all the more why her friends were being so critical. Sure, Preston was small and quaint, but the whole point was to leave the madness of the city behind and find somewhere sweet and laid back to chill out in. She was more than pleased to be here... despite the growing loneliness.

"Here we are." She tried to sound upbeat as they approached Petty's shabby, weatherworn façade. She pushed at the paint-scuffed door. "Don't be fooled by the look of it. This place has the best seafood you'll ever—"

"Jesus, Bebe. Is this all Preston can offer for a night out?" Jayrah's scathing words caught the attention of two men standing near the door. Bebe recognized one as Victor Phelps, the guy who owned the gas station on the far side of the causeway. He squinted at her through his cigarette smoke. A bald, rotund man stood smoking with him. Bebe knew he was the local butcher, but his name escaped her. His piggy little eyes ran over the women with open curiosity rather than any salaciousness. Her companions bristled and rudely swished past, startling the men into taking a step back. Bebe blushed, mumbled an awkward hello, and dipped her head to quickly follow.

Once inside, Bebe directed them into the lounge bar where they could grab a booth and order food. It was quieter than the back rooms where the locals gathered around the jukebox and pool tables. From the sound of it, there was a big crowd back there tonight.

The lounge bar served food and had proper waiters and soft background music. Bebe was looking forward to a fantastic fish dinner and a catch up on *Valley* gossip.

"Let's order a bottle of bubbles to celebrate something or other. What do we have to celebrate?" Suzzee squeezed into the corner seat and reached for the wine list. "Oh look, they have a decent selection. Who knew."

Bebe noted Suzzee was focused on the prices rather than the labels. Her anxiety notched up a little. She couldn't afford a drinking spree, especially at those prices. She had to be careful with her money, as she had no idea how long she'd be working. It was a boon to stay for free at Aunt Arlene's place while she sublet her studio apartment, but she needed to shore up her savings drastically.

"Let's drink to Bebe's birthday." Jayrah grabbed at the wine list.

"That's not for another month," Bebe protested.

"It's why we came down here, doofus," Jayrah said. "It was the only free time all of us had."

"Due to double booking, your birthday has been officially moved to today." Suzzee confirmed the plan.

"Oh. Thanks, guys."

"We knew you'd never come to us so we came here." Pebble giggled. "It's impossible to dig you out of this clam hole. Are there even any lesbians for you to flirt with?"

"Yeah. That's a great beach. It's hardly Fire Island, but surely *some* dykes come out here to use it?" Jayrah asked.

"I'm...I'm not sure." Bebe really didn't know. She hadn't thought about it.

"It's a pity you don't do boys," Suzzee said. "Small town boys are the best for a quickie. All the mind-numbing boredom concentrates the testosterone into pure fucking fuel." Suzzee laughed at their disgusted faces.

"Okay, let's order a bottle and drink to Bebe getting older and to a girls' night out in New England's foremost recessive cell pool." Jayrah took up the wine list again.

"I like it here. Honest, guys." Bebe twisted in her seat looking for a waiter, relieved when she saw a white jacket pop up behind the bar. "Excuse me, could we order some food, please?"

The last thing she needed was for her visitors to get stuck in the booze and forget about food.

❖

Clara sank the last stripe but couldn't pull back enough for the eight ball. She straightened and watched the cue ball roll up and kiss the cushion as if she'd planned it. She grinned over to where Ronnie slouched against the bar, a bottle of Bud at his elbow. He winked back. The game was as good as over. They would sail into the next round, but then again, they had pulled soft opposition in Victor's Gas Stop.

Although she looked cool, Clara was disconcerted. Playing against Victor always left her feeling odd. He still couldn't look her in the eye, even after four years, and it wasn't as if she held a grudge. Hell, nobody was to blame, least of all him. Clara fought to release the tightness in her gut. Often these days she was caught unaware with a rush of anger at Frances and the way she had left things. Clara hurt for the misplaced guilt Victor and half the town carried. She wanted to leech it off them and carry the burden all by herself, but that was a silly and self-gratifying sentiment. Esme would be first in line to knock it out of her. She mentally shook herself and concentrated on the game.

Victor had three more balls to make. She reckoned he would make at least one and hopefully leave Ronnie to drop the eight ball and move Dearhearts along in the competition. The Gas Stop always flunked out early. Victor was cross-eyed, for God's sake.

The door behind the bar connected through to the main diner. Every time the staff swung through, raucous female laughter followed and pierced the noise of the back bar. Her pool game more or less over, Clara allowed her curiosity to peak. She perched on a stool by the bar and ordered another beer for herself and Ronnie.

"Hey, Holly," she called to the barmaid. "What's going on next door?"

"Some chicks in from New York spending a fortune on booze." The young girl shrugged and clattered the till. "They ordered a whole platter of scallops and clams then hardly touched it. Chef was pissed." She slapped a handful of coins on the counter. "Probably *creative* types," she said sounding thoroughly bored.

"Creative types" was the local lingo for a particular set of seasonal visitors. They poured in at the start of the season under the premise of making art, but spent most of the summer swimming in booze and brash behavior. Clara was surprised; it was a little early for creative types to be dropping by.

Benjamin, the waiter in charge of the lounge bar, breezed through the staff door bringing another squeal of female laughter with him. He was bursting with news and headed straight for Holly.

"You'll never guess who's next door," he blurted.

"Who?" Holly was totally disinterested.

"Guess."

"Who."

"Guess." He was incredibly excited.

"Oh, fuck off and tell me," Holly snapped.

Clara hid her smile at Benjamin's miffed expression.

"It's only—Shush!" Benjamin nudged Holly sharply in the ribs and tried to look busy as she cursed him roundly. All the while he shot furtive glances over Clara's shoulder until she wanted to turn around and see what he was looking at. Before she could twist in her seat, a young Asian woman popped up beside her elbow. She stood far too close considering the bar wasn't crowded. Her perfume jarred on Clara's sinuses to the point she wanted to sneeze.

"Hey, another bottle of cava here," the woman called out, not bothering to see if anyone else was waiting to be served.

"The Jacob's Creek?" Benjamin jumped to attend while Holly glowered.

"Whatever. There's nobody serving at the other bar," the woman said. In the mirror that ran behind the back counter, Clara could see she was on the receiving end of a brazen check over. She bristled. The woman was clearly drunk, and Clara didn't like being leered at, not even by a pretty woman. Not that it was an everyday occurrence. Even so, it was unmannerly behavior, as Esme would say.

The woman leaned further into the counter, deliberately pressing her breasts against Clara's triceps.

"And bring more ice," she ordered Benjamin.

"Hey. If I wanted tits on my arm, I'd drink plutonium." Clara scowled and shifted in her seat. She got a spiked look in return, then the woman wheeled away.

"Do you know who that is?" Benjamin whispered furtively. Clara and Holly shared a blank look, and Clara snorted dismissively.

"One of the Three Graces," she muttered into her beer, "but which can it be? Rudeness, Inebriation, or plain old Lewd."

Benjamin was not deterred. "That's Suzzee Wang."

"Who?" Clara frowned.

"She plays Berry Ripe in *Valley of Our Fathers*." He tsked at her stupidity.

"*Valley* is a steaming pile of crappola," Holly delivered her opinion and stalked away.

Benjamin ignored her and continued to inform Clara. "I can hardly believe it. At least I'm almost sure it's her. I'm going to fawn all over her and ask for an autograph, then see what she tips me."

"Berry Ripe? What kind of stupid name is that?" Clara looked Benjamin in the eye. "Do you really think some ridiculous soap star would come all the way to Preston to drink cheap wine in a dump like this?"

"Well, she came in with Arlene McCall's niece, and *she's* got something to do with television. So why not?" He sniffed. "And the Jacob's Creek is not cheap; it's our slightly overpriced midrange cava. Though the way they're knocking it back, it might as well be cream soda."

"Arlene McCall's niece is here? Where?"

"In the lounge bar with her B-list celebrity friends." Benjamin sounded extra smug as he moved off to fill his order.

Clara's interest was piqued. She slid off her seat and headed for the corridor that led to the restrooms. It connected both bar rooms and from there she could see through to the lounge.

Three young women sat in a booth, rocking with loud laughter. As she watched, the one who'd pressed up against her managed to magnanimously overfill everyone's glasses with bubbling wine. It spilled all over the cutlery and plates, soaking the tablecloth. With shrieks and shrill obscenities, the other two leapt up before the wine could drip onto their laps. For such a small group they made a hell of a lot of noise. They were loud and colorful and oblivious to everything and everyone but themselves and their gratification.

A door clicked behind Clara. She turned as Bebe Franklin emerged from the ladies' restroom. She looked demure yet stylish in a short cream dress and eggshell blue cardigan. *Pretty.* The thought leapt into Clara's head from nowhere and startled her. Quickly, she tamped it down. Then she noticed the unsteady gait and flushed, discomfited features. Glazed blue eyes shone out from a sweaty, troubled face. Someone had met her limit head on, and the limit wasn't budging. Clara felt a surge of smug censorship. She glared at the intoxicated young woman that Esme held in such high regard, and was annoyed at her for being with the rowdies in the lounge.

Despite herself, she also noticed Bebe on a very different level. Clara's inner lesbian perked up. Her gaydar pinged loudly and repeatedly, warning her of incoming babe. The insistent alarm disturbed her slumbering libido. It uncurled and stretched luxuriously like a lazy cat, arching its back and flexing its claws. The involuntary reaction annoyed Clara. True, she wasn't exactly dead from the neck down, but from the neck up she was not amused with Bebe Franklin and the company she kept, one little bit.

Jeez, look at her. Clara glared openly. *She can't even walk straight.*

❖

Bebe wobbled as she left the ladies' room. She pushed her glasses back up the bridge of her nose and extended a hand to run along the wall and guide her back to the lounge in more or less a straight line. The colorful swirls of the carpet lurched before her eyes and made her stomach twitch. She didn't feel so good. It had been ages since she'd drunk this much alcohol, and her tolerance level must have zeroed out. The food they'd ordered had arrived long after the second bottle of sparkling wine, and by then she'd felt too chewed up to appreciate the beautiful seafood platter. She had done her best, but acids swilled in her belly like sea surf, making eating less than a joy.

She stepped forward carefully in what she hoped was a demure, sober-like manner, and made her way slowly along the hall, her fingertips grazing the flock wallpaper. Someone was hovering near the reception desk, probably a waiter. Maybe she could ask for the bill. Maybe she should ask him to order a taxi and try to get her friends out of here while they could still walk. A fourth bottle had already been opened, and Bebe knew she'd end up in a heap if she didn't call it quits while she had the chance.

Yup, ask the waiter to order a cab. She turned to do just that. *A fast cab...with open windows.* Bebe looked into the coldest eyes she had ever seen. A gaze so arctic it could freeze the human heart to a shuddering stop at five hundred paces. Bebe didn't have five hundred paces; she had barely a yard between herself and the iceberg in the crisp white button-down shirt and faded denims.

She recoiled against the wall, wincing as she banged her hip. What had she ever done to tick off this strange and foreboding woman? Maybe this was the manager. Were her friends being too raucous? Making too much noise? Maybe she should suck up and say what a great time her guests were having. Bebe swerved around to do just that.

"Mm...Ah. I was...ummm..." Once again, she was pinned by that flint-edged stare and her vocabulary self-combusted, turning to ash in her mouth. Bebe flushed hotly. Very hotly. So hot her ears hurt. The rush of rampant embarrassment triggered a memory. This was the woman who'd offered her the tissue when she'd had the nosebleed. She had seemed pleasant enough then. Bebe had been disconcerted when she'd rushed off and abandoned her. It had taken her ages to wriggle out from the attentions of Officer Doyle.

"Um," she tried again. Something was wrong here. The woman watched her silently with a look of unparalleled scorn.

Okay. Maybe I'll just go back to the table and wait for Benjamin. He was nice. Bebe knew her face was a most unbecoming beet red.

Her cheeks and throat scorched with it. She swerved back on course for the lounge. Best to get away as fast as possible. She was equally upset and cowed by the hard look, but determined to retreat with as much flair and dignity as possible.

Bebe drew in a deep breath, straightened her spine, and lifted her chin. One careful step at a time she walked as majestically as she could toward the lounge and her braying companions. *Look, lady, I don't know what your problem is, but I am having a great time, so there.* At least she hoped that's what her body language was saying.

❖

The copper curtain of hair swayed heavily against Bebe's shoulders as she lurched forward. Clara couldn't help but admire its luxurious sheen under the harsh corridor lighting. For all her tasteless behavior, Bebe was tasteful to look at. Despite her chilly attitude, Clara ran an appraising eye over a body that managed to be very, very curvy in all the best places. She knew how to dress with class. Her eyes lingered on Bebe's plump posterior and shapely calves that curved to tapered ankles and extremely stylish sandals. Clara watched Bebe weave away, quietly fascinated by the two-foot length of toilet tissue trailing from her left heel.

"If Arlene McCall was here, she'd rattle that one's ears with a stern word or two." Ronnie wandered up and stood behind Clara. "We won, by the way. We drew Belle's Pharmacy for next week."

"Better practice then. They're good," Clara said. She found it hard to equate the drunken behavior she'd just witnessed with the young woman Esme was so fond of. One last glance into the lounge bar saw Bebe squeeze back into her booth and manage to knock over everyone's glasses at the same time. Wine sloshed over the table and onto her companions' laps.

"Beebs! You fat ass! Look what you've done."

Bedlam ensued. With a wry smile Clara headed for the back bar, breathing deeply on the subtle smell of Night-scented stock. It trailed her up the hall, billowing with every step she took across the gaudy, threadbare carpet.

CHAPTER FIVE

The pool competition was over, the jukebox cranked up, and a full-on Friday night kicked off in Petty's back bar. Clara stood propped at the counter half listening as a regular bent her ear about his soil problems. He had too much nitrogen in his vegetable beds and wanted to know how to rectify it.

"Do we have any more cava?" Benjamin called across to Holly. "The Jacob's Creek is done."

Holly pulled a bottle of Freixenet from the chill cabinet and slapped it into his hands, leaving him to uncork it.

"Has that group not gone home yet?" she groused. Benjamin shook his head.

"They moved in here when the music started up." He nodded at a nearby booth. Clara sneaked a quick glance. The group from next door had indeed moved into the livelier back bar and were steadfastly ignoring every lusty glance sent their way.

Benjamin had managed to point out the celebrated Suzzee Wang to anyone who would listen, and now the women were the center of much covert attention. Doyle was on the sniff, circling like an excited truffle hound. But so far no one approached them. They gave out a city slicker aura of intimidation that kept even the most ardent of bachelors cautiously prowling the peripheries. Their drink of choice was far too flamboyant for the shallow pockets in Petty's back bar. Nobody would be sending over a bottle of that expensive looking wine in the hopes of an introduction.

Clara smiled quietly; given what she knew about Bebe's sexual orientation, it was highly probable her friends leaned in the same direction. In fact, she would have bet a dozen bottles of cava none of the boys would get far tonight.

Before the smile could fade from her lips, an acidic perfume seeped into her comfort zone. It was overwhelming and offensive enough to flavor her tongue with a chemical coating. A quick sideways glance told her another of Bebe's posse was standing almost on top of her, even though the bar was far from crowded. This one was blonde and petite, her hair and clothes were overly orchestrated and far too fussy for a pit like Petty's. Again, insolent eyes openly appraised her, and Clara stiffened. What was with these women? She ignored the woman completely and gave full attention to the man with the soil problems.

"Hey, I need napkins here." The rude bellow drowned out Clara's conversation. Benjamin nearly fell over to oblige. The woman turned and left without a word of thanks.

"Why do you bother when they're so rude?" Clara asked Benjamin.

"Because that *is* Suzzee Wang and Bebe got me her autograph," Benjamin replied smugly. "Bebe's a doll. I like her." He drifted away to the far side of the bar.

Clara watched as the woman returned to Bebe's booth with a smug, triumphant look. She'd been on some sort of reconnaissance mission Clara decided. And it somehow concerned her. Suddenly, she was as interested as any of the local guys to find out what the women in the booth were talking about. But unlike the guys, Clara did not want to be the focus of their attention. Her soil chemical advice given, she slid further around the bar to a new perch closer to Bebe's booth but angled so she was out of the occupants' line of sight. From there she could pick up a smattering of conversation over the thrum of the jukebox. It was blatant eavesdropping, but Clara couldn't stop herself. She'd picked up bad habits from Esme over the years.

"...she was yakking on about soil, and her fingernails are dirtier than the look she gave me. Definitely a gardener." The petite air polluter was reporting back to her table. "See, Bebe? There are queers here."

"Bebe, you need to get yourself a gardener." The famous Suzzee Wang spoke up.

"Oh, but I've got a gardener," Bebe burbled happily. "And guess what, he's called Mr. T and he's worked for my Aunt Arl—"

"The gardener at the bar." Suzzee interrupted with exasperation.

"She means you need to get laid, Einstein," a third woman with a loud, domineering voice stated bluntly. Clara lurched in her seat and glanced around anxiously. Luckily, Benjamin was well out of earshot and Doyle was nowhere to be seen. She zoned in on the conversation again.

"Pffh. Ack," Bebe spluttered over her drink.

"Jayrah's right. You need servicing and soon, before your panties rust up."

"Shut up, Pebble," Bebe said, mortified.

Jayrah? Pebble? Where did these people get their names? Clara was livid at being the object of such a salacious conversation. *There ought to be a law that allows eavesdroppers to sue.*

"It's true, Beebs. You need some action in the summer bedding department," Suzzee said.

"Ouf. Pafh." Bebe choked. How the hell she made a living with words was beyond Clara. Snorts of laughter came rolling from the booth, drawing even more curious glances from the bar patrons.

"Go on, Bebe. Get your buds out for the gardener."

Bebe's face blazed, and she giggled with embarrassment.

"Yeah, let her poke around in your petals…"

"…and ruffle your bloomers."

They were all in stitches now. Clara's face burned. She'd heard enough. She slid from her seat and stomped toward the exit.

❖

Urged by her friends to investigate this new local attraction, Bebe slipped from the booth on the pretence of going to the restroom. She was disappointed to find the sexy gardener's barstool empty.

Then she noticed a dark haired woman stride toward the door. A plaid padded jacket covered her broad shoulders and strong back. Her jeans hugged a very nice backside. She was taller than Bebe, which was good. Bebe liked them tall. And she had the type of slim hips Bebe fantasized wrapping her legs around.

Fueled by the boozy talk and her own sad little fantasies, Bebe stood buzzing as the object of their lewd jokes walked away. If she looked in the door glass maybe she would see the woman's face reflected back. It would be nice to have a face to go with that sexy bottom. The glass pane flashed in the overhead lighting as the door thrust open, and in the reflected angle Bebe's eyes locked with the same arctic glare that had blasted her in the corridor earlier.

Once again, a blizzard howled past her ears. She froze to the spot, her stomach shrinking to the size and temperature of an ice cube. The woman wavered for an instant, as if the locked stare had thrown her, too, then she pushed on through the door, a look of utter disgust on her face.

Bebe felt skinned alive. As if every raw little secret she'd ever had was laid out before the scathing gaze of this stranger. Every worthless, undermining, self-loathing thought she'd ever had oozed out and coated her in a suffocating unguent of self-disgust. She was an unattached, unattractive woman, with no creative talent and employment issues. A squawk of laughter from her booth jarred her. Oh yeah, and her work colleagues were all waiting for her to belly up, like the dead fish she was. She wished the weekend over and her friends gone. She wanted to be alone with her silly self-affirmations and chronic positive thinking. Not to mention her sniveling self-pity.

❖

Clara walked home along Three Mile beach. She liked the serenity of the shoreline at night. It was so tranquil under the starlight with only the occasional cry of a black-head gull strafing the waves. The rhythmic roll of the Atlantic became hypnotic in the darkness. She forgot about the bar and the pool competition and tried less successfully to forget Bebe Franklin. There was something about her that slid needle thin under Clara's skin. It pricked at her attention and made her think jagged, stinging thoughts. Clara was not normally so moralistic; she did not like that Bebe brought out an angry, censorious side of her. Clara didn't want to be priggish. And she didn't want to be around Bebe either. Esme's constant attempts to push them together was behind her churlishness. Bebe Franklin was her magnetic opposite, and the harder Esme pushed, the more Clara twitched and twisted away.

The salt air lifted the hair from her forehead and ruffled her curls. She drew in deep, refreshing breaths after the sour heat of the bar. She was satisfied she had rooted out her problem with Bebe; the answer was as before: stay away.

Up ahead, a lone night fisherman stood at the edge of the surf. As Clara approached she made out the unmistakable figure of Tom Ray. A big, burly man dressed in smeared yellow oilskins and thick rubber boots. Salt water streamed off him.

"Hey, Tom. What's it looking like tonight? Any luck?" She already knew the answer. Tom never caught anything and always blamed the weather.

"Nah. High pressure system coming in. Guess mud season is over." He turned to watch her approach. "I saw Frances."

Clara's step faltered. "Oh. Where?"

"Over at your place. Well, near it." He nodded in the direction of Clara's house. It was last in a straggly line of squat holiday shacks. It stood farther back from the rest, skulking among the sand hills, guarded and private.

"Okay." Clara quickened her step and cut diagonally across the beach toward the dunes.

"Thanks." She turned to call back, but Tom was already waist deep in the surf wading out toward the horizon, heading into the liquid darkness. She watched for a second as he stomped on until his head dipped under the breaking waves.

His skiff had overturned in a mean swell just north of the bay forty-one years ago. Some evenings he returned to fish where his body had washed ashore. Clara knew he could never stay for long.

He was compelled to return to the water. He was a fisherman through and through. His remains may have been buried in his family plot, but the sea was his true coffin.

Clara continued homeward. She could see the top of her shingle roof over the grass-tufted dunes and she quickened her step. Instead of walking around to the front path at beach level, she ran up the last dune and crowned it. She stood and looked down on the single story wooden shack. Painted in the traditional blues of Preston's shoreline, sun and wind had scoured the paintwork clean and weathered it to a silvery blue, the shingle roof as gray as a gull's wing. She waited with bated breath. There was no movement below. No light in the window. No rocking chair gliding quietly on the porch. Nothing looked out of place.

She scuffed down the dune to the picket fence and walked up the crushed shell path to the porch. In a few weeks the yard would be awash with sea holly, oyster plants, and yellow horned poppies. Now there were only clumps of dry gray foliage and windblown twigs. Her home was well worn and lived in, if not by her, then by the elements. It was set further back from its neighbors and it sat squat among the dunes like a chubby little picnicker. From the top porch step a dip in the sand hills gave the most wonderful views of the bay and the Atlantic rollers piling in. The boards creaked a welcome at her footfall, and the shack sighed as the heat of the day seeped from its planked walls.

Tonight was one of those mystical nights when the wind was behind the tide, and the roar of the surf rumbled through the house timbers. On nights like this her floorboards tremored and the house walls groaned, and if she felt fanciful enough she closed her eyes and dreamed she was in a Spanish galleon or perhaps the belly of a whale. She always slept well on stormy nights, her dreams rolling around her like stones in the tide. Clara desperately needed more storms before her sleep deficit drove her to the breaking point.

"Frances," she called. The porch swing creaked and dune grass rattled in the wind. "Frances?"

She stood and waited. She didn't need to push at the screen door to know the house was empty. She could feel it. Clara slumped down on the top step, the magic of the night and all hope of a sound sleep lost.

"Why, Frances?" she spoke into the darkness. The night air blew heavy with salt and the rustle of maram grass. "Why won't you talk to me?"

❖

"I can't believe you did this. You're all crazy and immoral... and have excellent taste," Bebe whispered, gazing in rapture at the beautiful negligee. It was nestled in a glossy black designer box, swathed in copious amounts of pink tissue paper.

She didn't know why she was whispering, except she felt very naughty and excited at the same time. The box lay open on the coffee table and coral tissue spilled over onto the floor. The most exquisite negligee Bebe had ever seen lay pooled in its center, the diaphanous champagne-colored silk shimmered under her adoring gaze. It would look gorgeous with her coloring. She held it up to the morning light. It glowed like angel's wings.

"Think of it as an early birthday present," Jayrah said. Her bleary hung-over eyes looked up from behind her coffee cup. "Pebble picked it out. Good thing, too. You need serious bait to hook that cutie gardener. Just don't sashay past when she's using a chainsaw or she'll lose a limb."

Bebe blushed and played with the newly attached gift card. "Ride on lawnmower," was scrawled across it.

"You're all incorrigible. We're not even sure she's gay," she said. She did not want the cold, proud woman from last night to be the raison d'être of this wonderful gift. It dulled the gossamer slightly.

"Stop trying to wriggle out of it. She's as bent as my Rolex," Pebble said. "Go for it, Beebs."

"Look, you're both stuck out here in the middle of nowhere. She might be glad of a little fling," Suzzee said, as tactless as ever. She dropped three Alka-Seltzer tablets in a glass of water. "I bet the locals diddle with the tourists all the time."

"Suzzee!" Bebe tsked. It seemed her gift came at a price. She had to get out there and do something dirty in it. Bebe hadn't done anything even remotely mucky for several months...well, a little over a year. Apparently, her six-week stint with an inhibited typesetter didn't count.

Bebe buried her face in the silk and breathed in its expensive newness. It must be mighty boring in New York for her dodgy love life to garner such interference. Her friends were looking for a distraction. Bebe felt like a rat in a love laboratory. It was a feeling she knew all too well. She was often the subject of her friend's bizarre experimentation. Every once in a while Pebble would turn her eye to the sorry state of Bebe's romantic existence. Like a true wardrobe mistress, she riffled through the musty old closet of Bebe's sex life. Every item, no matter how dross or moth eaten, was held up to the light of day for a stitch-by-stitch critique and detailed dissembling, with help from Jayrah and Suzzee.

Some ex-lovers survived. Usually those who could be accessorized for other occasions, while the rest were dumped in a trash bag for charity. It didn't take long to sift through Bebe's unfashionable collection of dull ex-girlfriends, clumsy one-night stands, and blunted sexual allure. Her trash bag was always full.

The silk lingerie felt cool and deliciously decadent under her fingers. It was definitely worth her friends meddling if this was the payoff. Bebe had never owned anything so sinful.

"So when do you think you'll see her again?" Jayrah asked. "At Petty's?"

"Oh, umm, I don't know if..." Bebe squirmed remembering the frosty glare.

"Look, she's a gardener. Find out who she is and get her around here to do some work. Lord knows you got acres out there." Jayrah jutted a thumb at the window.

"And you better be swanning around in that thing when she arrives." Suzzee nodded at the negligee. She reached across the breakfast table and snagged the last bagel.

"*And* heels. Wear those slutty gold sandals I made you buy." Pebble giggled at the look on Bebe's face.

"I can't do that," Bebe spluttered. Apparently, the negligee came with user instructions. "It sounds all lewd and tacky. I mean, seriously, guys, she might be straight. She's one of those cool types I find impossible to read." *And by cool read polar.*

Bebe hadn't the heart to tell her friends she was absolutely certain the sexy gardener was not likely to be seduced by Bebe in see-through fripperies. In fact, ole igloo eyes probably wasn't gay at all.

Jayrah sighed long and hard.

"Beebs, if she painted her ass rainbow and wore a neon strap-on, you'd find her hard to read. Just do as we say and you can't go wrong. Either she notices you and you're in, or she doesn't bat an eyelid and she's as straight as the road to hell. But at least you'll know how she swings once and for all. Okay?"

"Okay." Bebe wasn't at all convinced. The glare she'd received last night was not reassuring. Besides, she already had a gardener. One who came with Aunt Arlene's endorsement. She wasn't going to screw that up.

"Okay," she said, nodding firmly. Her friends were leaving right after breakfast. She would appease them, and then after they'd left, she'd pack away her embarrassing love life, along with the beautiful negligee.

CHAPTER SIX

C unt."
Bebe sighed and tried again. "No. Cont-tent-ment. Contentment. Come on, Darling. Try for me. There's a good boy."

"Cunt."

"You're doing it deliberately, aren't you?"

"Tennnt...mennnttt." Darling cracked his beak with evil-eyed relish.

Bebe gasped. "Oh, Darling. You nearly had it. Cont-tent-ment. One more time, you clever boy. Come on. Con...tent...me—"

"Cunt."

"That's it! I'm through. You can roll in your own filth for all I care. Dirty bird!" Bebe stalked away from her feathery nemesis before she wrung his scrawny neck.

Reluctantly, she went back to her laptop and the work she'd been avoiding all morning. Attempting to teach Darling a new affirmation was pure distraction, and she knew it. With a puff of resignation, she read back over what she'd written so far.

```
        A1 - Title Sequence
           - Titles End


1 - INT. STRIP JOINT DRESSING ROOM
Berry Ripe in a rhinestone Rodeo bikini. She
faces Rodriquez Diablo. She is angry.
```

BERRY
That's blackmail, you pig!

Rodriquez laughs cruelly:

RODRIQUEZ
Did you really think there'd be no
consequences, Berry? Being a renowned
orthopedic surgeon by day and an exotic
dancer by night?

Rodriquez throws her sequined Stetson at her:

RODRIQUEZ
Or perhaps I should call you Wild Ride Sally
from the Big O ranch?

Berry runs at him and pounds his chest with
her fists:

BERRY
You'll never get away with it!
I won't let you. I won't let you.
I'd rather die!

Rodriquez laughs cruelly:

RODRIQUEZ
You can't stop me, Berry. Can't you see? At
last I have you. You're mine! Mine!

Rodriquez laughs cruelly and grabs Berry in a
crushing kiss.

Camera fix on Berry's eyes as they flutter
closed in surrender.

Fade.

"Oh God, it's such crap." Mournfully, Bebe scanned the lines. *I hate* Valley of Our Stupid Fathers. *They should turn it into a reservoir. Hey, I wonder if Carter would buy that idea—*

"Hello? Miss Franklin?"

She looked up at the call to see a large Hispanic man hovering by the kitchen door.

"Teodor?"

She'd telephoned him yesterday to remind him that Arlene wanted him to come over in early May and do a general clean up. Bebe rose from the kitchen table and went to shake his hand.

Okay, so Mr. T wasn't the sexy gardening girl with the chilling eyes, but he *was* Aunt Arlene's regular man and a damn good gardener according to Esme. It suited Bebe just fine not to follow her friends' instructions. She was far too lily-livered to contact the woman from Petty's, if she ever found out who she was or where she worked.

"I'm pleased to meet you, Teodor. Thanks for coming over so soon."

"Please, everyone round here calls me Mr. T." He gave her a big grin and pulled a piece of paper from his back pocket. "I got the list. You okay if I grab my gear from the truck and get started?"

His grin widened into a big, happy smile that made Bebe feel everything was going to be all right. It was such a relief that the hassle of looking after such a large garden was so easily taken care of.

"Yes, please. Do whatever you need to. Would you like a cup of coffee?"

He shook his head. "No, thank you. Best get started. I'm gonna be trimming the hedges so it'll be noisy for a while, okay?"

"Go for it."

With the garden in Mr. T's capable hands, Bebe returned to her own work problems. Her next teleconference with Carter was only four days away, and she needed more on paper if she was going to sell him her idea.

"Bebe! Call an ambulance now!" Esme stuck her head through the open kitchen door and disappeared again almost as quickly. Bebe started to her feet, grabbed the cordless phone, and ran out after her.

"Esme, what is it? What's—Oh my God."

Mr. T was lying on the path by the side door to the garage. Esme was on her knees beside him.

"What happened to him?" Bebe cried. "Is he electrocuted?"

❖

Clara and the car behind her pulled over to let the ambulance pass. It raced along the causeway road heading toward Preston.

Someone's in trouble. Superstitiously, she tapped the wooden luck beads dangling from her rearview mirror. *Wonder if we'll get a call? How morbid am I?*

"Step on it!" Temperance popped up beside her. Clara swerved sharply into oncoming traffic.

"Jesus. You nearly gave me a heart attack!" She pulled back into her lane as cars sailed past with angry toots. "Can't you warn me or something?"

"If you want the dead to knock, hold a séance."

"It's rude to hurl yourself into a moving vehicle. I could have had an accident."

"Stop whining and follow that ambulance."

Clara cursed but followed. She was on her way to Esme's, the rear of her truck laden with Sugar Snack tomato plants.

"This is ridiculous. I feel like a vulture, trundling around town after an ambulance. What if people see me?"

"They'll think you care about your job."

"They'll think I'm a ghoul. Just tell me what's happening. Why am I doing this?" But Temperance had already vanished. "Damn it, Temperance. The sooner you pass over, the better."

Clara was nervous now. Temperance had done this to her before, directing her to Bebe's fender bender. Had something else happened? Clara sped up a little.

She caught up with the emergency vehicle as it hit Main Street. People stopped in their tracks to watch the flashing lights pass. It headed east, toward the end of town where Esme lived. Street after street, corner after corner, Clara's concern grew as the ambulance zoned in on her aunt's residential area. Her alarm heightened when the ambulance turned onto Hope Street where Esme lived, but it cruised past her house and rounded the corner.

With a puff of relief, Clara pulled into Esme's driveway and watched the ambulance drive out of sight. Despite Temperance's dictates, she was not going to follow it any further. She started unloading the first few tomato plants, then ambled around to the back door wondering if Esme knew about this latest excitement. The door was locked. Clara set the plants down and fumbled in her pocket for the key. It was strange for Esme to be out when she knew Clara was on her way over. This, combined with an ambulance in the neighborhood, unnerved her all over again. She instinctively knew something was going on and that Esme, as ever, was in the thick of it. Esme had a nose for spectacle.

Through a gap in the yard hedges Clara watched the ambulance lights flash down Mercy Avenue. It came to a halt partway down— in front of Arlene's house!

Clara took off at a gallop. She sprinted past her truck and hurled herself around the corner. A knot of neighbors clustered on Arlene's front lawn watching the paramedics jump into action. Clara increased her pace, her feet pounding the sidewalk. Esme was bound to be involved. *Please let her be okay.*

Esme's silver head popped up in the crowd. She was talking to a paramedic and gesturing toward the garage, totally in charge. Clara's pace slackened slightly as relief flooded her. Esme was okay. She continued her jog, buzzing with adrenaline. What the hell was going on? Had Bebe managed to detonate the ancient boiler after all?

Clara arrived just as Mr. T was brought out in a wheelchair and hoisted into the back of the ambulance. The doors were slammed and it took off at a more sedate pace than it had arrived. Clara joined Esme who was talking calmly into a cell phone.

"Yes, Minerva. The ambulance has just gone…He's fine…" Minerva was Teodor's wife. Esme was letting her know he was on his way to the hospital. "I found the EpiPen in his bag and gave him a dose…He was conscious all the time…Yes…Yes, he could talk. He told me where to look…Uh huh…If you leave now you'll probably get there before the ambulance." She looked up and smiled at Clara. "No. Clara's here. She'll be happy to drive his truck over and put the keys in the mailbox…Stop worrying, Minerva. He'll be fine. Bye." Esme ended the call.

"What the hell happened?" Clara was finally able to ask.

Esme linked her arm. "Come in and have a cup of tea and we'll tell you all about it. It's getting chilly out here."

Clara noticed Bebe hovering at Esme's other elbow. Her face was pale, her eyes large and fretful. She glanced quickly at Clara before coloring up and looking sharply away. She seemed very uncomfortable. Esme steered them through the dispersing bystanders cheerfully deflecting questions, until they reached the rear of the house. The back door was open and Bebe's laptop sat on the kitchen table. A half-eaten sandwich and a cold cup of tea sat beside it. Bebe plopped down disconsolately before her computer. She stared at the blank screen for a moment before snapping the lid shut. Clara watched her warily. She looked very upset.

Esme motioned for Clara to take a seat as she busied herself with the kettle.

"Clara, let me *finally* introduce you to Bebe. Clara's my niece, Bebe. She runs the family firm, Dearheart Funeral Directors."

Clara murmured hello and watched carefully as Bebe answered with a vague mumble and avoided all eye contact. From the high color on her cheeks, it was obvious she remembered their earlier meetings. Between the nosebleed in the street and the drunken episode at Petty's, neither was a particularly auspicious occasion. Clara was uncomfortable, too. She hadn't intended visiting Arlene's house while Bebe was here. She hadn't intended meeting Bebe at all, yet here they were sitting awkwardly at the kitchen table, a solid wall of embarrassment between them. Now that they were face-to-face, Clara felt more than a little contrite about her aloof behavior. Perhaps she shouldn't have been so openly judgmental. Which was worse—Bebe and her friends being drunk and incredibly raucous or Clara being sober and incredibly rude?

Clara deflected her awkwardness by asking, "What happened to Mr. T?"

"He came around to trim the hedges…" Esme tailed off as she hunted for the tea caddy. "Arlene arranged it before she left." She located the tea container and dropped four heaped teaspoons into the heated pot.

"I didn't know he had a peanut thing," Bebe said miserably, still staring at her laptop lid.

"Peanut thing?" Clara frowned at her.

"Allergy," Esme said. "Teodor has a serious peanut allergy. Luckily, he always carries his epinephrine injector with him."

Clara looked in question at the half-eaten peanut butter and jelly sandwich abandoned on the table.

"You gave him a pb and j sandwich?" she asked Bebe incredulously.

"No. That's mine. I ate that," Bebe answered, flustered at a perceived accusation.

"So? You kissed him?" Clara asked uncertainly. It was the only logical outcome she could think of. She bit back a grin even as she said the words.

"What? No! I shook his hand. God. Kissed him! Pfft." Bebe finally looked at her, eyes brimming with dismay at the thought of kissing Mr. T.

And she makes her living with words? Clara's eyebrows rose. She looked across to Esme who, while sympathetic for Mr. T's plight, had a twinkle of merriment in her eye. It seemed Bebe could do no wrong in her book.

"I shook his hand. Could that do it?" Bebe asked.

"I very much doubt a handshake was the cause," Esme said. "He somehow started an attack himself." She poured boiling water into the teapot. "I knew he was coming over today and I wanted to check if Bebe was okay with the list we drew up. I popped over and he was flat on his back by the garage wall. We called the ambulance just to be on the safe side."

Clara looked across at Bebe who sat in a pool of abject guilt.

"Do you think he'll sue?" Bebe took off her glasses and rubbed the bridge of her nose. She blinked woefully at Esme.

Clara found herself staring intently at her eyes. They were a beautiful color. Vacation brochure blue, like sunny skies and Caribbean seas. Clara could swim in that blue. A slow, lazy backstroke in ever decreasing circles, drawing closer to the inky whirlpool of iris. Bebe's eyes were warm and expressive, not the cold, washed out Atlantic grays of Clara's eyes.

With the sunlight pouring through the window, her hair flamed like bright copper. It reminded Clara of saucepans hanging in shiny rows on a kitchen rack. A burnished red gold curtain that swung heavily against the creamy curve of her cheek—

"Won't it, Clara?"

Clara started. Esme and Bebe were both looking at her. She'd missed the question.

"Sorry…what did you say?" she asked Esme.

Esme gave her a quizzical look.

"Just that no one will be looking at a lawsuit. This is Preston, not the city, and Bebe was never informed of his allergy. Lord knows he gives himself an attack at least twice a year. Minerva will scold, but that's about it."

"Yeah. True," Clara said, looking out the window at the wide expanse of Arlene's lawns, the crowded flowerbeds, and the large vegetable plot just about to get underway. It was an enormous garden, well laid out and lovingly tended, and a lot more work than Esme's.

"Though I'd rather be sued than scolded by Minerva. She has a viper's tongue," she said distractedly, roughly calculating the man-hours needed to keep the garden ticking over on essentials alone. Bebe would need to find a replacement gardener very soon. Minerva was a jealous, spiteful woman. When she found out Bebe had contaminated her husband by merely touching him, it was unlikely she'd let him return. Minerva was a religious zealot, besotted with divine vengeance. Bebe would be cast as an evil young temptress and Teodor's latest brush with "death" as a warning for her portly, genial husband to avoid adulterous thoughts. Bebe would definitely have to find another gardener until Arlene returned to make the peace.

"You'll have to help find a replacement gardener," Clara told Esme.

"Maybe we could help out ourselves?" Esme said.

But already Clara was shaking her head. "I'm crazy busy, and it's too big a garden. But I may know someone who could help. Let me check him out and get back to you." This she directed to Bebe who nodded with relief.

"Thank you," she said.

Clara rose to her feet. She didn't want to stay for tea after all. Those blue eyes unnerved her, and she had tomato plants lying all over Esme's back path, never mind Mr. T's truck to return.

"I need to go deliver Teodor's truck." She used it as an excuse to take her leave. She could feel Esme's scowl burrowing into her back.

"I'll catch you later," she said, unconcerned at Esme's dismay. With a polite good-bye to Bebe, she made her own way out.

❖

Clara's guess was right. The next morning Bebe called Mrs. T to see how Mr. T was doing and was left with scorched ears and moist eyes. Apparently, the Devil would be needing fleece lined thermals before Mrs. T allowed her husband anywhere near Bebe Franklin again. She made it sound as if Bebe had sat at an upstairs window with poison darts and a blowgun.

Bebe stared into space. What was she going to do now? She needed to find a new gardener quickly before Aunt Arlene's garden became a jungle, or worse, a litter box for every cat in the county. She reached for the local newspaper and flipped to the want ads; if they ran a professional services column she could spend the morning hunting down a new gardener.

Her head was buried in the newspaper when an acrid, unpleasant smell made her nose twitch. Smoke! She looked up aghast; wafts of smoke hung in hazy layers across the living room like a soft sea fog. Bebe leapt to her feet. Where had it come from? Oh God, was something on fire?

In the kitchen, Darling squawked and scuffled agitatedly in the gap between the cupboards and the ceiling. Bebe fully expected to find a pot left smoldering on the stove, but nothing was burning and the smell of smoke actually receded in the kitchen.

"Here, sweetheart," she called to Darling, relieved when he flapped down onto the window ledge. Bebe grabbed him before he hurt himself against the glass. He was surprisingly docile in her hands, for once comforted by her presence.

"Good boy, Darling." Bebe gathered him up gently and set him in his cage, tossing in a treat to pacify him.

The smoke was not originating from the kitchen, so Bebe returned to the living room. That room was clear as well. Bright sunshine beamed through the large picture windows and dust motes swirled in the air. There was no sign of smoke tendrils. Bebe wondered if she'd imagined it. She lifted a cushion from the couch and sniffed it; a faint sooty sourness clung to the fabric. The smoke had been real. She knelt by the chimney and peered up into the gloom. There was no smell of burning, but then she hadn't lit a fire since arriving. The windows were open. Could smoke have blown in from outside? She went to the kitchen door. Several yards up someone had lit a small bonfire in their yard. Weak wisps of smoke rose in a straight column. That had to be it. Somehow smoke from the neighboring fire had blown into her house. Though it was a weak effort for a yard fire, and there was hardly a breeze to blow it toward her. Perhaps the wind had turned, or the fire had burned right down? She had no other options; that had to be it.

Bebe opened every window on the ground floor and sat for several minutes watching fresh air stir the living room curtains. She did one more circuit of the house before shutting the windows tight. The mystery hadn't been satisfactorily resolved and left her with nagging doubts, but she had more immediate problems. She desperately needed a gardener. With a coffee mug in one hand and the local newspaper in the other, she sat at the kitchen table to keep a disgruntled Darling company and focused on the classifieds.

❖

A few days later, Bebe was no further forward. The classifieds had a few numbers, but she was unsure about what to ask for. What type of work needed to be tackled first? And what was the local rate for gardening work anyway? Because she'd derailed Mr. T and her aunt's schedule, Bebe was going to have to pay for the substitute gardener out of her own thin purse. She couldn't believe her cruddy luck.

She shook out the pages of the local paper and sipped her latte, wedged into a cozy corner table at the Bean There Drunk That coffee house on Main Street. Her head was buried in the want ads when the door tinkled as another customer entered.

"Bebe. How nice to see you. May I join you?" Esme bustled in, weighed down with overflowing shopping bags.

"Of course, Esme." Bebe moved her handbag and cleared the seat next to her. Over the past weeks she had come to see Esme as a friend rather than someone her aunt had badgered into keeping an eye on her.

"What a beautiful day. Summer is on the way. " Esme dropped into the seat. She signaled at the waiter, who immediately brought over a filter coffee. "Thank you, Samuel."

"No problemo, Ms. D." He wandered away again.

"You're a regular then." Bebe grinned at the special treatment.

"Oh, he's one of my ex students. When you've taught several generations in a small town like Preston, you get special treatment. Especially if the kids liked you," Esme said, settling into her seat. Bebe had an idea all the kids liked Esme Dearheart.

"And you're right," Esme continued. "I am a regular. Clara usually waits for me here while I do my Wednesday shop, but she's waylaid this morning. She'll stop by soon for lunch, then we're popping over to the garden center."

"Garden center? Damn, that's where I should have looked." Bebe's head jerked at the simplicity of it all. "I bet there's a ton of part time gardeners advertised there."

"Part time gardeners?"

"Mr. T isn't allowed back."

"Ah." Esme nodded wisely.

"So I need to find a new gardener. There's bound to be a service list at the garden center. I'm so dumb. I never thought to look there."

Esme looked dubious. "Has Clara come back to you with any possibilities?"

"Not yet." Bebe pretended interest in an elderly couple leaving. She hadn't expected Clara to get back to her. It was clear Esme's niece had taken an instant dislike to her.

"Perhaps I could persuade Clara to help," Esme said. "She's fantastic at all those heavy jobs. It would be much better than bringing in a man from the mainland. You'd need references and the like, and that takes time. Especially when you're new to the community."

"I need someone fast, Esme. The grass sort of sprung up overnight. And the hedges are a mess. And there are flowers everywhere, which is lovely, but some are dying off and I'm not sure if I should leave them to rot away or dig up the bulbs or deadhead them—"

"Leave them for now, dear. I'll come over and give you a hand with the flowerbeds. Arlene keeps some bulbs in the ground and lifts others. The seed heads she mostly collects for next year. I know what's what." Esme reached over and patted Bebe's hand soothingly. "There's really nothing to get so worked up about."

"Oh." Bebe bit her lip. She hadn't thought about Aunt Arlene's plans for next year's seedbeds. Now there was a possibility she could screw things up for the following year, too. This gardening thing was all so meticulous and organized. She was bound to destroy it.

"Don't worry. I'm sure that between us we can do most of the light stuff if Clara takes over some of the heavier chores," Esme said. "Oh, here she is, right on time. Let's ask her."

"Ask me what?" Clara approached, looking from Esme to Bebe and back again, her eyes slick with suspicion. Bebe gave a sickly smile and swallowed. She felt awful about the sleazy conversation she'd shared with her friends. It was all right when you didn't know who you were drunkenly sexually objectifying. Horrible when it turned out to be the favorite niece of your newest friend. Thank goodness neither of them knew.

Her gaze lingered a little too long on Clara's face. It was pleasant to look at. Her features were square and strong, and her left cheek had a secret dimple that only showed when her lips twitched. Mostly they twitched in annoyance, but once, Bebe had sworn there was nearly a smile. Clara's eyes were a pale, weathered gray rimmed with dark, spiky lashes. She had the same elegant sweep of eyebrow as Esme. Her hair was collar length, dark and unruly, and curled in any direction it wished. She wasn't beautiful, but Bebe found her face fascinating. *I wish she liked me. I wish I knew how I ticked her off so monumentally.* The distressed little thought drifted through her head before she could catch it and shove the silly thing aside.

"Mr. T isn't coming back for the foreseeable future," Esme said.

Bebe pulled her gaze from Clara's face. Instead, she focused on the pulse that fluttered against the tight skin of her throat.

"So I wondered if you could help Bebe with the garden?" Esme continued. "With the bigger jobs?"

Clara stiffened. Bebe noticed at once and was mortified.

"No!" she blurted, embarrassed at Clara's discomfort with the suggestion. She was a little too hasty with her rejection. Esme looked at her in surprise, while Clara sat down and sullenly watched her as she tried to rectify her gaffe. "No. I mean, really. It wouldn't be fair. You need Clara for your own garden. I'm happy to find someone else. Honestly," she said, her face flamed and her eyes widened with manufactured sincerity.

"Well, *I'm* not happy with that, Bebe." Esme sounded stubborn.

"So Minerva struck you off Mr. T's 'To Do' list." Clara stated rather than asked.

"She called me a poisonous copperhead snake." Bebe hogged the front seat on her very own guilt trip.

"Ouch." Clara barely concealed a smile. The dimple popped on her left cheek.

"I think we should help Bebe out." Esme turned to Clara, obviously expecting full support.

"Thank you both, but I'd rather get a regular gardener. I'll need one until Aunt Arlene gets back and fixes things with Mrs. T," Bebe said. She was not going to be moved on this. No way did she want eye-candy Clara bending over in her garden, ruffling her bloomers, or poking her petals, or cross-fertilizing her whatevers. Her cheeks blazed. The woman didn't even like her.

"I agree. You need a proper gardener." Clara sided with her, earning a dismayed look from Esme. "And I think I found someone who could help out."

"And who exactly would that be?" Esme asked.

"Billy Hoff."

Esme snorted. "That nincompoop? He nearly killed Raymond White's mimosas with the weed-whacker. Stripped the bark right off them at ground level. Raymond was livid."

"It was a mistake. He's usually okay," Clara told Bebe, playing down Esme's criticism.

Bebe shrugged indifferently. "I thought mimosa was a champagne cocktail."

"He also dumped rhubarb leaves in the compost bin. Ruined the lot of it. No. He won't do. He's next to useless," Esme declared, deliberately turning her back on Clara and fixing Bebe with a steely look. "Bebe, *I* will help you in the garden until we find someone suitable. Not some idiot who will put a rake through his foot on the first day."

Bebe blanched. "I can so see that."

Clara was not amused at Esme's volunteering. "You can't do that—"

"And neither it seems, can you," Esme interrupted.

"No, really. I'll get a man in." Bebe tried again. She didn't want them falling out over her self-made predicament. "I'll find one on the garden center services board."

"You'll get no one unless I vet him first. Arlene would never forgive me," Esme stated, tapping her forefinger on the tabletop. "And Billy Hoff is *not* on the list."

Clara sat back in her seat, arms folded, her face closed. Esme sat ramrod straight in her chair. Bebe's gaze flicked from one to the other. She was confused at the standoff. Why on earth should her garden woes cause such discord between these two? There was a subtext here she was totally failing to read.

CHAPTER SEVEN

"You're exhausted." Clara glared at Esme. "Have you been over at Arlene's again? I thought I told you to take it easy. What about your heart?"

It had been a week since the conversation in the coffee house. Esme had emphatically ignored Clara's advice to hire Billy Hoff as a stopgap. Instead, she seemed determined to work in the garden with Bebe most afternoons, returning sweaty and exhausted by dinnertime. Clara knew Esme was doing this out of pure mule headedness. That she was still annoyed Clara had not volunteered her services, or even given a plausible explanation as to why she had refused. In Preston, people helped their neighbors. It was the right thing to do. But what could Clara say? *I overheard Bebe and her friends calling me sexy. They told her to grab me for a summer fling...and it scared me.*

She knew given half the chance Esme would be in there with them, goading Bebe on. And that was exactly what Clara wanted to avoid, Esme's misdirected matchmaking. City-birds like Bebe wanted a distraction to liven up the small town boredom of places like Preston. Clara could never be a passing romance for anyone; she was a one-woman gal. God, how she knew that for a fact! She just wished Esme would accept it, too.

"Look at the state of your hands. Why weren't you wearing gloves?" she scolded her. Esme's fingers were covered with small cuts and scratches.

"I set them down somewhere and lost them." Esme stiffly rotated her shoulders, grimacing with the effort.

"What were you doing?" Clara said. "You're stiff as a board."

"Oh, that half planted rockery. It's not draining right. I thought we should remove some of the rocks and dig in more sand."

"What?" Clara was aghast. "I thought you were helping with the light stuff, like weeding and dead heading, not moving a ton of rock like some…some Tonka truck. Stop it at once before you get sick."

Clara was angry. She knew Esme was taking on these heavy, awkward jobs to force her into volunteering. It was out-and-out manipulation. Esme had a slight heart attack several years ago and it terrified Clara that she was overdoing it now. It also made her furious that Esme was abusing these fears to bully her into gardening for Bebe.

"It's not going to work, old lady," she said. "You'll end up in Bangor Hospital with nobody but yourself to blame. And I will make a point of visiting you *every* day just to stand at the foot of your bed and tell you what a jackass you are."

"Oh, Clara. Why won't you help her? She's a lovely girl, and Arlene's a good friend to you, as well as me. It seems churlish not to help." Esme tried the plaintive approach. Clara scowled, uncomfortable with the direct question. She had no real reason to refuse, apart from a feeling of discomfort around Bebe that she didn't want to examine too closely. She did not want to go near Bebe Franklin; the very thought made her guts quiver with nervousness.

"Please, Clara. For Arlene's sake?" Esme was playing the last of her lowdown dirty cards. "It would be such a nice thing to do. Bebe needs help, and I promise to find another gardener as soon as possible. Only someone Arlene would approve of, not a machete-wielding fool like that Hoff boy," Esme said and picked at a newly formed scab on her finger until it bled. She sucked in her breath as if in pain.

Clara watched the tiny ruby bubble squeeze out of Esme's index finger and sighed. She was beaten. Esme would always get her own way because she was a master manipulator. But Clara was far from happy. She'd seen a side of Bebe Franklin her aunt didn't know existed—a selfish, brash side that made Clara want to keep her distance. If Esme insisted she close that distance then Clara would have to come up with some other strategy that allowed her to work alongside Bebe but manage to keep aloof from all her shallow city nonsense.

❖

Clara recognized Arlene McCall's station wagon. She didn't recognize the curvy denimed bottom sticking out of it, though she had a good idea who it might belong to. It didn't stop her from looking.

She hunched down further in her seat and drummed her fingers on the steering wheel. Esme was taking forever, as usual. No doubt she had bumped into a crony in the garden center and was yakking away. Clara glanced at her watch. She would be late back from lunch and Ronnie would bitch.

Bebe Franklin heaved another fertilizer bag from her cart into the back of the Mitsubishi. It was an excruciating spectacle. It wasn't that the bags were particularly heavy, just awkwardly shaped and covered in slippery plastic. Bebe used both arms and a knee to drag the bag up into a bear hug before wobbling over to the car and lugging it into the back. Then she collapsed across it and somehow shunted it into place before reeling back to the cart for the next one. It was a cumbersome maneuver, and knowing Bebe's track record, a catastrophe waiting to happen.

Clara drummed her fingers harder. Still no sign of Esme. Everywhere she went she found someone to gossip with for hours. Bebe was on her third sack. Her top half was buried in the back of the car shoving bags around. She leaned so far in the toes of her sneakers scratched the asphalt. Her bottom wriggled. Clara's hand moved to the door handle. She should go over and help. There were several more bags to load, and at the rate Bebe was going it would be nightfall before she finished. Clara slammed the truck door and strode over.

"Here, let me." She grabbed a bag from the cart and tossed it into the back of the station wagon. Bebe looked at her in amazement.

"Oh. Thank you," she said, pushing her glasses back in place. Her hair was mussed and her face shone with sweat. "You make it look easy."

"It's in the grip. I'll toss and you tidy, okay?" Clara threw in another bag and waited for Bebe to do her part. "Are you planning on digging all this in?"

"Yes." Bebe was bright eyed with enthusiasm. "It's mostly for the vegetables and the big back border. It was one of Mr. T's jobs."

Clara heard herself harrumph like a grumpy old woman. *I'm growing more like Esme every damn day.* "It's backbreaking work." *And you can barely lift the bags. Esme's right, you'll never manage the garden.* "Have you got a gardener yet?"

"Not quite. And please don't tell Esme you saw me get this stuff, okay?"

"Why?" Clara tossed a bag.

"I know it's hard work but I want to do it myself. If Esme gets wind of it she'll insist on helping, and I'm worried she's overdoing it. She looks so exhausted these days and I try to make her do the lightest work possible, but she'll hear none—"

"You're preaching to the choir. I know how she is." Clara threw the last bag in the back of the station wagon and reached in to straighten it, along with the others. Bebe hadn't done a very good job. "How will you unload all this?"

"One at a time. Even if I have to drive around with a car full of fertilizer all summer." Bebe's smile was infectious. Clara scrabbled for the antidote. She didn't want to share a joke or even a smile with Bebe. She wanted no friendship or closeness between them whatsoever. She reminded herself that she was a sour, humorless, battered human being, the antithesis of sunny, strawberry blond Bebe Franklin, and that helped keep her lips glued in a straight line.

"I suppose it's a plan," she said and wiped her hands on her jeans. "I better get back."

"Thank you again," Bebe said. With a gruff good-bye, Clara walked back to her truck. From the corner of her eye, she could see

Esme coming out of the garden center. Best to grab her and go if Bebe wanted to keep her secret, she decided.

"Here I am." Esme clambered into the truck and set her shopping at her feet. "All done. Do we have time for lunch?"

"Bean There?" Clara asked, putting the truck in gear and moving off.

"Yes. Will we get a table at this time—Oh! Is that Bebe?"

Clara grunted distractedly and drove on.

"I wonder what she's doing here. I didn't see her inside." Esme craned her neck to look back as Clara trundled on toward the exit. "She's got a load of fertilizer," Esme exclaimed. "I told her I'd arrange that. What's she up to? Oh stop, Clara. Let's ask her to join us for lunch."

"I can't stop. There's a car up my ass." Clara pulled out onto the causeway road and turned for Preston. Esme settled in her seat and gave her a disappointed look.

"You don't like her, do you," she said.

"I don't even know her."

"Why are you so peevish about her?"

"I'm not peevish. I am far from peevish. I've barely spoken to her and you keep pushing—"

"So that's it. You think I'm matchmaking even though I've told you time and again I'm not," Esme said.

"It's not that," Clara lied. "I've told you I'm busy, yet you keep pressuring me to do her garden."

"I'm not pressuring you. It was an honest request for help." Esme looked out the window. "Forget I even asked."

"I already said I'd help when I have time." Clara knew she sounded snippy but didn't much care.

"I don't understand you."

"That's because you're not listening to me."

"Oh, I hear you well enough." Esme sniffed. "And I hear a fool. I don't know what nonsense you have in your head about Bebe, but she's a lovely girl."

"I never said she wasn't." Clara kept her opinions to herself.

"Kind, mannerly, smart. Sweet on the eye. You could do a whole lot worse and have d—" Esme broke off.

"Have done? Were you going to say have done?"

Esme stayed silent and continued to gaze out the passenger side window.

"Is this about Frances?" Clara's voice was tight. They never spoke about Frances. It was their unwritten rule.

"It's time you sat up and looked around you. Life's passing you by, Clara, and it's not healthy. That's all I meant."

"Next it will be platitudes about Frances not wanting me to sit around moping. How she'd want me to go looking for her replacement."

"Don't be ridiculous." Esme's voice was full of cool, school marmish authority. "Frances would never want that," she murmured almost inaudibly.

They drove on in moody silence, the bonhomie of the morning in tatters. After several minutes Clara found herself searching for a peace offering. "You took forever back there. Who did you meet?"

"There's a new sales assistant. She's called Sandy Bergson and she lives over in Rockland with her parents. Her father's a denturist and her mother works part time in real estate. She's just graduated in ceramics and this is a summer job. She's single, and I think she'd be perfect for Ronnie," Esme said, her good humor bouncing back as she rattled off Sandy's checklist.

"What's a denturist?"

"Makes false teeth."

"Ah. And why would you point her at Ronnie? Did she short change you?"

"Don't be trite. It doesn't suit your glower. I noticed she had a motorcycle T-shirt, and she's tall."

"That's it? That's the science of matchmaking. Tall with a T-shirt?"

"It's all in the gut." Esme rat-a-tatted her flat stomach with the palm of her hand. "I have my own gifts, Clara. You had best respect them."

Clara snorted and pulled into the last free parking space before the Bean There Drunk That diner. "Bestow your gifts on Ronnie all you want. I can look after myself."

❖

In the fourth round of the Town Traders pool competition Dearhearts were pitted against the Lucky Shrimp bait shop. They were a tough team but not unbeatable, except Clara hadn't practiced and it showed. Her last shot was sloppy and had left the table wide open.

"Strugggggglinng..." Benjamin sang as he sailed past with a loaded tray. She slouched against the wall and watched the opposition mop up. Ronnie sat at her side sulking. Clara was fed up and wished the game was over. She turned away from the easy winning shot and noticed Bebe sitting by the bar chatting with Benjamin.

"You played like shit," Ronnie groused.

"Ah shaddup. I'll buy you a beer," she mumbled and wandered over to the bar fishing a ten out of her pocket. She stood next to Bebe's barstool.

"Hi," she said awkwardly, curious at Bebe showing up at the local watering hole. Apart from the good food, Petty's was hardly a tourist trap. Before she could say anything more, Doyle breezed over and straddled the barstool on the other side of Bebe.

"Hey there. Let me get you a beer." He waved Benjamin over and ordered before Bebe had a chance to respond.

"Benjamin," Bebe called after the barman. "Cancel that beer, thanks." She turned to Doyle. "I'm okay with my Coke, thank you, Officer Doyle. I'm just about to go, anyway."

"Call me Frank." He tried to hide his dismay at her polite refusal.

"I'm fine with my Coke, Frank. Thank you."

She turned immediately to Clara. The relief on her face at having other company for a distraction was obvious. She had Clara's sympathy. Doyle could be pesky with the ladies, but he was usually easy enough to derail. He had no follow-through if his first attempts got the brush-off. Clara could see him sitting forlornly behind Bebe, unsure how to catch her attention now that his offer of a beer had been rejected.

"Hi, Clara." Bebe promptly turned beet red. "So…did you win?"

Doyle gave a loud derisive snort, but they ignored him. Clara nodded over to a woebegone Ronnie.

"Does that look like the face of a winner?"

Bebe flicked him a look. "Was it really that bad?"

"A total rout. And only myself to blame, as Ronnie keeps reminding me. I didn't practice enough. It was a busy week."

"Oh dear," Bebe said. "If you're busy things must be bad."

"Huh?"

"Well, if *you're* busy then people are dying." Bebe was floundering on this particular conversation point and Clara decided to unwind a little and rescue her.

"Yeah. It's better that way. They sue if I bury them and they're not dead." Clara was pleasantly surprised at how easy it was to talk nonsense with her. "That was a lame funeral parlor joke, by the way. We're not noted for our humor."

Bebe seemed to relax, her awkward blushing calmed and her face regained its normal creamy complexion. No sooner had Clara congratulated herself on her conversational flair than an uncomfortable silence welled up between them.

"So…you like Petty's?" Clara struggled to keep the chat going. Her eyes fixed on the curve of Bebe's cheek then drifted to her mouth. It was cherry ripe, moist, and very lovely. She didn't want to order her beers and quickly move away. She wanted to linger and make clever small talk so as to slyly look at Bebe. When had she become as foolish as Doyle? The tension left her body. It was nice just to relax and chat a little. How could there be any harm in that? She was only being polite, and Esme would approve.

"Benjamin told me Friday night was popular with the locals," Bebe said. "He nagged me into coming back for another visit."

It occurred to Clara that Bebe was indeed a local. She was certainly not a passing tourist. Bebe had family here. She was minding her aunt's house for most of the summer. Of course she wanted to fit in. Clara squirmed remembering her frosty behavior toward Bebe and her friends. Had her rudeness made Bebe avoid the place? She felt ashamed. Bebe must have recalled that awful night, too, for she took a massive gulp of her Coke and gave an embarrassed splutter.

"Usually I go for a long walk in the evenings, but tonight I decided to see what was going on here," she said, mopping her mouth. Clara considered this. Was Bebe lonely? She remembered Esme had suggested as much. Perhaps she should call around and help unload that fertilizer. Esme was right. It was churlish of her not to help, and the longer she held back, the worse she felt about it. The chores still to do were hard ones, and Esme looked ragged these days. Clara noted the cuts and scratches on Bebe's hands, just like Esme's. She was working just as hard.

"How's it going with the garden?" she asked. "Did you unload all the sacks?"

"I have only three left in the trunk," Bebe said with pride. "The garden is surprisingly okay. Your aunt is a very hard lady to please as far as part time gardeners go." Bebe gave a little smile. "But we're coping. We have to slow down soon as I have a deadline looming and I need to concentrate on that. And Esme has shown me how to keep on top of the light stuff. In fact, I've found out I actually enjoy gardening. It's a hobby I never considered before and now I'm hooked." Her smile broadened into a dazzler and Clara's breath hitched.

She had to help. There was no way Esme and Bebe could manage the bigger jobs. Suddenly, she didn't feel bullied by Esme anymore. It was obvious they really did need her and it was not just a matchmaking ruse on Esme's part. She'd avoided volunteering all this time, yet now she wanted to help out. Deep down she had a grudging respect for Bebe and all her hard work. And maybe it was time to cut Esme some slack and do as she asked for once. Plus, with any luck, Esme was concentrating on Ronnie's love life these days. Let him suffer for a change.

Bebe's lips closed around her straw in a pert, pink O, as she sucked up the last of her Coke, and Clara's gut jellified.

"What'll it be?" Benjamin called over the boom of the jukebox. He gave Clara a wide, smug smile. She guessed he'd won money on the pool game she'd just handed over.

"Two of the usual. Do you want another Coke?" she asked Bebe, who shook her head and slid off her stool. Her shoulder bumped against Clara's, and Clara wanted to lean into her. She put a hand on Bebe's forearm to steady her, then pulled back abruptly, flustered by the begging touch. *What's wrong with you? First you hate her; now you want to talk all night.*

"No, thanks. It's getting too loud in here. I think I'd better be going." Bebe shrugged on her jacket. "Bye."

Clara watched Bebe leave, annoyed she couldn't think of a way to keep her talking. She was as sad a specimen as Doyle. She wanted to make up for her earlier frostiness and wasn't sure how to, except by doing grunt work in Arlene's garden.

Bebe was friendly and polite, but there was an underlying awkwardness that neither of them could quite work around, and Clara knew she was responsible for it. She was annoyed she hadn't the panache to smooth out a new start.

"What's keeping that beer?" Ronnie appeared at her side as Benjamin delivered their drinks.

"Clara was chatting up Bebe," Doyle said.

Clara's head whipped round. "Not funny," she snapped, wiping the smile from his face.

"Hey. He's only messing with you. It's obvious she likes you." Benjamin tried to placate her.

"I didn't mean anything, Clara. A guy's gotta try, right?" Doyle said before slouching off.

Ronnie took a slug of beer. "Benjamin's right. She's been eyeing you all night."

"I was not chatting her up." Clara was obstinate. "It's not like that." There could be no doubt. She owed it to Frances.

"More fool you, then." Ronnie shrugged. "Wish a woman looked at me like that once in a while." He strolled away.

Benjamin still hovered. "Time rolls on, Clara. Nobody meant any harm and Doyle's an idiot. We all know that."

"I wasn't chatting her up. I said it's not like that." Clara scowled at her beer bottle and picked at the damp label.

"It should be like that, Clara. Don't feel bad. Frances has been gone almost four years," he said as gently as possible given the crowded bar and the thundering rock and roll. Clara kept picking at her label, refusing to raise her head and meet his eyes, then another customer hollered, and with a sigh Benjamin went to take his order.

Her shoulders relaxed once he moved away. Frances was not gone. That was part of the trouble, but Benjamin would never know that. Frances was out there, and her damning silence cut like a knife.

Clara waited long enough to half finish her beer, then took off. She knew her early exit would be put down to grumpiness at losing the match, but she didn't care. Everyone knew she was grumpy anyway.

She'd been thinking about offering Bebe friendship, that's all. Friendship. It annoyed her that people assumed she was hitting on her, the only other lesbian probably within a fifty miles radius. It annoyed her that people thought she would do that at all.

❖

Roses, roses, roses. The air was thick with roses…and vanilla, and crisp, clean linen off the wash line, the scents swirled around her as light and fluffy as spun cotton candy and Clara was the stick.

"What is it you want, Temperance?" Clara pulled the orange juice carton from the refrigerator and poured a glass. "I can smell you."

"Smell me? Are you insinuating—"

"It's a nice smell. Sweet. Mostly musk rose."

"Oh." Temperance sounded pleased. "Anyone in particular?"

"Dunno, maybe Narrow Water."

"That's a hybrid." Temperance sniffed, semi insulted.

"And a rambler, like you, old lady. When are you going to rest in peace, hmm?" Clara couldn't help but smile. She swung her fridge door closed to find Temperance standing directly behind it, lighting up her kitchen with a kaleidoscope of pink and white diamante lights. "What's up? You look worried."

"I am, Clara. Something's wrong. I'm worried all the time for Darling."

"Bebe seems to be doing a good job. He's still as happily obnoxious as ever."

"Don't be flippant. I sense things you can't, and I'm not happy. Will you go over and check on him for me?"

"Is this a setup?" Clara's suspicions rose. "Have you been talking to Esme?"

"Of course not. She can't see me. She doesn't have the Dearheart gift. Do you honestly think I'd be standing here talking to you if I could have a conversation with Esme?"

"True."

"I'd get some sense out of her. This isn't about you and your arrhythmia of a love life. Though Lord knows a good kick up the ass might get your heart pumping right," Temperance grumbled. "This is about my Darling. He's unhappy. Something's not right at Arlene's."

"I know, I know. Your ether's all out of whack and Darling's off his peanuts." Clara sighed in mock martyrdom. "Look, I'll drop by at some point this week, okay? Esme asked me to check out the hedges, and the rockery is not draining ri—"

"Good." Mission accomplished, Temperance was gone in a snap.

"You're welcome." Clara took her juice into the living room. "Feel free to drop in anytime and tell me what to think, feel, do, and say."

❖

Bebe and Esme met regularly over morning coffee to check out the latest list Bebe had culled from the want ads and garden center service boards. Esme sucked her teeth and tutted her way down it, scratching out names until, much to Bebe's consternation, no one was left. According to Esme, most of the hopefuls didn't know their Albiflora from an abalone.

One man, for instance, was an ex con, and "parole board or no, he was not getting within a hundred yards of an attractive young woman living alone." Another was a purported flasher and he "was not getting within a hundred yards of an attractive young woman living alone." The third had a well-known penchant for knives and skinned road kill for a hobby, "and he was not going to get within a hundred yards of..." Bebe got the picture.

"Well, I'm at my wits end." She crumpled yet another list and pitched it at the kitchen trashcan. "We need to pick someone soon, Esme. The hedges are running wild."

"Clara will help." Esme patted her hand. "She promised me she would." Her eyes gleamed with satisfaction. "Her mornings are free from next week on and she said she'd maybe call by on Monday."

Bebe frowned. Clara had been so adamant about not having any spare time. She had said as much the last time she'd seen her. Nevertheless, Bebe perked up. Finally, the capable, hardworking Clara would be onsite to sort out the bigger jobs, and maybe unload the last sacks from the car. Bebe's back was breaking. No matter how hard she and Esme toiled over flower borders, vegetable plots, and lawns, the undone jobs overshadowed everything they did.

She remembered the pool competition on Friday night. Clara had been relaxed and vaguely social, not frosty or affronted like on other encounters. Bebe had been flustered at first. Frank Doyle's bludgeoning attempt at charm had thrown her, but thankfully, Clara had been around so he had been easy to shake off. Bebe was glad of their chat for other reasons. It was nice to become better acquainted with the elusive Clara Dearheart.

Bebe had been secretly spying on her while she played her pool game. She had watched the T-shirt stretch across Clara's shoulders and ride up her back as she stretched for a long shot. She had cast sly sideways glances as her denim-clad bottom bent over the table. She had had leery thoughts that would have had Suzzee and Jayrah cheering.

When the game was over, Clara had come to chat, and Bebe panicked. What if her thoughts paraded across her face? She was useless with secrets, especially her own. She'd spent the next ten minutes wriggling on her stool in guilt and embarrassment, painfully aware of Benjamin's smug looks. He was gay. He knew the score. She had the hots for Clara Dearheart and that was that.

Her mind drifted to the champagne negligee lovingly folded in her bottom drawer. Clara might call by on Monday morning, Esme had said. Would Bebe ever be bold enough to follow her friends' seduction instructions and just happen to be wearing it while Clara toiled in the garden?

"I'll tell her to call you and arrange something." Esme's words pulled her out of her reverie. Bebe looked up to catch Esme giving her that same sly look she had seen on Benjamin's face.

❖

"Berry Ripe's life is in tatters. Her flaky mother has run off to Mexico with a toreador. Rodriquez is blackmailing her into his bed, plus she's facing a massive lawsuit over a surgical botch job on the president's son."

"Let's not forget the bomb making factory next door to her private practice."

Bebe sighed into the phone. "Yes. We have Jayrah to thank for that little gem."

"Okay, so what's Berry gonna do?" Suzzee asked.

"Kill herself. As simple as that." There was a hitch of breath at the other end as Suzzee digested this.

"At last. I love it! How does she die? Can I choose? Please. Please."

"If you want. As long as I can work with it. If you give me grief then I'll just do it my own way." Bebe was stern.

"She falls on a chainsaw."

"Suzzee—"

"Wait, wait. Drowns with stones in her pocket."

"Too Woolf."

"Head in the oven?"

"Too Plath."

Suzzee snorted. "Well, cutting her wrists is too Julius Caesar, and so clichéd."

"Caesar was stabbed in the back by his friends."

"Oh, how cool. Is that a maybe?"

"No. It's got to be suicide, not murder. I've already started this episode. It's got to be with Carter next week."

"He'll be doing a Caesar on us," Suzzee said rudely at the mention of Carter's name. "Backstabbing bastard."

"No. He'll do a Brutus on us. Brutus was the guy with the knife. But as I've had a target on my back for months it will come as no surprise." Bebe was calm in her acceptance of the inevitable. Two months in Preston's tranquil heartland could do that for a troubled soul. She knew beyond all doubt she wanted out of New York and out of *Valley of Our Fathers*, the sooner the better. But she needed to plan it carefully before she jumped. "So what's it to be? Choose your exit."

"I suppose a gun is the easiest." Suzzee sounded dubious. Belatedly, Bebe remembered Suzzee's cousin had been shot dead in a store robbery several years ago.

"To be honest that was my choice," she said. "But I'll understand if—"

"No. It's all right."

"Are you sure? What about your parents?" Bebe said, deciding the gun idea sucked.

"It's all right. They know it's only make-believe, Bebe. Plus I already told about the job in L.A. They don't care about Berry anymore. They're in love with Tanya Foo of the L.A.P.D. now."

"You signed! Congratulations, Suzzee."

"Well, almost. And I told Jayrah, and guess what? She's been offered a new job, too. Isn't that great. We're all bailing out at the same time. What will you do, Beebs?"

"I'm glad for Jayrah. What's her new deal?" Bebe ignored the question. She had no idea what she would do next. No one was offering her jobs.

"I'll let her tell you."

Bebe guessed Suzzee hadn't a clue what Jayrah was doing.

"It's time we all started out in new directions," Bebe said. She was glad her friends were choosing to jump rather than be pushed. She'd been sitting on that ledge forever. It was good to take control of the long drop down.

"How's it going with the gardener, by the way?" Suzzee asked out of the blue.

"It isn't. I chucked the idea on the compost where it belonged." Bebe wrinkled her nose as if she could smell the actual compost. "I don't think I'm the seductress type." She didn't mention her embryonic plan to be just "happening" to wear her sexy negligee whenever Clara came over next week. She was still uncertain and didn't want to discuss it with Suzzee. She would only manage to sully it somehow.

"You're too traditionally romantic."

"Oh?" Bebe was surprised at this. She'd never really thought about it. She was also surprised at the lack of reproach in Suzzee's voice at her latest romantic copout.

"Yeah. You want someone special to fall in love with you. And so you should, because you're worth it. You *deserve* love. You deserve happiness."

"Wow. That's nice of you, Suz."

"Really?" Suzzee sounded delighted. "I'm practicing my Tanya Foo. She's the touchy-feely type underneath a tough exterior. Always giving out heartfelt advice to people who get snuffed two scenes later, sort of thing."

"Oh. Well, you got it nailed." Bebe rolled her eyes. When would she learn?

"You should go for it anyway, Beebs," Suzzee said. "What do you have to lose? So she'll see you in your nightie, it's hardly an arrestable offense. Not even by Preston standards."

Darling screeched loudly and began rattling the bars of his cage, peppering the floor with sunflower husks and other debris. Bebe frowned at the mess.

"Suz, I have go. Darling has—"

"Okay, bye then." Suzzee hung up without further ado, leaving Bebe staring at the phone.

"Death by gunshot it is." Bebe replaced the receiver. "This is one scene I'm going to attack with creative relish."

She went to the kitchen closet for a broom to clean up Darling's mess. "Tanya Foo's" heartfelt advice made her smile, and the news about Jayrah's new job was hardly surprising, though Bebe had always assumed that out of all the writers, she'd be the first to go. She'd call Jayrah later tonight for all her news.

Bebe halted.

Smoke crept out from under the kitchen closet door. Gray and thick, it streamed through the gap at the bottom of the door like liquid. The closet held buckets and dusters, mops and brooms. There was nothing flammable stored in it. Bebe reached out a trembling hand. She couldn't believe it. She touched the wooden door. It was cool to her touch, no heat. The smoke swirled around her ankles and squirmed across the floor low and menacing like swamp gas. Her grasp tightened on the handle. It was dangerous to open a door on a possible blaze; she knew that. But she didn't believe this was a fire. It was mystery smoke, just like before. It was freaky and weird, and it was not real. She closed her eyes—and yanked the door open. Darling screeched.

Bebe opened her eyes and looked at the contents of the closet. She looked at her feet. The kitchen floor was littered with the dust and shells from Darling's cage, nothing more. There was no smoke. Nothing. Bebe looked around her. The room was absolutely clear. A small bead of blood trickled onto her top lip, and she fumbled in her cardigan pocket for a clean tissue to press to her nose. She was stressed to high heaven.

"Darling," she said quietly. "Is this house haunted?"

CHAPTER EIGHT

B ebe pulled the champagne negligee up over her head and tossed it on the bed for the umpteenth time. *No. I'm not doing it. I'll never carry it off. I have all the womanly wiles of a walrus.*

Darling squawked from the banister railings outside her open bedroom door.

"And you can shut up. These things can't be rushed. You'll get fed all in good time." She caught sight of her naked body in the dressing table mirror and pinched at her waistline. "Hey, Darling. Do you think I'm losing weight?" He squawked again, louder, and ruffled his feathers with impatience.

"Okay, okay. Breakfast time. You're such a bossy boots." She slipped back into the negligee, delighting in the cool feel of the silk against her skin. She was pleased the extra work in the garden was toning her body. It gave her the boost she needed to be daring. She did look great in the sexy new nightwear. All she needed was the confidence to carry it off. And today her Affirmation happened to be all about confidence. *Today is auspicious. Today I take another step toward changing my life.*

By the time she reached the kitchen, Darling was already there perched on top of the door watching her every move with interest. She refreshed his water and filled his bowl with feed before popping bread in the toaster for her own breakfast.

Outside, the weak sunshine was obscured by fast moving clouds. Bebe flicked on the radio and then the kettle and watched the sky darken.

"It's going to be a good day for staying inside and writing, Darling. Look at those clouds." The wind was heightening. "No. Not again!" Bebe dashed for the toaster too late to save her cremated toast. "Damn it. See what happens when you daydream."

She examined the dials, but they were set to normal. "This toaster's junk." The bread was burned black and a plume of acrid smoke filled the kitchen with a sickly smell. Bebe quickly scooped the slices onto some paper towels.

"This stinks," she told Darling. "It's for the outside trashcan." She slipped her bare feet into her gardening boots—they were a permanent feature by the back door these days—and scurried across the backyard to the trashcans. Halfway there she had a better idea. The toast could go on the bird table. Maybe the wild birds would appreciate the taste. She veered left and made for the garden.

❖

It seemed strange to drive down Hope Street and not stop at Esme's door. Clara turned the corner onto Mercy Avenue and continued to Arlene's house. The wind was vicious this morning, blasting her truck with powerful gusts and the sky glowered with rain clouds. There was no way she could trim hedges in this weather.

Clara pulled into the driveway. She had the keys to Arlene's garage, and all she had to do was collect Esme's shears and check that the hedge trimmer was in good working order for later. If the station wagon was unlocked, she would unpack the rest of the fertilizer bags. This was only a lightning visit, and she wanted to do it without disturbing Bebe at such an early hour.

It was six a.m., so Clara was surprised when she heard Bebe's voice as she walked up the path to the side door of the garage. The wind was loud, but as she got closer, Bebe's words became clearer over the blow.

"Oh no! No. Ouch. Ow...Ow! Get off me."

Clara broke into a run. She rounded the corner and jarred to a halt.

Bebe stood under an ornamental rose arch in the most impractical nightwear Clara had ever seen. It was a floaty, flimsy affair that danced around in the wind. Her scanty ensemble was accessorized with a pair of black rubber boots.

"What the..." For a second, Clara couldn't understand why Bebe was standing there, looking so surreal. Then she noticed her long hair was snagged in several places by the fierce thorns of the Nightlight roses that climbed over the arch. As she watched, another gust whipped more long strands up into the jagged overhead stems, cruelly snarling them. Held firmly in place by her hair, Bebe tugged at the rose branches with one hand while trying to keep her nightgown in place with the other. The wind played tricks with her, swirling and curling and teasing her mercilessly.

"How the hell did you manage this?" Clara came forward to help. Bebe's face flamed on seeing her.

"The toast burned and I was leaving some out on the bird table. The wind caught my hair on the way back. I've been stuck here for ages." She sounded miserable, her hands grappled with her inadequate covering, trying to keep herself decent. "I'm freezing."

"Let me see." Clara came closer to check the tangled hair. Bebe looked so distressed and forlorn, and Clara fought to keep her face serious and quell her incredulous laughter. She had never seen such a preposterous situation.

"You've got yourself in a right old mess. Hold still," she said gently.

"And where would I be going?" Misery colored every word.

Several clumps of hair were well and truly enmeshed through the leaves and thorns, making it impossible for Bebe to even turn her head. She was going nowhere fast unless she wanted to rip her hair out by the roots. Clara tried to tease out the knots. Bebe winced with each torturous tug. It was impossible to release her easily. The jagged thorns lacerated Clara's hands. Nightlight roses were the purest evil to work with.

"I'm afraid I'll have to cut some of this free." Clara pulled out her pocketknife. It wasn't amusing anymore. This was a real mess. "I'll try and cut more plant than hair."

"Oh," Bebe whispered. Crimson faced, she tried desperately to push her swirling silk into submission and preserve a little modesty.

Any hair that wasn't captured by the roses blew all over the place, lashing at both their faces. It danced wickedly on the wind and flew in Clara's eyes, until her head swam with Night-scented stock, and clove, and amber, and all the hazy and sensual smells she associated with Bebe. They bloomed with the subtle heat of Bebe's skin. Her hair was damp from her shower and tendrils stuck to the back of her neck in tight curls. Clara's fingers brushed against the softness of Bebe's nape as she lifted the weight of the hair in her hand. Her fingers shook and she swallowed hard, gulping down that heady scent until it fluttered in her belly. Bebe's scent had been haunting her since they met.

"My hair's going to be ruined, isn't it," Bebe said softly. "Hacked to bits."

"I'll try to be careful," Clara murmured. Bebe's hair was her glory. Its color glowed like embers, its texture as subtle as silk. It would never be ruined; it was too splendid. She was close to Bebe now. They stood practically nose-to-nose, and Clara's coping skills were falling apart. Her fingers were clumsy and her mind stupid and sluggish. The intimacy was overwhelming her. Her fingers meshed in the cool, damp thickness of Bebe's hair.

"I'll only cut what I can't untangle," she said thickly.

She was super conscious of Bebe's fluttering nightdress and the full, hard tipped breasts only inches from her own chest. Tight, raspberry nipples pushed against the skimpy material. They jutted full of self-importance and a cheerfulness that wasn't apparent in their owner. Clara felt her face overheating and inched back, afraid she might inadvertently brush against them and electrocute herself.

The thorns were vicious and held tightly onto the heavy tresses of Bebe's hair. The autumnal shades of her hair were woven through the glossy greens and antique yellows of the Nightlight roses. The effect was beautiful yet tragic and reminded Clara of a pre-Raphaelite painting. Her very own Ophelia stood before her crowned with wreaths of thorns and roses, and blinking back tears. Clara wanted to wrap her arms around Bebe's shivering body and reassure her it would be all right, that her beautiful hair would grow back, each and every strand.

"Do you have a tissue?" Bebe asked. "I think I'm getting a nose bleed."

Clara scrabbled about in her pockets and thankfully found a clean tissue. She thrust it at Bebe. Bebe held it to her nose, her other hand fighting with the wayward negligee. A gust of wind plucked the silk from her fingers, dancing the hem up around her waist. Clara's heart lurched at the flash of a titian triangle, vibrant and fiery against the smooth vanilla of Bebe's thighs. It was too much. Her belly burned, then turned molten. She bolted around behind Bebe to spare both their blushes and bring her heartbeat under control. It thundered hot and hard in her ears. Her legs quivered.

"Keep still." Her words rasped out of a very dry throat.

"I am." Bebe's voice gritted back. "What else is there to do?" They were both stressed.

From the relative safety of this new position, Clara nimbly worked the hair loose. The swirling scent, the soft hair caressing her face, that tantalizing glance of Bebe's sex, and ruby nipples stretched against champagne silk all jumbled into one big lusty swirl of colorful confusion in her head, until she thought it would burst.

Nearly done. Just hang in there. She stood on tiptoe grimly stretching for the last thorny snarl on an uppermost branch. Just one remaining tangle and—

A gust lifted Bebe's negligee revealing a soft, plump bottom. Milky white, soft as cream, smooth, delicious, lickable. Clara's legs nearly buckled out from under her. With shaking hands, she carelessly hacked away the last captured curls, leaving a tuft of hair sticking out from Bebe's scalp at an odd angle. Then she turned and ran. If she stayed one minute more around Bebe she would explode like a Firecracker seed head.

"Just checking the bean poles," she called over her shoulder as she loped toward the vegetable plot at the rear of the yard.

Bebe didn't wait around either.

With a muffled thank-you, she gathered her silk negligee tightly to her body and dashed for the house.

❖

Frozen to the bone, Bebe took another shower to warm up and wash the plant debris out of her hair. With vehemence, she crumpled the champagne negligee into a tight ball and threw it in the trash. It was plucked and torn by the thorns, and she hated it now. She stood before the bathroom mirror and examined her hair, and burst into tears. Not because she looked like a scarecrow, a visit to the hairdresser would fix that, but because in order to check her hair she had to look in the mirror—at her stupid face.

Self composed and dressed in comfortable sweats, Bebe shuffled around the house avoiding the windows. She wasn't sure what Clara could find to do in the garden on such a windy day, but after the earlier debacle, she did *not* want to be caught spying on her from behind the curtains.

She was a total fool. It had taken her hours to work up the nerve to put on the negligee. She had wanted to look alluring, and mysteriously sexy...but from a very safe distance. Instead, it had typically turned out clownish and catastrophic. She hoped her friends would never ask how it went. She knew she wouldn't be able to keep the mortification off her face. She would lie. She would tell them the gardener had moved away, emigrated, died.

Bebe sat on the couch with her laptop on her knee. All the living room windows were opened, and despite the wind blowing in from the bay, the house still held the acrid smell of burned toast. No matter how hard the curtains flapped and the blinds rattled, the stink lingered. It annoyed her that she'd allowed the toast to burn. The toaster oven had a mind of its own. No matter what way she set the dial, she had to practically stand over it or else it incinerated everything. She should never have taken her eye off it this morning.

Berry Ripe's swan song was open on her screen and Bebe's mind was as blank as the page. This was crucial. This episode had to be punchy enough to mollify Carter into accepting that Suzzee was leaving, yet good enough to please Bebe that she had written her last episode to the best of her ability and that it would somehow enhance her thin résumé. And it had to be ready by next week. Carter had bought the blackmail idea, much to her surprise. But then anything she thought was garbage usually floated his boat so it really wasn't much to brag about. The more she worked on *Valley*, the more de-skilled she became. It was long past the time to go.

The thought of leaving felt curiously appealing. She had some savings, and if she was careful she could probably get by until something new came along. What that something was, Bebe had no idea. Arlene had offered her a roof over her head for as long as she wanted, and that was a definite bonus. She liked Preston; the pace of life suited her.

She took a deep breath. This was it. This was her swan song, too. Carter would see helping one of his stars leave as an absolute betrayal. She was going into the tailspin alongside Berry Ripe.

So far Bebe had only a list of unconnected ideas all swirling around in her head trying to take form. Now all the pent up shame and humiliation of the morning focused it. She sat pensively for several seconds, formulating her new strategy, her nose wrinkling against the sharp stink of burned toast. Then, with a new determination, and a huge feeling of release, her fingers began to fly over the keyboard.

The hedges whipped in the wind like a row of cancan dancers. They badly needed trimming. Clara set her mind firmly on checking twine and canes and cable ties, and refused to think about Bebe Franklin and her soft curves, or the milky pallor of her flesh against that dramatic titian fieriness.

Half an hour later she realized she was ravenous. It surprised her. She had skipped breakfast, but that was her usual start to the day. She was seldom hungry. Her appetite had been suppressed since Frances's death. Esme swore if she didn't feed her Clara would fall down the cracks in the sidewalk she had lost so much weight. She checked her watch. Esme would be up and about now. Maybe she could call over and see if they could share breakfast.

❖

Eggs, hash browns, refried beans. Esme looked at the cleared plate with raised eyebrows.

"This is a change. Usually you pick and poke at your food until my heart is broken." Esme took the plate away. "I made ice cream yesterday. Want some?"

Clara considered this. "This early in the morning? You really are trying to pack the calories into me."

"And why not? You need them, and besides, it's a fresh batch of homemade."

"What flavor?" Something snapped in her. She needed extra sugar today. Her blood levels were all over the place. Clara sat back in her seat and relaxed. She felt animated and energized.

"Vanilla," Esme said.

"Can I have it in a cone? Like you make it in the summer."

Esme smiled happily. She filled a wafer cone with a generous scoop of homemade vanilla ice cream.

"Did you remember to check Arlene's bean poles?" she said. She indented a small dip in the vanilla with the handle of a spoon and filled it with a blob of her homemade raspberry syrup. "This wind could flatten them."

"Yes. I checked everything. Nothing's going to collapse in Arlene's garden." *Well, maybe me.*

Clara took the cone and eyed it appreciatively. It held happy childhood memories for her. Esme made wonderful ice cream, and her fruit syrups were sheer heaven.

"But did you see Bebe?" Esme asked.

Clara's suspicions were immediately on alert. "Did you tell her I was calling by this morning?"

"Of course I did. I didn't want her thinking she had an intruder rummaging around in the garage, now did I?"

"You told me not to disturb her," Clara said.

"Yes, but there was no reason she shouldn't know you'd be there at some unearthly hour."

So Bebe knew she would be there. Was that the reason for the fancy negligee? Surely nobody slept in a contraption like that? And it had all gone woefully wrong under the rose arch. Roses grow thorns for a reason.

Clara examined the creamy mound of vanilla, frosty and smooth, with its little apex of sweet red syrup. She closed her eyes and ran her tongue in a broad sweep along the underside against the wafer rim. Vanilla exploded on her taste buds. Another broad lick, this time to the topside, swirling her tongue around the syrup-tipped center. With a murmur of satisfaction, she gently tapped on the raspberry button with the tip of her tongue. Each tap extended the sugary mixture up into a long point. Delicately, she swirled it into her mouth, and with a grunt, she sucked up as much of the entire concoction as she could manage into her mouth. Her tongue and lips were bathed in it. The sugar high hit her with a whoosh. She swallowed the entire mouthful with a blissful sigh.

Clara opened her eyes to find Esme watching her with morbid fascination.

"What?" she said.

Esme shook her head. "Look at you," she said and tossed a napkin. "It's all over your mouth and chin. Whatever were you thinking?"

CHAPTER NINE

Bebe's feet sank in wet sand. She was glad she'd worn her boots. It meant she could walk closer to the incoming tide. The wind picked up, flipping her new hairstyle and stripping out the hairspray the stylist had drowned her in. It felt good to be out in the cooling evening air. All her worries were momentarily snatched away by the wind. She could relax and stretch her legs into a brisk stride.

The beach was one of her favorite daytime walks. She'd never come down after dark before, always imagining it would be spooky with the rushing waves and rattling dune grass. It was sort of spooky, but only if she let it be. Instead, she concentrated on a domed starlit sky, hung with a quarter moon. The crunch of damp sand under her boots harmonized with the tumbling waves and growling wind and somehow included her in the magic of the nighttime shore. With each step her body felt more refreshed and her mind more focused.

She was leaving *Valley of Our Fathers*. She was going to walk away, but before she did she would deliver as promised. She was a professional, and as much as she disliked Carter, she would honor her contract no matter how difficult he made it. After that she had no idea what to do and that was the fly in the ointment. The cautious inner voice that made her wildest wishes seem silly, now coaxed her to play it safe, to swallow her pride and hang on in *Valley* until the bitter end. Bebe was desperately trying to ignore that voice. It felt defeatist and self-marginalizing, but to completely quell it she needed to have a structure for her future.

Where would she go? What could she do? What she really wanted but was almost too scared to formulate, was to stay in Preston and write. She wasn't sure if that meant the obligatory novel she, and everyone she knew, had tucked away on their hard drive, or maybe working as a freelancer for local newspapers and magazines. She'd spent all afternoon going over her finances seeing when she could afford a career change. According to her figures, it was possible if she took up Arlene's offer to stay on in Preston a while longer. The studio apartment would have to go. No more fast city life for her. But on a night like this out here on the coast, that didn't feel like such a wrench. She loved Preston with its clean, vigorous air and tight community. Somehow it felt like the right place to be.

Up ahead she saw a greasy yellow blob by the edge of the tide. It soon took on the outline of a shore fisherman dressed in old-fashioned oilskins. As she drew level he looked over at her with open curiosity. She smiled back. Hesitant at first, he nodded and smiled cautiously, a flash of white against the black bush of his beard.

"Hi." She slowed her step. "Any luck?"

"Umm. Hah. No," he answered, looking at her strangely. "Too much of a blow tonight."

She wondered why he bothered if it was too windy, but thought it rude to ask. Maybe he just liked fishing in all weather, no matter what the outcome.

"It's a beautiful night," she said. "Despite the blow."

"That it is."

She stood beside him and they both looked out over the bay for several seconds.

"See that inlet over there? By the big rock." He pointed out a few miles north along the shoreline where the headland hooked a sheltering arm around the bay. Bebe nodded. "That's where the old boatyard used to be. My little skiff was built there in nineteen twenty-seven," he said proudly.

"Goodness." She tried to sound suitably impressed. "Does the yard still operate?"

"No. Not since the war. My dad gave me that skiff. Peapod she was."

"What do you mean peapod?"

"It's the shape. Tapered each end. Looks like a peapod." The next twenty minutes were spent with her new friend explaining the little open boats the locals used for pot hauling and line fishing. She learned about their seaworthiness and construction, and the local yard that used to build the best on the New England coastline. Bebe enjoyed standing toe to toe with the creeping tide line, looking out over the choppy swell and listening to the enthusiasm in the fisherman's voice. He talked a flood, as if something inside him had gone pop and all these words fell out.

See? There's a magazine article in there somewhere about a lost boat-building industry. This place is just full of stories, and I could write them all. She shot him a sideways glance, curious at his old-fashioned wet gear. It didn't seem to be very efficient. He was soaked through, and water dripped incessantly from the sleeves and hem of his oilskins. His face and floppy sou'wester were saturated. His big, bushy beard was encrusted with sand and slithers of seaweed. He must have been standing full face in sea spray, Bebe decided, though the conditions seemed a lot calmer now. A small crustacean wriggled out from his beard and scuttled toward his chest. Bebe started.

"There's...I think." She pointed at his beard and he looked at her questioningly. "I think there's a crab in your beard," she said. He reached up and plucked off the tiny crab examining it with a big, hearty laugh.

"Bait!" he chortled, and tossed the little creature into the tide. Bebe blinked at the peculiarity of it, but what did she know about shore fishing?

"Well." She bundled her jacket collar around her neck. "I better get going. It was nice to meet you..." She didn't know his name.

"Tom," he said with a big grin.

"Tom." Bebe smiled back. His grin was as engaging as his conversation. "I'm Bebe. I'll see you around."

"That would be nice. Goodnight, Bebe. Thanks for the talk."

Bebe trudged toward the dunes, pleased with her decision to go on an evening stroll, and pleased with meeting someone so interesting. Tom was a nice man. She hoped to catch up with him again. The idea for a local article on boat building was already circling in her head and it excited her. She knew the kernel of a good story when she saw it.

❖

Clara slumped on her porch chair and sipped her malt whiskey. The dune grass cracked against the rails of her picket fence, a fanciful effort to delineate her property from the encroaching sands. The wind hissed through the thicker clumps of maram grass and created a riotous symphony with the creak of her chair rockers and the clack of the bamboo wind chimes.

"No point huffing about it. Huffing does no good." A second set of creaking runners joined hers. The wind had stripped away the musk rose scent before she could catch it and realize she had company.

"It can if it's done right," Clara answered, not looking to where Temperance sat rocking beside her. Temperance popping by only meant trouble of the migraine variety. Clara felt her body tensing all over. She wanted to be alone tonight. She needed time to think. She did not need ephemeral visitors.

"Well, then, I guess you're the champ." Temperance sniffed and the air around her cracked and sparkled.

Here comes the tunnel vision, Clara thought miserably, her head aching already. She concentrated on the mournful face of the moon, partially turned away from the earth, as if vexed with all who resided there. *Perhaps the moon huffs, too.*

"What do you want now?" The sooner she dealt with Temperance's requests, the sooner she'd be gone—once she got her way, that was. "Does Darling need his water changed, his cage cleaned, what? Perhaps a new tinkle toy?"

"Huffy *and* snitty, that's you."

"Dead *and* annoying, that's you. What is it you want, Temperance?"

"I can't get into my house. Every time I try I just…can't. Why is that?"

Clara shrugged. "I don't know. I only see the dead. It's not like I know the rules."

"There are rules?" Temperance looked troubled.

"You'd break them even if you knew them."

"I want to go to Darling, but there's something about that house…Oh, I don't know what it is! I start out to go there and I always end up someplace else, like here, talking to you. Do you think I deliberately come looking for you? It's all very annoying."

"You bet it is."

"Well? Will you drop by and check Darling for me?"

Clara shifted uncomfortably. It was awkward around Bebe. Her opinion of her was changing by the minute. Neither did she want to become a pest like Doyle and hang out where she might not be wanted, checking on a stupid parrot. "Bebe's looking after him just fine—"

"Oh, for goodness sake, it's not as if she bites. Though that might do you a world of good." Temperance's words sucker punched her. "It's time to stop acting the widow, Clara. The dead don't need it."

Clara stared at her, shocked.

"Have you been talking to Frances?" She found her voice.

"No one has been talking to Frances. Frances *won't talk.*" Temperance's words still had acid. The old woman was angry. "Let her be and get on with your own life. It's no good nagging me to move on when you won't move on yourself."

"Frances and I are none of your business. Not when you were living, and not when you're dead."

"You never saw that woman clearly when she was alive, and you're not seeing her clearly now."

"I'm not seeing her at all." Clara jumped to her feet and strode from the porch down onto the crushed shell path. She walked out into the dunes following the path toward the beach. Temperance had annoyed her. She hadn't said anything new. Lord knew she'd been vocal enough when she was alive in that brash, arrogant way the elderly have when they believe they've seen and done it all.

Esme too, in her own way, was always pushing for Clara to let go and move on. But she didn't want to, she wasn't ready yet, and at the end of the day, it was *her* heart that set the agenda for her mourning, not other people's discomfort with it.

But am I still mourning? Or am I just stuck? Recently, the grief that dogged her days had transformed, as if a cloak had slipped and underneath stood an ugly, squirming pile of guilt. And beneath that again, she could feel anger at Frances bubbling gently away, and it frightened her. She was scared to even look at it, and that made her angry with herself and everyone who called attention to her mourning. Everything was changing and she didn't know why it was happening or what had caused it. And she wasn't ready for it.

She emerged from the dunes deep in thought, practically mowing down another walker who crossed her path.

"Oh!" Bebe leapt in alarm and clutched her chest.

Clara caught at her arm.

"It's me. I'm sorry. I didn't see you there." Over Bebe's shoulder, several yards back along the beach, Tom Ray frowned over at them.

"You scared the life out of me," Bebe gasped. "It's spooky enough without people looming out of the dark."

"Sorry," Clara said. Tom continued to watch with concern. It surprised Clara. Usually, he paid no attention to the living, wrapped up in his little cocoon of fish and salt water.

"Where on earth did you come from?" Bebe asked.

"I live back there." Clara indicated the beach shacks with her thumb.

"You live in a beach shack? How cool is that! I've always thought they looked so cute." Bebe came alive with interest.

"Do you want to come back for a nightcap, or coffee or something?" Clara found herself mumbling the question but desperately wanting Bebe to say yes. She felt low and confused and decided she must be in need of company this evening—the corporeal kind.

On other nights when she felt like this she would go knocking on Esme's door under some silly pretext or other. Inevitably, Esme would see the state she was in and invite her to stay over, and Clara would hide in Esme's guest room. She always slept well at Esme's house. In her own bed she was plagued with insomnia.

Tonight Temperance had tipped her back into that desperate place, and it was far too late to go and hound Esme. But tonight she had literally bumped her into another rescuer of sorts. Bebe Franklin had increasingly fascinated her, and she so wanted to make amends for her earlier bad behavior. She desperately hoped Bebe would say yes to her invitation. An hour spent talking to someone over a drink felt like the best antidote for her brooding depression. Tonight Clara didn't want the dead for company.

"I'd love to," Bebe answered, and Clara's body hummed with relief.

Together they turned toward the dip in the dunes and the straggly path that led to Clara's shack. Bebe waved at Tom Ray. He raised a hand in return before giving his full attention to his fishing line.

"I don't want Tom to worry about me," Bebe said then walked ahead, leaving Clara in her wake, rooted to the spot.

❖

Clara poured Baileys over ice and took both glasses back to the living room where Bebe stood examining her bookshelves. Her head was tipped at an angle reading the spines. Her hair hung in a heavy, lustrous curtain past her shoulders. The soft lamplight rippled across it in shifts of burnished gold to deep bronze. Clara watched her silently, still shaken by what had occurred on the beach.

She can see ghosts. She smells beautiful, and the first time I saw her was at a car crash...well, fender bender, hardly life threatening. Her hands shook slightly. Was Bebe a ghost, too?

No. She couldn't be. Esme talked to her, and Benjamin, and Mr. T, and...and the whole town in fact. Everybody seemed to like her. No. She couldn't be dead. *It's simply my own fear. I don't want her to be another ghost. I don't want her haunting me like this. I want her to be warm and alive and...here.*

"Here." She handed over a glass and watched keenly as Bebe took a very mortal sip. "How do you know Tom?" she asked as casually as possible, watching Bebe swallow, her eyes fixated on the cool column of throat.

"I don't. I just met him tonight and talked with him for a while. He seemed lonely. He told me some great fishing stories about the old days. His family have always been Preston fishermen."

Clara nodded. She still couldn't understand how Bebe could see Tom and not recognize him for what he was. It had never occurred to her that Tom might be lonely. She never perceived much emotion in the spirits she met. They seemed happy enough. They passed the time of day and then passed over. No more to it than that, was there? Yet Bebe seemed sensitive on a level Clara had never acquired. Why was that? What was she?

"You have a lovely home, Clara," Bebe said.

"Do you want to look around? It will only take about three minutes. The place is tiny." Clara grabbed at social niceties rather than muse over Bebe's mysteries. "These shacks were originally built in the fifties for summer use. I've added insulation and heating so I could live here all year round."

"Lucky you. It looks so cozy." Bebe glanced again at the off-white walls lined with bookshelves, and seascapes, and nautical bric-a-brac. "Do you sail? You seem to love the sea."

"Everyone around here sails, or kayaks, or fishes. We're all descended from fisher folk, after all." Clara raised a hand and swept the room in a grand gesture. "As you can see, from the front porch we step directly into the main living area, complete with a wood stove for those cold winter evenings," she said in a mock realtor spiel, glad they could be lighthearted. "The door at the rear leads to a small but well appointed kitchen, and the bijou bathroom, formerly an outhouse, lies beyond that. The door to your right takes us to the master bedroom. Okay, the only bedroom. Which is not en suite, as the main bathroom is only three steps away through the freezing kitchen. A real joy in the depths of winter. Feel free to roam, but be careful not to get lost."

"Don't worry. I've got a compass toggle on my zipper." Bebe waggled the decorative zip tab on her fleece pocket.

"I see you came prepared."

"How long have you been living out here? The view must be spectacular." Bebe wandered toward the kitchen deciding to ignore the bedroom. It felt too snoopy and uncomfortable to take a peep, though she would have loved to.

"The dunes obscure a lot of the view, but that's okay as it keeps the shack private from the beach. If you go up higher, behind the house, you can see the whole bay," Clara said, following her as far as the kitchen door. "I bought this place about fifteen years ago when they were cheap as dirt. My dad thought I was crazy, but they've more than quadrupled in price since."

"Smart move. It's fabulous." Bebe was glad Clara stood back and allowed her to investigate on her own. She could glean a lot about Clara's character from her home, and if she was honest, that interested her more than décor and real estate prices.

The kitchen and the bathroom beyond were neat and tidy and every bit as small as Clara had admitted. Both were entirely practical spaces with no lurking luxuries to give clues as to their owner, and Bebe was looking for clues. The bathroom was tiled in a quality white and gray veined marble. Clara used a good brand of unscented, organic toiletries. Her towels were thick and soft, and arctic white. It was a cold room in look, if not temperature. A splash of color would have made a world of difference. But sometimes indifference colored a home more.

The kitchen was clean, orderly, and did not belong to a cook. Everything was as plain and practical as the bags of dry pasta dominating the food shelves. Bebe longed to load the cupboards with colorful labels and containers brimful of spices and herbs, and bolstering homemade sauces. The refrigerator would bulge, the stovetop bubble, and the vegetable rack would groan under the weight of homegrown potatoes, leafy greens, bright peppers, and fiery chilies. And the wonderful aroma of cooking would fill every corner of the small house. This was a kitchen begging for something to happen, and Bebe ached to pull on an apron and explode in it. If a kitchen was the heart of the home, then Bebe wanted to spill herself into this one until it brimmed over with happiness.

"Told you it was tiny." Clara stepped over the threshold and crowded the remaining space. "Not enough room to toss a salad."

"Oh, I don't know. If you knew what you were doing this would be just fine." Bebe ran a calculating eye across the work surfaces.

"I take it you do know what you're doing in a kitchen?" Clara asked, as if decent cuisine was some kind of universal mystery known only to the initiated.

"Yes. I love to cook. The kitchen in my apartment is not much bigger than this, but I can easily cater a dinner party for eight people. I could feed more, but they'd have to sit in the stairwell."

She looked over for a reaction to her joke, but Clara wasn't listening. Instead she was watching her curiously. Slowly, she reached out a hand and touched Bebe's cheek. Bebe could feel her flesh tingle and grow warm under Clara's fingertips. Before the heat could bloom into an ugly blush, Clara flushed first. Her fingers trembled and she gave a sudden, sheepish grin.

"Sorry. Just checking something." She made to pull away, but Bebe tilted her cheek into Clara's palm, and she paused.

"What is it?" Bebe's heart was thumping so hard she was surprised the kitchen pans didn't rattle. Heat pulsed between them. They were a continuous circuit linked through Clara's fingertips in a never-ending electrical arc.

"Just…something." Clara's thumb whispered past the corner of her mouth and then her hand dropped away. "A fleck of Baileys cream."

"Oh. Thank you." Bebe was confused. There was no Bailey's on her mouth. She had only just checked herself over in the bathroom mirror. Had Clara simply wanted to touch her? Her pulse fluttered at what it might mean. Did Clara find her attractive? Did she think Bebe had an agenda this evening, because any thoughts of seduction were well and truly buried at the bottom of Bebe's trashcan along with a champagne negligee and a big dollop of mortification.

Clara moved back into the living room and Bebe followed, still uncertain. They sank into deep armchairs and sipped their drinks. The room settled around them and Bebe's unease soon dissolved in the ambiance, like the ice in her glass. Clara had no agenda either. Tonight was all about olive branches and burying their embarrassment, and Bebe silently thanked her for that.

A quiet lull slipped over them as cozy as cashmere. A vintage clock gently ticked on the mantel, the distant rush of waves a rhythmic whisper. Ice tinkled in their glasses as they drank. The hush was almost hypnotic and growing more intimate by the second.

"Do you like Preston? It must feel comatose here compared to New York." Clara broke the silence, groping for a safe topic of conversation. She sat back hoping Bebe would seize on the question and allow Clara's nerves to settle. She felt ridiculous for thinking for even one moment Bebe was not a living, breathing, wonderful human being. How stupid to feel compelled to touch her just to be sure. But she was glad she had, her fingers still hummed with pleasure. Bebe pulsed with life and energy and things that made Clara feel full of hope and peace. It had been years since she had been interested in anything or anyone outside her own meager sphere. Now she was alert; she was enervated. Bebe had seen Tom Ray. There was no denying it. Why? What was it all about? Clara would have to talk to Tom about it. This was something new to her. Her father had never mentioned anything about outsiders seeing spirits. As far as she was aware, only a few of the Dearhearts had the gift, though she was pretty sure Bebe had no idea she had just made friends with a man drowned over forty years ago.

"Who is Frances?" The innocuous question snapped Clara's attention. She followed Bebe's gaze to a photograph on the mantel. "Frances and Clara" was engraved onto the wooden photo frame, along with a date. They smiled and raised champagne glasses in salute to the camera. Colorful balloons floated in the background and glitter confetti covered their table.

"Frances was my partner. That was Esme's retirement party four years ago."

"Oh. She's very pretty." Bebe fell quiet. Clara tensed awaiting a barrage of questions. Eventually her shoulders relaxed when she realized they were not going to come.

"She died shortly after that photo was taken," she said. She wanted Bebe to know at least that much. It was only manners.

"That's sad." Again, Bebe did not follow up with a string of intrusive questions, and Clara was grateful.

"Do you have anyone back in New York?" Clara wasn't sure why she asked. She knew the answer.

Bebe gave an unladylike snort and immediately colored.

"No. I'm...I'm not really looking. I have some big career decisions coming up, and the last thing I need is another person to factor in. It's hard enough deciding what I want to do for myself." It was a remarkably sensible and honest answer, and Clara liked hearing it.

"So what are your plans?" she asked, happy to follow this line of conversation, finding herself genuinely interested. "It sounds like you have a few options to chew over."

Bebe managed to bury her snort this time, but barely. Clara hid a smile. She was enjoying their talk.

"Apart from ditching my full time job? None. No options. No plan Bs, no fallbacks, and no backups. Besides holing up here and waiting for an epiphany. Not the best of escape plans, but I really need to get out of where I am." She took a sip from her glass and the ice cubes clinked. "Have you ever felt you were being slowly mummified with each hour that passes?"

Clara nodded. She knew. She sat quietly as Bebe continued.

"Well, that's what my job is for me," she said. "I'm becoming more and more de-skilled every day. And it undermines the rest of my life too, I suppose, because everything I do is wrapped around my work and the people I meet through it. I feel like a walking, talking blank page, and if I don't start to write my own life story soon then people will just graffiti their opinions all over me, and that's all I'll ever be, walking, talking graffiti. I know I'm not making much sense..." She tailed off, embarrassed.

"I understand," Clara said. This was interesting. It resonated somewhere in her own life. She used to love what she did. Every day was full and vibrant. But since Frances's death, it had all fallen away. She was hollow, simply going through the motions, mechanically moving through her day and slowly running out of steam. Everyone around her sensed it and had strategies to shunt her along, as if all she needed was a good shove through the grief and out the other side where it would all be all right.

"Why do you hate your job?" Clara's own opinion on the awful soap show was suddenly not as important as hearing what had gone wrong for Bebe.

"You mean apart from it being terrible?" Bebe gave a rueful smile. "It's the sort of writing that turns me into a dry husk. There's no creative joy in it. It doesn't inspire me or project me onto the next fantastic idea. There's no flow on the inside. Instead, I'm writing my way into a creative cul-de-sac. I'm such a bad fit for where I've placed myself."

"So coming out here gives you space to think." It was sort of an obvious statement, but Clara wanted to keep Bebe talking now that she was opening up to her. Esme had dropped hints Bebe was unhappy. Now Clara wanted to know more. She wanted to make up for her weeks of indifference.

"Yes. Preston is like the cool side of the pillow to me. You know…when you wake up troubled in the middle of the night, and you just turn the pillow over so it's so cool and restful against your cheek, and before you know it you've drifted back to sleep. Does that sound silly?"

"No." Clara thought about it. "No. It sounds like you found somewhere truly peaceful, and that's the hardest place to find."

"Yes, I think I've found something special out here. But everyone has their own ideas. Benjamin plagues me silly about New York. He can't wait until he's saved enough money to move there, and here am I, running in the opposite direction." Bebe checked her watch. "It's later than I thought. I really need to get going."

Clara helped her shrug on her jacket. "At least let me walk you part of the way."

Bebe shook her head. "Thank you, but I came out to chase the cobwebs away and grab a little think time. I'm only ten minutes from home. I'll be okay."

Put such a way, Clara had to respect the request for solitude, but she did walk Bebe down to the beach. With a wave good-bye, she watched her until she was out of sight, her hair a ghostly halo in the weak moonlight, the tidewater already filling her footprints.

CHAPTER TEN

Bebe began to notice a difference in the garden. Once a week she crossed the causeway to grocery shop at the mall. When she returned with a trunk full of shopping she might find the hedges trimmed or the lawn mowed and its edges cut into crisp, straight lines. Borders were mulched and replanted hanging baskets swung from hooks.

The first time it happened she had telephoned Esme and asked her to thank Clara, but Esme was as surprised as she was. Clara had not informed anyone of her intentions. She had simply shown up and did whatever work needed doing. Esme seemed a little put out by this development, and Bebe guessed this was because she had not engineered it.

After that, Bebe became used to odd jobs being done here and there, in no particular order, and at no particular time. The only common denominator, and one that vexed her greatly, was that the work always took place while she was away from the house. She assumed Esme's gossiping allowed Clara to time her visits around Bebe's comings and goings. At first she felt hurt that Clara might be avoiding her, but soon realized Clara was squeezing time out of her busy schedule for the garden work. This made Bebe feel awful. She did not want Clara making Herculean efforts over her never-ending chore list.

She wished she could see her and thank her, but since Dearhearts bombed out of the pool competition, Bebe had failed to bump into Clara at Petty's again, and walks along the beach always found the little shack empty, its owner not at home. Eventually, her *Valley* deadline took over her life, and shopping excursions and beach walks took second place to her writing.

Berry Ripe's demise from *Valley of Our Fathers* came with a discrete off camera pistol shot. It was better that way. An open-ended exit would allow Carter room to maneuver. Suzzee Wang might be gone, but Berry Ripe could still be reinvented with a new actress and a cosmetic surgery storyline plugging the hole in her head. Stranger things had happened in *Valley*.

Bebe took a deep breath and hit Send. Her final episode winged its way to Carter. It might as well have been her Last Will and Testament. Her letter of resignation would go tomorrow. No point giving Carter a double heart attack.

"Good-bye old life, hello new. Wherever you are."

She went to make a celebratory cup of tea when a movement in the garden caught her eye. Clara was digging in the back borders. Bebe checked her watch. It was nearly one p.m., lunchtime. Her hands twitched on the countertop.

She had lain awake most nights, lost in panicked, spiraling thoughts about *Valley* and her job, and what she would do next. She would try to clear her mind of this jumbled morass, blanking it out and trying to imagine a peaceful, happier place, but somehow she would always latch on to Clara Dearheart and pick apart every little morsel she knew about her. Once Clara was in her thoughts, everything else receded, her anxiety stilled, and she eventually fell asleep curiously content.

Through the kitchen window she watched as Clara pressed her boot to the shoulder of the spade and broke open the soil. She was planting something. Bebe could see boxes of greenery stacked behind her. Curiosity got the better of her. She wanted to see what was happening. What she really wanted was to say hello.

"Hi." She walked across the grass to where Clara sweated. "What are you planting?"

Clara looked up. She was flushed with exertion and had a smear of dirt on her left cheek. It stopped just short of her mouth. Bebe found herself watching that mouth as it shaped words back at her.

"Have you just arrived home? I didn't see Arlene's car," Clara said. Her mouth curled naturally at the corners. Her mouth was made for smiling, yet so seldom did. Bebe was fixated on it. There were probably a lot of things that mouth should do but didn't. *Like laughing, and kissing, and whispering into that sensitive spot just below my ear.* The hairs along her forearm rose.

"It's at the shop for a service," she answered. "You don't have to call when I'm out, you know. It's not as if you're in the way. I'd never have known you were here."

"I wanted to give you peace and quiet. I know you have a lot of writing to do. Esme said you had a deadline." Clara raised a hand to her dirty cheek. "Have I got something on my face?"

Bebe realized she was still staring.

"Just there." She pointed. "A little bit of dirt." She cheered up. Clara was not avoiding her. She was actually being thoughtful by giving Bebe space.

"What are you doing?" She changed the subject, pointing at the dug up border and the boxes of plants at Clara's heels.

"Planting Tansy. This is the Golden Button variety." Clara nudged the box of tall, straggly plants with a mud clad work boot. "I know they don't look like much now, but they have a pretty yellow flower and ants hate them. It will clear them out."

"Ants don't like Tansy? Why's that?"

"It's poisonous, and ants are smart," Clara said. "Please keep away from it," she added, almost as an afterthought.

"I'm hardly dumber than an ant." Bebe was pleased that they were chatting so easily. It made her feel a little braver, so she said, "Look, I'm about to make lunch. Would you like to join me? It's just a sandwich." She tried to look nonchalant.

They'd had such a nice time talking over a nightcap at Clara's house and Bebe wanted to return the hospitality.

"I'd love to join you for lunch." Clara's reply surprised her.

"Great." She'd half expected a polite rejection. "Come down when you're ready."

The next surprise was Clara setting aside her spade and walking with her across the lawn to the garden path.

"Um. You're not allergic to any foodstuffs are you?" Bebe asked anxiously. "Peanuts or anything?" She was startled by Clara's soft laugh.

"No. Don't worry."

They crossed the patio to the backdoor and Clara stepped out of her muddy boots and followed Bebe into the kitchen.

"Clara! Oh, Clara! Oh. Oh. Oh." Darling squawked loudly at her entry. Bebe blushed furiously. It sounded so licentious.

"Hello there, big boy. Did you miss me?" Clara tickled his neck until he displayed his wing feathers and did a swaying dance on his perch for her, crooning a garbled tune.

Bebe giggled. "He likes you."

"He does, for some reason," Clara said. "He always makes a squawking fuss when he sees me. I see he's finally settled in with you."

"Oh, he has his moments, but mostly we bumble along. He likes it when I sing, but he's not so keen on learning his affirmations."

"I heard about that." Clara grinned. "Temperance used to sing to him. It soothes him."

"Mm. He likes to join in and sing along. Well, sort of. He also mimics random words I say from time to time and comes out with the weirdest sentences." Bebe opened the fridge. "I'm making an egg salad sandwich." She fidgeted with the fridge contents until she had all her ingredients. "Is that all right with you?"

She made a killer sandwich and was eager to show off and spoil Clara a little.

"Yes, thank you. Has Esme asked you to start collecting eggshells?"

"No. Why do I need to do that?"

"As a natural slug deterrent. They don't like creeping over the rough edges. And they attract birds. Good for the compost, too."

"Eggshells attract birds?" Bebe filled the kettle and took it over to the stove.

"Yeah. Birds peck at the shells for added calcium. It helps them lay stronger eggs. And if there are any slugs around, the birds will eat them too. It's a natural—"

"Ow!" Bebe pulled her hand from the stovetop and looked at her palm in dismay. Darling screeched and rattled his feathers in alarm.

"What is it? Did you burn yourself?" Clara leapt from her chair.

"Yes." Bebe held up her reddened palm. She rushed to put it under the cold water faucet. "The stovetop is roasting hot, and all the burners are on full."

Clara turned the stove off. "You went out and left the burners on? That's dangerous, Bebe."

"No, I didn't have the stove on this morning. I had cereal for breakfast." Bebe examined her hand. She didn't bother to explain cereal was now her regular breakfast as the toaster oven incinerated her bread no matter what setting it was on.

"Hot. Hot. Hot." Darling was still squawking.

"Hush, Darling. The stove was red hot but I didn't turn it on. I know I didn't."

"Shut up, Darling. Here. Let me see." Clara appeared at her elbow with the first aid box. "Keep it under longer." She pushed Bebe's hand back under the running water. "Well, a stove can't just turn itself on," she said.

"Honestly," Bebe said. "I didn't use it at all today. In fact, I didn't even use it last night. I microwaved leftovers for dinner." She could see Clara was only half listening as she examined the ointment labels in the first aid kit. "I hate this kitchen. The stove turns itself on and the toaster oven won't turn itself off."

Clara found what she was looking for. "This will sting."

They sat at the table and Clara took Bebe's palm in her warm fingers and applied the ointment.

"Aaah!"

"Told you."

"Telling me doesn't stop it from hurting," Bebe snapped, pulling her hand away.

"You're as bad tempered as your grandma. She was a redhead, too." Clara grabbed the hand back. The flash of grumpiness said a lot. The similarity between Temperance and her granddaughter stood out very clearly, and both were dominating her thoughts a lot recently. Clara suppressed a smile.

"Grandma Temperance was the sweetest dear." Bebe scowled as more ointment was smeared onto her palm.

"She could be forgetful, too." Clara began wrapping the hand in clean gauze. "I remember she often left appliances on until Arlene banned her from the kitchen completely."

"She was nearly a hundred. Of course she was forgetful. *I* am not forgetful, and I did *not* turn that damn stove on. I know I didn't."

Clara taped the bandage and let go. Bebe immediately pulled her hand away in a huff.

"Stoves don't turn themselves on," Clara said.

"Then there's something wrong with the electricity in this house. There's been mysterious smoke twice now, and I could never find the reason for it."

"Smoke? Did you check the boiler?"

"Of course I did. I even got the boiler man out." Bebe fidgeted with her new bandage. "But there was nothing to show him. The smoke disappeared as quickly as it came. Between the toaster oven incinerating everything and now the stove switching itself on at random, I think the damned house is haunted."

Clara packed away the first aid kit and glanced around the kitchen.

"Nah. This house isn't haunted," she stated with some authority. It felt far too normal. No strange smells, no sparkles. This house was clean from spiritual energy. Not even Temperance could pop up here, and she was desperate to plague the place.

"Like you'd know." Bebe moodily examined her dressed hand. "Thank you." She waved it at Clara. "Will I be able to work in the garden with this?"

"Should be okay. Chose your jobs wisely and keep it clean. I'll look at it again in a day or two, okay?" Clara pushed the first aid kit back into the cupboard. "Now, about lunch. Let's head out, my treat."

Bebe's eyes shone at the invitation, and Clara felt a surge of pleasure that she had offered. She was growing to enjoy Bebe's company. And after all, it was only polite to invite Bebe out considering she hurt her hand making a sandwich for the both of them. It also felt good they were getting along so well. God knew Clara had been mean minded enough where Bebe was concerned. She was thoroughly ashamed of herself now. Esme was right. Bebe was a lovely young woman.

❖

"Cooee!" Esme called as soon as Clara and Bebe entered the diner. "What a surprise." She seemed inordinately pleased as they bundled into her booth, moving her shopping from the seats to make room. "Imagine bumping into you two here."

"Imagine," Clara said dryly. "Such a small town."

"You can't cast a shadow but it lands on somebody's toes." Esme smiled at her.

"I was making lunch when I managed to burn my hand." Bebe showed off her bandages. "Clara suggested we come here instead. Less dangerous."

"That looks nasty." Esme tutted.

"It will be fine if she keeps it clean." Clara sounded a little brusque.

"How on earth did you do it?" Esme asked.

"It's the weirdest thing. I burned it on the stove, yet I know for a fact I hadn't turned it on. Did Aunt Arlene ever say anything about the stove being dodgy?"

"Dearest, I very much doubt she'd have allowed you over the county line if she thought she had unreliable electrical appliances in her home." Esme placed a soothing hand on Bebe's arm. Clara snorted in amusement.

"We talked about this. I did not turn that stove on. In fact, I haven't used it for nearly twenty-four hours." Bebe was greatly offended by the suppressed laugh.

"I didn't mean to laugh. I apologize." Clara's cell phone chirped. She squinted at the caller ID before moving away to answer.

"The whole house is cross wired or something," Bebe said, turning back to Esme.

Clara returned a few seconds later. "That was Ronnie. I'm afraid I've got to go."

"Is everything okay?" Esme asked, her voice indicated that when Clara was called away all was not well for someone, somewhere.

"Yeah. I'll catch you later. I'm sorry about lunch, Bebe. Maybe another time?" She looked genuinely rueful. "Soon?"

"Yes. Definitely." Bebe tried to hide her disappointment, but her gaze followed Clara all the way out the door.

When she turned back, Esme was watching her intently. Her cheeks bloomed and Esme's eagle eyes narrowed. Bebe blinked under the stare. She felt like a timid mouse cowering in the undergrowth, easy pickings for a snoopy old bird like Esme. Sure enough, Esme swooped.

"And how is it working out with Clara, dear? The garden does look lovely."

"Oh, she drops by from time to time, but I hardly ever see her. She's very kind to help out. You both are. I don't know where I'd be without you both." Bebe tried to deflect. "Both of you."

"Clara is a lovely young woman. But I worry for her. It's not right for her to be so reclusive."

"It must be hard, though," Bebe said. "She must miss Frances a lot."

"She told you about Frances?" Esme was in like a shot and Bebe realized she'd wandered into a well-oiled trap. She cleared her throat before continuing.

"We bumped into each other on the beach a few nights ago… literally…and she invited me back to her house for a nightcap. It's lovely out there by the water. I've always wanted to see inside one of those sweet little shacks." Again, she tried to move onto less personal ground.

"They're very picturesque."

"Yes," Bebe said, relieved her ploy seemed to have worked. "Yes, they are. Beautiful."

"And she told you about Frances?"

And Esme was back on track just like that. Bebe was unsure how to manage this conversation. "I saw a photo of Frances."

"Ah." Esme sounded strangely satisfied.

"Clara said it was taken at your retirement party. It looked like great fun. When did you—"

"A strange girl," Esme interrupted her.

"Strange?"

"Not a good fit for Clara. But that's easy to say in hindsight, I suppose."

"What do you mean?" Bebe shifted in her seat, uneasy, yet riveted.

Esme sighed. "I mean I'm a snoopy old busybody, and it's not right to talk to you like this. It's just that Clara still grieves for her and, Lord forgive me, but I'm not sure Frances was ever worth it."

"Oh."

"Maybe I shouldn't have said that. It's just that Frances and I were never fond of each other. She didn't take to any of the Dearhearts, truth be told, until…well."

"Until?"

"Until it suited her."

The conversation blundered to a halt. Bebe felt awkward and thankful it had stopped. She was out of her depth. She didn't want to talk about Frances. She'd only recently discovered the existence of her, and it had put Bebe firmly in her place as far as Clara was concerned. Clara was *not* available. Nobody could compete with a ghost.

"Well, she seemed to make Clara happy," she said at last, in a quiet voice.

"Yes. She seemed to."

A waitress approached and Esme picked up the menu.

"What would you like, dear?" she asked Bebe.

Clara. Bebe ran her eye down the list. *I'd like Clara, please, despite her ghosts.* "The turkey sub sounds nice," she said.

CHAPTER ELEVEN

Bebe waved good-bye until Esme's car turned the corner, then she unlocked her front door. She was glad to be back home. Lunch with Esme had been pleasant despite the disappointment of losing Clara's company so soon. They had discussed the garden, the summer season at Preston, and nearly everyone who came in and went out of the diner. Esme knew everybody, and their table drew frequent visits. The flow of friends allowed Bebe to sit back a little as Esme caught up with local news and gossip. Her mind drifted to the conversation about Frances. Not that she thought Esme disloyal in having a negative opinion of Clara's deceased partner. It was clear Esme's relationship with Frances had been strained. Rather, it gave Bebe an insight into Clara's life she felt she should not have, at least not until Clara felt free to share with her, if ever.

Bebe shucked off her sandals and walked bare toed across the oak floor through warm oblongs of sunlight shining through the windows. It was time to make her calls. She had worked all morning on the demise of Berry Ripe. Now she should let Suzzee know it was done, and Jayrah, too. Though she was unsure how that conversation would go. It would be a shock for Jayrah having two friends exit in one episode—actor and writer.

"Darling, I'm home. What's our special word for today? Is it Harmony? Huh? Is it Harmony?" She hung her coat in the hall closet.

"Come on, say Harmony. Haar-mon-neee." Not a squawk or flutter greeted her.

"Darling?" Bebe went looking. He was not in the kitchen or snoozing in his open cage. He wasn't perched on the telephone, or strutting along the mantelpiece, or even plucking the cushion tassels to pieces. It was too quiet.

"Where are you?"

It took several minutes before she managed to locate him on top of a tall, cherry wood bookcase. There were barely six inches between it and the ceiling, yet he had squashed himself into the far corner, against the cornicing. Bebe tiptoed precariously on a dining chair and tried to reach him. He sat huddled with his beak tucked into his neck. He looked like he was napping, but Bebe knew better. This was a sign of upset.

"Come here, my Darling. What's wrong? Come to Bebe, sweetness," she cooed, but he wouldn't budge. She ran back to the kitchen and grabbed a few treats to coax him down. After about five minutes of outright bribing, he uncoiled enough to snatch a tidbit from her fingers, then shrank back into his corner and refused to move.

"Okay. Look, I'm going to set some more treats on the coffee table here...see?" His beady eyes followed her around the room. "Then some more here, by the kitchen door, okay? And the rest are in your cage."

She couldn't believe she was trying to bribe the stupid bird down off the furniture, but he was a stubborn old coot. She could stand there waving dried fruit at him forever and he wouldn't move until he was damn well ready to. Lord knew what had gotten into him. He got moodier and moodier by the day. Yesterday she'd found him anxiously plucking at his chest feathers, when he realized she was watching he'd kicked over his water tray. She'd had to sing to him for ages to bring him out of his funk.

"Look. I'm turning on the radio to your favorite station, and I'll be right here on the couch where you can see me," she said.

She switched on the Latino music station he liked and went to collect her laptop from the upstairs study. She was on the third step up when she stopped. A burned out matchstick lay by her foot. Bebe hesitated, unsure. On the next step lay another. A few steps farther up several more matches were piled in a heap, each one of them burned away to a stub. Bebe's skin prickled. What the hell? Had someone come into the house to start a fire?

She pulled out her cell phone. Who could she call? The police? Clara? Esme? She peered up the stairwell. Could someone still be lurking up there? Nothing seemed different. If there was an intruder then the jaunty accordions and timbales of Guatemala had warned them well in advance that she was now home. Hopefully, a burglar would run for it. And apart from the matches had she any proof someone had actually broken into the house? She dropped the cell phone back into her pocket and continued to the landing gazing cautiously into every bedroom. Upstairs was empty and exactly as she'd left it. Damp towels spilled from the bathroom hamper, her slippers lay abandoned on the bedroom floor, the bed linen still bunched up and the pillows askew. It didn't look like anyone had been there. It didn't *feel* like it either. The house had the same energy as when she'd left it. So where had the matches come from? She descended the stairs wondering whether to check on the basement. Could an intruder be hiding down there with the old boiler and the recycling boxes? Threading carefully down the stairwell, she caught sight of a scrap of cardboard lying behind the couch. Bebe picked up the tattered matchbox. A few blackened matches dropped from it onto the floor. She threw a suspicious look at the bookcase where Darling stared down at her with acute interest.

"Was this you?" she said sternly. "Did you find an old box of matches and rip it to shreds?" Bebe shook her head. She could easily believe it. Wasn't he lurking guiltily in his newest hiding spot? He had found an old box of matches and torn it apart in boredom. It would be just like him to throw matchsticks all over the place then skulk off and hide. Lord knew, he was super sneaky. The other day he'd snatched her best bra from the laundry and wrestled with the elastic shoulder straps all afternoon. If he'd known how to turn on the stove, she'd have her kitchen poltergeist for sure.

"Darling, you gave me quite a turn, my boy-o. I thought someone had been in the house." Bebe tutted. Darling squawked and shook out his wings, as if annoyed at being reprimanded.

"Okay." Bebe sighed, collecting the burned matches and stuffing them back into the broken box. "We'll forget about calling the police this time, my little mischief maker." She tossed the box in the trash, relieved, for once, to have an easy answer. "But next time I go out, you're going into your cage. No more crazy time for you."

Bebe couldn't settle after that. She e-mailed Suzzee that the suicide episode was completed and with Carter, but she couldn't bring herself to call Jayrah just yet. She needed fresh air. This was the day Carter would realize that she was not, and never had been, on his side. Tomorrow she would send in her resignation and soon be on her way out of *Valley*, and it was making her feet itch.

She shrugged on her coat deciding to take a long walk to center herself. She felt half-giddy and half-terrified at the new direction her life was taking. Part of her regretted that Suzzee's agenda more or less decided her own exit point, but the truth was it gave her a chance to walk away with kudos rather than have Carter dump her like so much litter in his pockets.

Bebe headed away from the shore and moved inland. Now that summer had arrived, the beach was busy and she wanted solitude and peace to think while she walked.

The back road behind Preston was a steep, single lane blacktop, used mainly by commercial vehicles to reach the satellite masts above the town. The road was called Bayview, though the view of the bay was partial and bleak. The lane was about two miles long and ran upward and away from Preston's shoreline. Straggly hedgerows bordered wide fields sloping toward the causeway road on one side; on the other a few scattered dwellings sat in rows of twos and threes. Their shingle roofs peppered the hillside all the way up to the satellite masts.

It was a warm day and the breeze this high up was pleasant. Over the hedgerow she could make out the pastel building blocks of Preston in the distance and the strip of steel blue sea beyond. She pulled a stalk of Timothy grass and twirled it in her fingers as she walked. Blackbird families flitted away from her, and she could hear chickadees calling out a warning of her approach. With each step, she accepted she'd passed through an important waypoint in her life and was now cruising into unknown waters. But she was eager for change. She had initiated it.

Soon she reached the first of the houses, a row of three homes with neat gardens and modest family cars parked off road. Some had swings and plastic sandpits on their lawns. Others had orderly flowerbeds and ornamental shrubs. There was something appealing being this far back from the blare of the tourist town with its bright lights and noisy shorefront.

Bebe stood and looked at toys scattered across a front porch and imagined the school run. Maybe it could be too isolated, living out here. There were no sidewalks or streetlights, just wind and fields and a row of scattered houses for a neighborhood.

She walked on. The houses gave way to more hedgerows and fields. A half-mile on, she came across the foundations of two more houses. They had been burned down to the ground.

At one time these had been neighboring homes. Now they were no more than concrete squares with charred beams and siding scraped into piles. She could make out the twisted metal skeleton of furniture among the debris. Broken glass and crockery was scattered everywhere, the sad remains of someone's home. Even the fence posts, what was left of them, were blackened stumps slung haphazardly around the small front yards. It must have been a terrible blaze.

Bebe stood and stared. Compared to the cheerful houses she had just passed, this dereliction was harrowing. She could imagine flames roaring through the wooden structures, blistering the pretty paintwork, searing the garden until it withered and burned.

The breeze picked up and rattled the hedges until they hissed. Bebe sighed along with it. Before her, a ragged rose bush thick with aphids swayed in the blow. Its one and only magnificent blossom drooped onto the blackened earth that had once been a lawn.

Pink Parfait. Bebe recognized the rose from Esme's garden. Esme and Clara doted on the roses. *It must be awful to lose everything you love like this. To have it literally razed to the ground.*

"Poor people," she murmured.

"That one's mine." A chirpy voice came from behind and made her jump.

She spun around to face a large, cheerful woman. Bebe guessed her to be in her late sixties, but her round happy face took years off. Her clothes were haphazard, as if thrown on in a hurry. She wore a wide brimmed safari hat and a khaki windbreaker despite the warmth of the day. A floral nightdress peeped from under the hem of her coat. Her legs were bare and her feet were thrust into yellow rubber gardening clogs. She pointed to the ruins on the right. "That one there."

"It…it must have been awful," Bebe stuttered, a little stunned that such an eccentric lady had popped up out of nowhere. "Were you here when it happened?"

"The sparks from the other house set mine off. Caught the roof." She carried on talking as if she hadn't heard Bebe. "I was screaming and hollering. Turned on the hose, but it was no use. Just too fierce."

"How awful." Bebe felt nothing but horror for the poor woman. "Where are you living now? Are you going to rebuild?"

"Took the fire engine an age to get up here. Ambulance, too. I couldn't wait any longer." Again, the woman spoke over her, not registering her questions. Bebe began to wonder about her state of mind.

"Um. I'm Bebe Franklin. It's nice to meet you." She held out her hand.

"Jean. Jean Bury. I used to live there." She pointed to the wreck on the right, ignoring Bebe's proffered hand. "I had great roses. Wonderful roses. They grow well here. The soil's light. Good for roses, the soil around here."

Bebe was very concerned. Where had the woman come from? Why was she dressed in a nightgown with an old jacket thrown over it? She should not be wandering around the country roads like this.

"Where are you going to now, Jean? Perhaps I could walk part of the way with you? You could tell me about your roses—"

"Is that sirens? Thank God." Jean cocked her ear to the wind.

Bebe stood still and listened but heard nothing. Jean turned, and without another word, plunged through a gap in the hedge into the field beyond. Bebe peeped through the gap after her, but Jean had completely disappeared. Bebe stood at the edge of a potato field and looked about her. There had to be a track that dipped down to the causeway road. A shortcut the locals used? Jean must be tucked somewhere along it just out of eyesight. Bebe had no idea where she had gone, or how she had moved so quickly. She waited and watched to catch sight of Jean farther down the fields, but she never appeared. Bebe pushed back through the gap onto Bayview Road. She was worried for the woman, but what could she do?

With one last look at the burned out ruins, she turned and headed for home, her walk back far less relaxing than the walk out.

❖

The Mellor funeral was over by three thirty. Ronnie and Tony, the part-time driver, were jet washing the limousines. Clara stood in the chapel room in the back parlor where they held the services. She'd vacuumed the darkened oak floors. Now her attention was on dusting. Her duster flicked over the small podium and the chairs sitting in rows before it. Slowly, over the sharp citrus tang of the polish, she began to pick up the deeper, more subtle tones of bergamot and vetiver. Clara closed her eyes and breathed in. She felt drugged. Sugary and sluggish and very content.

"I thought you were leaving today, Joe." She opened her eyes and smiled at the elderly gentleman standing before her. He was dressed in a slightly dated, yet dapper suit. The air around him burned like an aurora borealis with serene greens and bright, sultry turquoises.

"Am too. Right this minute, in fact. Just wanted to drop by and say thanks for everything, Clara."

"You're welcome. It was a big send off."

"It was, wasn't it?" He sounded pleased. "I think every head I ever cut was here. It was nice seeing everyone together like that for the last time." Joe Mellor had been the town barber for thirty-eight years until his hands started shaking too badly. His eldest boy had taken over the business and Joe retired to hang out with his cronies, playing cards and chewing over small town life at the cafes along the boardwalk. He had a large family and many friends to help him while away his retirement.

"And why not? You were a big part of this town," Clara said.

"Ah. Don't know about that," he said, forever modest. His hands ran over his best suit, patting at unfamiliar pockets. "You're a good kid. I knew your father and your grandfather before him. Good people, the Dearhearts."

"Thanks, Joe."

"How are your folks?"

"Good. Mom and Dad love Satellite Beach. Their condo is close to Michael and his family."

"Your brother still working at Kennedy?"

Clara nodded. They stood smiling at each other.

"Don't be afraid to live a little, Clara," Joe said, turning serious. "I'm eighty-two, and believe me, life really is short." He gave a little nod and a big smile to show he wasn't really lecturing her. "Not that I'm complaining."

She smiled back, taking no offense at all. His face straightened back into familiar crease lines.

"Be brave, Clara. You need to be happy. Trust me, the dead don't need tears."

Outside, the automatic garage doors gave a high-pitched whine as they slowly dropped closed. Clara turned her head toward the sound. *We better get those doors serviced soon before they jam.* She glanced back to Mr. Mellor…and found herself alone. The room was quiet and austere as always, the ribbons of turquoise light had gone. Rows of hard backed chairs sat before the cherry wood podium with its vase of freesias, their scent mingling with the lemon floor polish and the ever so faint smell of vetiver.

She flicked her duster half-heartedly over a chair and decided to call it a day. She was tired and a little low. Overhead she heard Ronnie's foot tread as he climbed the stairs to his apartment and wished that she were home, too. Once upon a time this had been her home. The solid, stately house was overstuffed with memories and quiet comforts.

Clara's father had retired to Florida over five years ago when she had taken over the Dearheart funeral home. She had apprenticed to him after graduating in mortuary science, much as her cousin Ronnie was apprenticed to her now. Working alongside her father helped Clara realize why her family had started in this business so many generations ago. It also explained strange occurrences from her childhood, and gave her a better understanding of the Dearheart legacy and her eventual place in it.

The Dearheart home had been in the family for several generations. From the outside it was an august, austere building. On entering the ground floor, the somberness lent a soothing quality to the nature of the business conducted within. But to Clara this building would always be her childhood home.

As a child she had played on the stairs and upper corridors, crouching with her teddy bears to peep at her father through the banister railings. He always looked so kind and important in his somber suit talking gently to the tearful visitors. And as she peeked Clara could see the people the visitors cried for. They drifted vaguely through the rooms and hallways of the funeral home, examining things, hovering near loved ones, inquisitive yet content. Finally, they cautiously blew out the doors and onto the sidewalks of Preston, and then away. They fascinated her with their floating colors and vivid sparkling, brighter than any Christmas tree or trinket in her mother's jewelry box.

Clara never mentioned her sightings at the dinner table. She never drew crayon pictures of her ghosts at school, or told her parents what she saw every day on the streets of Preston and in their own home. She didn't need to. She knew her father could see them, too.

As she grew up, life became complex with converse realities for Clara. Spirits wandered the mall where she lounged in a knot of noisy teenagers. Others coasted through crowded streets, or strode across school playing fields weaving through running backs and wide receivers. She saw ghosts on the beach and boardwalks strolling alongside tourists. They cut across town parks and wandered through the traffic on Main Street. All were caught up in some magical moment of anticipation, a lull before their transcendence to somewhere that Clara couldn't begin to imagine. But she felt their energy and understood their excitement. And she drowned in their scents—the beautiful bouquets and fragrances that suffused her every cell when a spirit was nearby. In some special way, spirits signaled to her through balmy perfumes and exotic spices. It was a personal thing, derived from her love of flowers and gardening, learned by spending many childhood hours in her aunt Esme's garden.

Her father heard the hum of well-tuned engines when a spirit appeared. The hairs on his arms would thrill to attention and he would tingle all over. But then motor engines had been his passion. From hotrods to steam engines, he loved the growl of raw power and the subtle reverberation of gears and pistons. He once told her that her grandfather had always heard music. Sometimes a simple, elegant melody, sometimes rolling anthems, or huge, cresting orchestrations that thundered like tsunami. Her grandfather had played the piano, so Clara guessed music had been his medium, just as scent was hers.

Clara smiled at the thought of her father and his ghostly engines, and wondered at the music her grandfather had heard. He had died before she was born, so she would never know how it sounded.

Not every Dearheart had the gift. Only a few could communicate with the dead, and the dead didn't always want to talk. This spiritual affinity had passed down through the Dearhearts for generations and with it came the keys of the funeral home. Clara knew her aunt Esme was immune to it, as was Ronnie, despite his working at the funeral home. She had no idea where her own successor would come from, but they were a large, dispersed family and she was certain that in time someone would step forward with their scents, or engines, or wondrous music.

Most of the far-flung Dearhearts were unaware of the gift. It was a select family secret. Esme knew about it, and Clara would tell Ronnie soon enough. She would explain it as her father had to her—that the Dearhearts were spiritual facilitators. Their gift didn't exist for exploitation through the occult. They were quite simply undertakers, people who undertook the task of comforting the bereaved, but with the added assignment of comforting the deceased as well. They helped everyone concerned to move on as best they could. They understood the dead had schedules to keep, and sometimes business to complete before they could depart, but once they were gone they were gone. Throughout this process the Dearhearts were merely the smallest of cogs in the greatest of schemes. Frances had never understood that. A lot about the Dearheart gift had made Frances angry. In fact, in some small measure she had turned it into a curse.

CHAPTER TWELVE

C an't she hang or something?" Carter threw the script on the desk and leaned back in his chair.

"Hang?" Bebe blinked. This was not the conversation she had expected when Carter demanded her immediate presence. In fact, she was still disgruntled at having to come all this way in order to be fired face-to-face. It was an expense she could do without. Except Carter wasn't firing her, he was engaging her in a work conversation.

"B…but a gunshot is more dramatically effective," she as good as stuttered. "National suicide statistics say women use firearms more often than—"

"She hangs. We need to keep her face intact. Both of them, the two-faced bitch. She can hardly come back if half her head is blown away."

"Suzzee's coming back?"

His eyes narrowed. "Don't shit me. You know about L.A."

"She's coming back?" Bebe repeated, not rising to his bait.

"It's still under negotiation." He picked up the script and fiddled with the corner clasp. "Don't get me wrong, Bebe. I like the suicide angle. We'll go with it, but she hangs. Lots of things can go wrong with a hanging. She can survive it, if she wants to, that is. But keep her head in one piece. Okay."

"It won't be as dramatic as a gunshot."

"Then you better make it fucking dramatic." He checked his watch and stood. "You're my new wingman, Bebe," he said and walked out leaving her sitting there…employed.

❖

"I don't get it. Suzzee was wild about the L.A job." Bebe stirred her coffee and watched Jayrah tear the wrapper off her biscotti.

"Money talks. She has Carter's balls in a visc with this new job offer. She's been dropping hints about it left, right, and center. Now the Suits are waking up to the fact they have to pay big, big money to keep her. And they will pay, considering nearly all the storylines include her in some shape or form," Jayrah said bitterly. "That's what these last few months have been all about."

"Suzzee's cutting a new deal with Carter?" Bebe was hurt and angry. She had put her head on the line with Suzzee's exit script, and all for Suzzee's negotiating leverage? Jayrah gave her a sour glance.

"Not Carter. He's on the way out. Asshole thinks he can turn it around somehow, but he's the one who allowed Suzzee too much clout. He'll be made to pay for it. That and a heap of other bad moves he made. Idiot just doesn't realize it yet."

"Suz more or less asked me to write myself out of a job with her suicide ploy. What the hell was she playing at?"

"You're not the only one who stuck her neck out for her. But your scene worked. You're safe enough."

"Suzzee said you found something else?" Bebe asked delicately. She knew Jayrah was in a snit. Suzzee had played around with Jayrah's life, too. Big time.

"Yeah. I did. Now I'm not so sure I want it, especially if Suzzee's sticking around. It's more than just money, see. There's a rumor that *Valley's* rigged to win some primetime soap awards, and if that happens there'll be an advertising cash injection *and* a better time slot."

"You want to stay here for that?" Was Jayrah still stuck on Suzzee? It was hardly a progressive career move.

"Look, you've been buried in Toontown for too long and missed all the gossip." Jayrah became defensive. "New investment equals new producer equals no Carter. And I want to be in on it if there's a turn around," Jayrah said. "I got a track record here, Beebs. I'm not walking away and letting some newcomer ride on the back of all my hard work."

Bebe watched Jayrah fidget. Bebe had a track record here, too, though not one she was particularly proud of. Her friends were supposed to keep her posted on the gossip, and in a way they had. She knew who was sleeping with whom. She'd heard all about the latest cosmetic surgeries and adopted overseas babies. But the bread and butter politics had not been passed on to her. She had basically been writing herself out of a job while her friends scrabbled to stay onboard. And all this so Suzzee could score a better deal? *To hell with that. To hell with the lot of them.*

"I'm still leaving," she said.

"Huh?"

"I want out. I'll do the rewrites Carter asked for, then I'm out of here." She stood and grabbed her coat.

Jayrah gawped. "But everyone's talking about your fantastic suicide idea. You're on a winner there, Beebs. Stay and talk to me, maybe I can help with that."

Bebe shook her head and glanced at her watch.

"Gotta run. I have an appointment with my leasing agent."

It was a relief to exit the coffee house. Let them rot in their precious *Valley*, for all their whining and manipulations, it's where they belonged. It wasn't the right place for her. Okay, so Bebe had no idea where the right place was, but as she walked to the subway she realized that for now she didn't really care. She was on her way to see her leasing agent and sign off her studio apartment, effectively saying good-bye to the city. She was taking up Aunt Arlene's offer. In less than six weeks she would be her permanent lodger. It was the right thing to do. Bebe already knew Preston would give her the answers she needed. It was that type of place.

❖

Bebe's eyes flew open. The darkness was thick and warm. She lay perfectly still, straining for the sound that had awoken her.

She kept her breath shallow and controlled, though her heart hammered and her throat was dry. All was quiet. Maybe she'd dreamed it? No. There it was again, the rasping noise that dragged her out of her sleep. She heard it again. What was it? A papery sort of rasp. A strange, yet oddly familiar sound.

Rasp. Rasp.

Bebe sat up and switched on her bedside lamp. The noise came from downstairs. Was Darling up to more mischief? She'd put him in his cage at bedtime so how could it be him? Pulling on her robe, she stepped into her slippers and headed for the stairway, switching on all the lights as she went.

The noise was scratchy and intermittent. Rasp. Rasp. Carefully, Bebe descended the stairs, hesitating on the step where she'd discovered the burned matches. She realized what she was hearing—match heads being struck on the side of a matchbox. Only these matches never flared to life, they just rasped and rasped against the emery. Several strikes and then it would stop, only to begin again moments later. There was no pattern to it.

Unnerved, Bebe continued her search, turning on every light in every room. Soon the house was aglow and Bebe had found nothing. The noise had stopped.

She went to the kitchen and opened Darling's cage. He hopped out and bobbed up and down in a troubled little dance. Bebe continued to investigate with a curiously quiet Darling watching her every move from the top of the bread bin.

"What do you think it is, Darling? Huh? Pyromaniac mice?" She chatted to him for comfort more than anything else. Perhaps it wasn't matches? Perhaps she just had that idea stuck in her head?

"Maybe it's a branch scratching at a wall?" She peered out the window. "I'm damned if I'm going outside to look."

Twenty minutes later, Bebe gave up. The noise had stopped and she had no idea what had caused it. The house was still and Darling had nodded off again. Bebe switched off the lights and went back to bed but slept badly, plagued by dreams of roses and burning lawns.

❖

"Clara. Do you get any…feelings…when you're over at Bebe's house?" Esme asked.

When did it stop being Arlene's house? "How do you mean?" Clara went immediately on to the defensive. What was Esme fishing for now?

"It's just that Bebe came over for morning coffee and mentioned some things that had happened—"

"Oh. Like what?"

Esme gave her an odd look, and Clara realized she was overreacting. She fiddled with the tab of her soda can. Esme was stretching the silence, an old trick of hers. Clara resisted the urge to say something, any old thing. She traced an idle pattern on Esme's kitchen table. She'd be damned if she broke first—

"Okay. What did she say?" she blurted. She flushed slightly and it annoyed her that Esme saw it.

"She asked if Arlene's house was haunted," Esme answered with a steady, all-encompassing gaze. "Have you noticed anything?"

Apart from Temperance trying to stalk her parrot? "Ah. That. She's mentioned it before. The stove that turns itself off and on. Beelzebub's toaster oven. The mysterious smoke that comes and goes." She shrugged. "Believe me, Aunt E, that house is sound. There's nothing going on over there an ounce of common sense wouldn't sort out."

"As long as you're sure." Esme seemed content with that. Clara glanced out the window and focused on sunlight dappling the leaves of a Buttonbush. She was uneasy with the conversation, and not as sure as she stated. She hadn't told Esme that Temperance was still lingering. Nor had she mentioned that Frances was still around, missing in action, so to speak. She was not sure how Esme would take to Temperance hankering after her parrot. And as for Frances, Esme would be most displeased she had not moved along to some other place well away from Preston. But she could say with certainty that she had picked up no paranormal activity at Arlene's house, not even from Temperance, who scratched to get in it.

"How are the two of you getting along? The garden looks a hundred times improved." Esme's next question had her even more on guard.

"Fine. Just fine." Clara was abrupt, wary of a trap.

"Fine?"

"Yeah. Fine."

"Well, good." Esme's gaze drilled into her. Right through to the backbone.

"Yeah. Just fine."

They descended into a thick silence, and Clara fought hard not to twitch. She had so many triggers around the Bebe situation, and Esme knew how to pull each one. A polite silence pulsed through the kitchen.

"It's going okay." She finally capitulated. She hated Esme's trickery, but she fell for it every time.

"You like her, don't you?"

Clara twitched. "She's okay."

"Is she 'fine'?"

"You can be horrible sometimes. You know that?"

CHAPTER THIRTEEN

"Whatya doing?"

Bebe stifled her yelp of surprise and turned to face the young man asking the question.

"Oh. Hi…Hi, there. I was…I was just collecting some cuttings."

"Cuttings?"

"Well, yes. From the protea." Bebe pointed in the vague direction of a waxy silver leafed plant "I was told this was a good place to collect a sample for my garden." She waved the brown paper bag in his general direction, as if that explained the entire process of basically stealing from a public park. Bebe was unsure if it was morally correct, but Esme assured her Prestonian gardeners, including herself, did it all the time. It was almost a tradition.

"Neat." The young man seemed satisfied with the explanation. However, he showed no sign of moving away and even seemed prepared to stand and chat. Bebe hadn't heard him approach at all and was still feeling flustered at being caught red-handed in an indelicate horticultural act.

"I'm Marcus, by the way." He grinned and shrugged awkwardly, his cheeks glowed pink.

"I'm Bebe. Bebe Franklin. I'm looking after my aunt's house this summer and I know she adores proteas. I heard this was a good place to get some cuttings so I thought I'd give it a try."

"Hey, it's free and the dead don't mind." He had a charming grin and Bebe found herself relaxing. "There's some more over there if you want some. It's a different color though."

"Is it pretty? Do you come here for cuttings, too?" she asked dubiously. He did not look the horticultural type. He was tall and ruggedly handsome in an athletic way.

"No, but my friend Clara is always going on about the flowers here." He shrugged again and looked at the grounds, obviously seeing nothing remarkable in the well laid out lawns and multitude of flowerbeds.

"Clara? Clara Dearheart? I know her, too."

"Cool. I wondered why you could…" he tailed off uncertainly.

"I could what?"

"Nothing. Grab your stuff and I'll help you look for flowers. I remember Clara saying there were some good ones over by the vault with the Corinthian columns."

Bebe bent to grab her pruning shears and handbag. When she stood up Marcus was several yards away waving at her.

"Here," he called, a big grin splitting his face. "Got some yellow ones."

Bebe blinked in surprise at his agility, he must have moved like lightning.

She spent the best part of the afternoon hanging out with Marcus as he wandered around the cemetery with her pointing out possible specimens, most of which were totally unsuitable. But she enjoyed his company and his bright breezy enthusiasm for her chore and wondered why he was willing to spend so much time with a stranger rather than go hang with his buddies. Toward the end of her visit, she looked up to find him gone. He had been standing nearby and had now simply vanished. She was a little disappointed he had not said good-bye.

The shadows were growing longer as the sun settled into what promised to be a glorious balmy evening. This was the time of day Bebe felt most melancholy for company. She wished she had more friends here so she could maybe have a dinner party, or a barbeque, something to involve her and move her through these unsettling hours.

She gathered up her plant cuttings, all stored damp and secure in her cooler bag, and zigzagged along the gravel paths toward the cemetery gates, anxious not to be locked in. Her stroll took her under a copse of trees, into an area of the cemetery she had not visited before. A grave marker caught her eye. It was plain black granite with gold lettering, and why it stood out she was not sure. It was no more remarkable than any of its neighbors. It had fresh flowers and she supposed these had drawn her attention. She stepped over the grass to stand before it.

Frances Jane Plummer

Bebe was surprised. This was the grave of Clara's partner. A sadness came over her, for Clara's sake. She examined the bouquets on the grave. They were homegrown and not shop bought. Flowers from Esme's garden she supposed. As she stood there the breeze turned chill, and for an instant the light seemed to falter and dim. Bebe shivered, the hackles rose on the back of her neck, and a chill ran down her spine. She felt uneasy, as if she was not wanted there. As if something was chasing her away. Immediately she moved away from the grave and stepped out from the copse into the late afternoon sunshine. Her skin warmed and she felt cheered and a little silly at being spooked. Across the gravestones, about several hundred yards away, she could see Marcus. He had not gone after all. He stood looking in her direction, concern on his face. When he saw her emerge from the trees he gave a relaxed smile and waved. She waved back and headed for the exit.

❖

"There." Bebe hit Send. Her e-mail winged off into the ether. "Wriggle out of that noose any way you damned well want."

So far it had been a great morning. She was well and truly done with Berry Ripe and the rest of them. *Valley of Our Fathers* was now officially past tense on her résumé, and especially so after the long, tedious telephone conversation she'd had with Carter last night. His paranoia couldn't fathom that she was leaving his show without some other fat contract in place. They went their separate ways with her promising to deliver her rewrite, and his certainty that she was lying and had another job lined up with a rival show.

Hitting the Send button sealed her part of the deal. She was finally free. It was scary and exhilarating all at the same time, but it also felt incredibly healthy.

"Time for a celebratory cup of tea, eh, Darling?" She rose from the desk and stretched cramped back muscles. "Darling?"

She realized how quiet he had been. Usually, the minute she opened her laptop he began crowing and snapping his beak, and generally competing for her attention. He had been well behaved this morning, and now that she thought about it, that was suspicious in itself.

She found him in the kitchen, his red tail feathers sticking out of the bread bin.

"Get out of there, you scavenger. You were fed already. Greedy boy." As she went to shoo him away, it became clear he was not ripping open the bread wrappers but cowering in the safest hidey-hole he could find.

"What is it, my lovely? What's spooked you?" Bebe picked him up gently and cradled him. He ducked in under her chin and sat quietly against her breast.

Bebe threw a nervous glance about the kitchen and blinked in disbelief. The countertops were covered with dust, papery and thin, the color of pearl. A speck of gray floated past her face, as fluffy and delicate as a solitary snowflake. Then another drifted after the first, and another, and another, and several more. The air around her was filling up with soft gray particles, shifting in light flurries and swirling gently like the start of a snowfall. The countertops and utensil jars, cupboards and plate racks were coated in a layer of fine ash.

Bebe choked, a sudden tightness gripping her chest. She was breathing it in. She backed to the door. The ash fall came in heavier swirling eddies, smearing the kitchen window so daylight became dimmed. It carpeted the floor and she could see her shuffling footprints as she backed away. It was claustrophobic. Her heart thumped until it ached with fright.

"Okay, Darling. I think we need to get out of here." She coughed; her lungs were unbearably tight. She bundled them both out of the kitchen and into the living room, which was mercifully clear of any weird ash. She clung to Darling, who huddled in her arms.

She was several steps into the living room when the chimney breast began to rumble. The rumble grew louder and louder, a strange, ominous noise, as if a subway train would burst from the mouth of the fireplace at any moment. On and on it went, the rumbling growing, until it became absolutely deafening. Bebe ran for the door and clawed at the handle. Behind her, with a terrifying whoosh, a black ball of filth flew out of the hearth and exploded into the room. The air became a blackened, seething mass of lung-clogging soot. Bebe screamed. Darling screeched. She wrenched open the door and ran down the hall for the front door. Bebe yanked it open. Sunlight blasted her retinas. Fresh air poured into the hall, crisp and delicious to her burning throat. Darling shook free of her grasp and flew on awkward wings to the clear skies above, shrieking in panic. Bebe fell out the door after him, blinking in the sharp daylight, sucking in great gulps of clean air. She squinted into the sunlight to see Darling lopsidedly flapping toward town. His shrill, frightened cries alarming the local bird life until gardens rang with warning calls and small flocks took to their wings.

Bebe grabbed her handbag from the hall table and scrabbled for her car keys. Haphazardly, she drove toward the town center, one eye on the road and the other on the skies, trying to keep track of a screeching streak of red and silver.

"Clara! It's an emergency. Can you meet me in front of the town hall as soon as you can?" Esme's voice rang out over Clara's cell phone.

"What? What is it?" Clara pulled her truck into an illegal U-turn and pointed it back toward town.

"For some unearthly reason, Darling took himself off to Main Street. Now he's ensconced at the top of the town hall having a panic attack."

"A panic attack." Clara slowed down. Some emergency. She worried where Esme's head was at these days.

"You know he's agoraphobic." Esme's voice took on a determined whine and Clara sighed. She knew this voice well. "Bebe's with him now, but he's not responding to her. She called for help. I'm on my way."

"What do you expect me to do with an agoraphobic parrot? I'm a mortician, not Dr. Dolittle."

"He likes you, Clara. Don't be awkward. We need help. He could harm himself if Bebe can't calm him down. Arlene would never forgive me if something happened to him while she was on vacation."

Clara sighed again and imagined Temperance popping up before her at any moment badgering her to help. It's a wonder she hadn't done so already.

"Okay. I'll be there in five," she said. The path of least resistance was also the thoroughfare of sanity.

A group of about twenty people had gathered before the town hall staring up at the faux marble pediment. Preston's town hall was a disastrous neoclassical affair that some former council thought would lend substance to the market square. Instead, it was laughably out of place in the small resort, like part of a Hollywood film set that had never been carted away.

Clara noted most of the bystanders were locals, with a few tourists scattered through the throng. Prestonians were a nosey lot; they loved to be entertained by the mishaps of others. Vendors and customers alike stood in shop doorways enjoying the impromptu drama. Above them, Darling sat on the lower ledge of the pediment, glaring down at all and sundry, shrieking and displaying his wings in a show of aggressive anxiety. The little square reverberated with his exotic shrills and squawks.

Clara started looking for Esme.

"Clara! Yoo-hoo! Clara! Over here, dear." She heard Esme calling her and soon spotted her aunt near the front of the crowd. A fretful Bebe stood at her side gazing up at the wayward parrot.

Darling also heard Esme's familiar cry. He stopped his caterwauling for a moment and surveyed the people below with great intent, before crying out, "Clara! Clara!" In a perfect mimic of Esme's call. The crowd laughed in delight, and Darling moved into a swaying dance, lifting one foot and then the other. More laughter encouraged him to perform further. Now aware of the crowd focused on him, he continued to call, "Clara. Ooh, Clara. Ooh, Clara."

Clara felt her cheeks heat. She reached Bebe and Esme.

"Seems I'm in time for the cabaret," she muttered. "How will we get him down? He could be up there for days with all this attention."

"Officer Doyle has gone for a ladder," Bebe told her. Clara noted Bebe's face was flushed as well. They were both conscious of the looks they were getting. People recognized the McCall's parrot and knew Bebe was supposed to be looking after him. The suggestive quality of his calls had not gone unnoticed either.

"I'm so worried for him." Bebe was actually wringing her hands. "My poor baby. What if he—"

"Ooh, Clara. I'm coming. I'm coming. Ooh, Clara." Darling shrilled at full volume. The crowd around them exploded into laughter, and Darling danced even more.

"What did he just say?" A look of horror filled Bebe's face.

"Jesus, I'm coming. I'm coming," he squawked.

"He says he's coming." Clara's face was chalk white. She stared straight ahead, trying to shut out the giggles and tittering around her. Her ears burned with embarrassment. The crowd had almost tripled in size as passersby stopped to enjoy the spectacle.

"I'm coming. Bebe. Bebe. Bebe. Bebe. Bebe. Bebe...BEBE!"

"Get me a gun." Bebe's tone was stone cold. "I'll get the little bastard down."

"Bebe!" Esme tried to sound shocked. Clara wanted to throttle her more than the stupid bird if only for the twinkle in her eye and the tilt of a smile she couldn't quite conceal. "He's just a poor innocent bird."

"He's a duplicitous old buzzard. I hope a hawk snatches him," Bebe snapped.

Doyle arrived with an extendable ladder and a few other officers to steady it while he gallantly climbed the town hall frontage. The crowd buzzed with anticipation.

Seems Darling's not the only one who likes an audience. Clara glowered at Doyle, hunching further into her jacket and her shame. She noticed he hadn't the wit to bring a net and that cheered her up a little. Darling would dismantle him the minute he got within five feet.

"Shouldn't somebody tell Doyle that Darling doesn't like men," Esme said anxiously.

"Let him find out for himself," Clara muttered.

"All he has to do is push Big Mouth off." Bebe's eyes gleamed.

"Oh, Bebe! Oh, Clara! Bebe. Clara. Bebe. Clara. Bebe. Clara. Bebe. Red hot. Red hot—" Darling was on a roll and didn't notice Doyle's approach until the last minute. Doyle was on the last rung, only two feet away when Darling did finally spy him. He spread his wings and flapped them madly at Doyle's face.

"CUNT!" He screeched full volume.

Doyle fell back and lost his footing. He slid down several rungs before he scrabbled a purchase. The collective gasp from the onlookers added to the circus theatricality.

"Tent-Ment." Darling watched Doyle's ungainly descent with a cocked head and beady eye. His concentration broken, he took flight and disappeared around the back of the building.

"After him," someone called. The crowd moved to follow.

"A seagull will have him," someone else said.

"A seagull is welcome to him," Bebe muttered. Glumly, she followed the crowd.

"I'm calling Animal Welfare." Esme was on her cell phone. "This is clearly not a job for amateurs," she said, watching a humbled Doyle climb slowly down to the emptying square. Even his ladder holders had deserted him for the new Darling spectacle at the rear of the building. "Besides, there are minors in the crowd. We need to be NC-17 for a performance like this."

"Not funny, old lady." Clara scowled at her. A heavy arm fell across her shoulders. She glanced around at Ronnie.

"Well, cuz," he said with a huge smile. "That was the worst kept secret ever. Imagine being outed by a parrot."

"And you can shut up, too."

He shook her shoulders until she thought her head would fall off.

"I'm proud of you, Clara. I knew that girl liked you. Everyone is happy for you."

Clara didn't dare look up. The last thing she needed was to see the smug, knowing faces of the townsfolk. The past fifteen minutes had been mortifying enough. She seethed at feeling so exposed, and at the stupid conclusions people leapt to because of a dumb parrot. Part of her felt as if a shell had been prized off her back, but instead of raw nerve endings and tender flesh, she felt a curious lightness, as if she had dropped a weight she had been carrying around for years.

❖

Bebe finally caught Darling in the local park. She and Esme simply lined a travel cage with his favorite foods and waited all of five minutes. For a parrot that loved rooting around in the bread bin, a food laden metal receptacle was no problem. He was transferred to Bebe's car, where he promptly fell asleep.

"What on earth made him take off in the first place?" Esme asked as she filled the kettle. Clara and Bebe sat exhausted at her kitchen table.

"Oh, the soot fall freaked him." Bebe visibly jerked at the memory. "It sure as hell freaked me, too."

"Soot fall?" Esme was aghast.

"Yes. A huge one. God, Aunt Arlene's living room will be a mess."

Clara frowned. "Come on." She stood and nodded at the door. "Show me. We'll be back in a few minutes," she told Esme and followed Bebe out the door.

❖

"The carpets and upholstery can be professionally cleaned." Clara examined the sooty mess on the floor before the fireplace.

"It was much larger than that." Bebe looked at the sooty patch in disbelief. "It was massive. It was like an evil black avalanche. I thought I was going to asphyxiate."

"Yet you're not covered in any soot." Clara raised an eyebrow, certain this was going to turn into another ghost story. She glanced around; this house wasn't haunted, that she knew for a fact. It was boringly normal. There were no mystical lights and wonderful fragrances that could transport her onto her tiptoes here. Only the delicate perfume of the house sitter and that drenched her senses enough.

Bebe swung open the kitchen door and peered inside. She went on through and stood looking around her.

"What is it?" Clara came and stood behind her. The kitchen looked ordinary. What had Bebe expected to see? Clara didn't get what was spooking her about the house. Whatever was going on was becoming borderline unhealthy. Maybe she needed to speak to Esme about Bebe's fixation.

Bebe sighed. "Nothing."

"It has to be something."

"No. You wouldn't believe me anyway, and I'm not inclined to try and make you." She made to leave and Clara reached out and caught her upper arm.

"Try," she said. "I need to know what's making you so upset."

"Aside from that vulgar parrot?" Bebe flared. Her eyes glinted, and Clara felt her stomach contract. Before, she'd believed those eyes could get Bebe Franklin anything she wanted. Anything. Now she knew Bebe didn't work that way. She lacked artifice. Bebe played by the rules, and she expected others to do the same. It was a recipe for disappointment and disaster. Those baby blues would always show dismay rather than duplicity, and Clara found that endearing. She also found herself staring, and quickly looked away.

"Tell me what made Darling run. I promise not to be all judgmental."

"Because that's something you'd never do."

Clara reddened. "No. Because it's something I've learned to outgrow. I made a mistake." She was glad her tone was steady and level. Inside, her guts were whisked into a froth. Guilt could do that to a healthy digestive system.

"I'm sorry. I've had a lousy day…week, even, but I've no right to take it out on you." Bebe looked around the kitchen with a bleak stare. "I came in here and found Darling scared out of his wits. He was hiding in the bread bin. I lifted him out and then I noticed the air was filling up with ash. It was lying all over the countertop and messing up the windows."

The kitchen was spotless. Gleaming even. Bebe was an excellent housekeeper. She kept on top of all the chores.

"I had to run. I was choking with it." Bebe's face grew pale and her eyes darkened to a saturated sapphire. Clara was in no doubt Bebe believed she'd experienced this phenomenon. She scoured her mind trying to come up for a plausible explanation, but could find none. The kitchen surfaces shone smugly back at her.

"Then we went into the living room and the whole chimney started shaking. The soot came out like some huge pyroclastic explosion. I just ran." Bebe looked Clara straight in the eye. "I know Esme thinks I'm nuts. But the spookiest things happen in this house. I'm beginning to hate it. Something's not right." Her eyes clouded with worry and her plump lower lip trembled slightly before she pulled it in and distractedly chewed on it. Clara felt a bubble of desire burst somewhere in her chest and surge through her body in a delicious lava like glow. She turned away quickly.

"Let's deal with what we can for the moment. The living room needs to be professionally cleaned," she said. "We'll get someone in to do the furniture and carpets. Meanwhile, you need to get out of here for a while." Then her mouth started saying words she was unprepared for. "Leave Darling with Esme and come down to my place for dinner tonight. It's nothing fancy, just a barbeque. It's nice down on the beach in the evening and it will do you good to unwind a little." *What the hell?*

"I'd love to," Bebe said. She looked surprised and pleased at the offer.

"Good. Good." Clara swallowed a lump in her throat. *Everything she does is so simple and…and elegant.* "I'll go get some steaks… oh, and lobster. Local lobster is the best." She picked up a box of Darling's bird food. "You can tell Esme she's parrot-sitting."

CHAPTER FOURTEEN

Clara's hands were sweating and all she'd done was buy a few steaks and a split lobster. She had some greens in her fridge to throw together a salad. At least she thought she had. She stood frowning in the greengrocers, scanning the fresh produce. Perhaps she should get more fresh stuff just in case the salad leaves had wilted, or she hadn't as many tomatoes as she remembered.

What on earth possessed her to invite Bebe to dinner? She was a lousy hostess, a terrible cook, her house was untidy, and she'd barely have time to straighten it out. She hadn't lit her barbeque once this year. Did she even have enough coals to cook with? What about wine? White or red? Or perhaps Bebe preferred beer? She decided to buy all three.

"Forget that vinegar in your hand. Get the 2008 Cabernet Sauvignon. The one from the Alexander valley. It's there, to your left." Temperance appeared beside her, her floral aromas mixing with the wooden wine caskets of the wine boutique.

"This vinegar is twenty-five bucks a bottle." Clara tightened her hold on her chosen bottle, ignoring the forty-dollar bottles Temperance pointed at on the next shelf.

"If you're going for red then get the Cabernet Sauvignon," Temperance grumped. "Try something decent for a change."

"Go away," Clara said, conscious of the other shoppers around her. She didn't want to be seen talking to herself. There was already enough speculation about her after Darling's supposed denouement. She imagined eyes boring into her from all angles.

"Cabernet Sauvignon, 2008. Bebe has a palate. She's a McCall after all."

Clara thumped her original bottle into her shopping basket and moved over to a chiller cabinet filled with the white wine and rosés.

"The Riesling. At least get the white right." Temperance's scratchy voice rang in her ear. Clara reached for the Semillon. "Are you huffing at me, young lady? The least you could do is compromise with the Gewürztraminer. She likes German grapes. You'd think you'd at least get the nationality right."

With a defeated sigh, Clara picked out two Rieslings and replaced her bottle of red on the shelf. *White wine it is then. Anything for peace and quiet.*

"Do I need beer?" she asked. A man standing nearby looked over at her curiously. She turned away. No answer from Temperance. She had ducked out once she got her way with the wine. *I suppose that means no to beer.*

She went to pay.

Clara checked her watch. Bebe would be arriving soon. She was organizing a cleaning firm to see to Arlene's carpets and curtains. She hoisted her shopping bags into her arms and headed for the truck, her stomach still in knots. She was extremely self-conscious about the evening ahead.

"Beer makes her flatulent." Temperance was in the driver's seat when Clara opened the truck door.

"Do I really need to know that? And move over."

Temperance shrugged.

"You'll find out soon enough." She shimmied over awkwardly and Clara climbed in and set her grocery bags on the passenger side floor.

"Where were you earlier when Darling had his freak out?" Clara maneuvered the truck out into Main Street and set off for home. "It's not like you to miss a Darling moment."

"I told you. It's that house. Something is keeping me away from my own house!" Temperance slapped the dash in frustration. Clara threw her a sideways glance. The old lady was very upset.

"How do you mean? Maybe you're not meant to go there. It can't be good for you to be snooping around your nearest and dearest. I told you that before."

"You said there were no rules."

"I said I was unsure if there were any rules, but it wouldn't surprise me if there were. Hundreds of them, in fact."

Temperance contemplated this for a moment, then shook it off.

"Anyway. I felt his upset but I couldn't reach him," she said.

"Where were you?"

"I don't know. It's hard to describe. Like just before you drift off to sleep, then you're suddenly falling but something jolts you back and you feel all disorientated? Like that. Sort of. Only this doesn't last an instant. It can go on for days and days. It's very unnerving."

"Okay." It sort of made sense. Temperance, and souls like her, were balancing on a fine line between two dimensions. Who was she to argue with Temperance's experiences? She'd find out in her own time what it was like.

"I was so worried for him, Clara." Temperance was back onto Darling again. "It was so strange. I could feel him. He was frightened. Terrified even. Then he was suddenly having a whale of a time. He was happy and singing, and then he fell asleep well fed and content. I was with him in my heart even if I couldn't manage to get there in person…or spirit, rather." Temperance turned to face Clara. "I knew you and Bebe were with him. I felt that, and that was a tremendous relief."

"Well…good." The least said about Darling's escapades the better.

"I hear you and my granddaughter have been having sex," Temperance said. Clara's grip tightened until her knuckles shone white on the steering wheel. Temperance narrowed her eyes and glared at Clara. "You don't look like someone who's having sex. You look wound up tighter than a rattler, as usual."

"That is none of your business, old lady!" Clara glared right back. "And where did you hear such rubbish?" She knew exactly where the rumor had started and cursed Darling and his troublesome beak. She was surrounded by meddlers and rumormongers in all shapes and sizes.

"Everywhere. The whole town is buzzing with it. Clara Dearheart and Arlene McCall's niece are having a lesbian affair. It's on everyone's lips. And you're telling me it's rubbish? Well, it better not be. I happen to love that girl dearly. Don't you dare hurt her, or you'll have me to contend with."

"I'm not going to hurt her. It's all bunkum. Darling started it with—" But Temperance had already gone, her threat hanging in the air with the scent of summer roses and some fast fading pink sparkles. "Like I don't have you to contend with anyways."

Clara headed home to Three Mile Beach. She had perhaps an hour to light the barbeque, tidy her house, and throw together a salad…oh, and shower. Her guts clenched with nervous tension, and it annoyed her to be so silly over something as simple as inviting a friend for dinner.

Bebe had become a friend, she supposed. And what was so wrong with inviting friends to dinner? She scolded herself. Nothing. Nothing at all.

❖

"I hope you don't mind, but I brought some things for a salad." Bebe bustled in with a large grocery bag. "Have you marinated the steaks?"

Clara stood back as Bebe brushed past her at the door and made straight for the kitchen.

"Marinade?" she asked, feeling stupid that she hadn't thought of it.

"I thought not," Bebe called back to her from the kitchen where she'd started unpacking her bag and clattering about. "That's why I made this chili and honey paste. We can coat the meat with it then put it straight on the grill. Where do you keep your knives?"

"In the drawer to the left of the sink." Clara stood in the kitchen doorway deciding it was best not to enter the small space that now seemed so full of Bebe Franklin and her frenetic energy.

"You call these knives? I wouldn't cut air with these knives. They're blunt. In fact, this one has chunks missing from the blade." She looked over at Clara accusingly.

"I use it to shuck clams," Clara said, suffused with a sort of abstract guilt. "Maybe I should buy a new set sometime." She had never considered the state of her kitchen knives before and what she put them through. They cut things—bread, clams, wood—what else mattered?

"Humph." Bebe's head was already buried in the fridge. She dragged out all sorts of items. "I'm glad you have fresh lemons. I'm going to make a dressing. Could you crush some garlic for me?"

"Yeah. Okay." And just like that, Clara found herself standing hip to hip beside Bebe in her tiny kitchen preparing the first fresh meal she could remember making in years. It had been a long time since her home had been open to the simple pleasures of cooking and companionship. Takeout, microwave meals, and frequent visits to Esme's table were how she sustained herself these days. She ate to stop from falling over; it was as simple as that.

Garlic coated her fingers, its earthy pungency burst into the kitchen and mingled with the sharp zest of lemon and lime. She watched amazed as Bebe skillfully threw together a colorful salad in mere minutes, rescuing the limp leaves she had managed to toss together earlier. A fragrant mix of greens and reds and yellows tumbled into her earthenware salad bowl. The steaks gleamed on a plate, coated with a sticky aromatic goo, mouthwatering with promise. Clara's stomach flipped. She was hungry. And happy. Her back and shoulders relaxed. She hadn't realized she was holding herself so stiffly.

"I'm going to put the steaks on the grill." She lifted the plate and headed out. "We have lobster for starters."

"I'll bring it out." And Bebe was behind her, coming out onto the deck. The dunes rolled out before them, laced with the long shadows of crackling maram grass. Beyond that the sea rolled, slow moving and indigo in the setting sun. Delicate fairy lights twined along the wooden handrail, twinkling magically as dusk fell. Clara had plugged the lights in at the last minute and was pleased they still worked.

She watched as Bebe paused to take in the scene, the table set so prettily for her with its sunset backdrop. The edges of the tablecloth lifted slightly in the breeze, and the cutlery and ice bucket with its bottle of chilled Riesling gleamed silvery in the lowering light. Clara poured wine into mismatched crystal wine glasses.

"This is so lovely," Bebe exclaimed and Clara smiled.

"It's been a long time since I entertained," she said, relieved that so far it was going well. She went to check on the barbeque and put their steaks on the grill. Behind her Bebe fussed over the salad bowl and their lobster entrée. A warm breeze ruffled Clara's hair and she raised her face to the sunset and closed her eyes, allowing the simple pleasure of the moment to run through her, filling every cell of her being. She felt genuine, bone-deep contentment, sure that she was in the right place and doing the right thing. How long had it been since she had last felt like this? She looked at Bebe preparing their plates; her hair glowed in the last rays of daylight and her skin shone like satin. Clara wanted to tell her she never did this anymore, had friends over or entertained; that the deck with its pretty lights, and white tablecloth, and glimmering crystal was really an illusion. This was not her reality. This house was too empty to fill with words and laughter. But somehow tonight that had changed. Tonight it was real. She wanted to tell Bebe how everything sort of…increased when she came close. How walls expanded, how windows widened to pour in light and clean, fresh air. How Clara's whole world grew when Bebe looked at her, and she grew right along with it in proportion to Bebe's smile, or word, or glance. How her mind became focused, how she felt taller, stronger, happier, more whole. But she didn't know how to say any of these things, so she silently watched the golds and pinks of the setting sun slide over the bare skin of Bebe's arms.

"Cheers." Bebe reached for her glass of Riesling. "Here's to peace at the end of a Darling day."

Shyly, they clinked glasses in a salute to a beautiful evening they had created for themselves.

❖

"More wine?" Clara uncorked the second bottle of Riesling. The first had been easily sipped away with the delicious meal. Now they sat under a dome of constellations watching for shooting stars. Their talk was minimal and general, safe topics like books and movies.

"Let's celebrate good endings and even better beginnings." Clara toasted Bebe's decision to leave *Valley of Our Fathers* and stay on in Preston freelancing.

"It's utter madness in the current economic climate," Bebe said. "But I can honestly say I feel fantastic. As if a migraine has suddenly lifted off me. I didn't realize just how oppressive it all was."

Inwardly, Clara applauded Bebe's strength to call it quits and take a chance. The fact it kept her in Preston longer was an unexpected bonus she was frightened to inspect too closely. She took her seat alongside Bebe and they relaxed, looking out over the moonlit bay.

"This has been a wonderful evening," Bebe said. "The wine is fantastic, by the way."

"It came recommended."

"Did you and Frances live here? It's a wonderful home."

This had been the closest they had come to personal talk. Clara shifted. She took a breath and thought it through. This was what she wanted, for their talk to become more personal, more intimate. She wanted to ask Bebe so many ridiculous things: What would she write about in Preston? Did she know she saw ghosts? Did she really like Clara the way Ronnie said she did? No. Scrap that last question. Clara's face flushed. She refocused her thoughts. In return, she wanted to tell Bebe about her time with Frances and the life she had been living since her death.

"Frances didn't like the beach much. It was too touristy in the summer and too cold in the winter. The storms blow in from seaward and the whole shack moans like an old donkey. She thought it was too small, anyway." She was surprised to voice what she always considered a curmudgeonly side to Frances. The shack was in a wonderfully private area of the beach, and with her winter upgrade it was toasty when the woodstove was lit.

"It's the perfect size for two. I'd love to live out here. It's beautiful." Bebe held her face up to the soft night breeze. "Smell that air all salty and clean. It's perfect."

Underneath the salty breezes and smell of warm sand, Clara could pick up an undertone of Night-scented stock, Bebe's smell. It was her spiritual scent, and Clara would always associate it with her.

A moth landed on Bebe's hair and Clara lifted a hand to brush it away. Her fingers strayed into the silken coolness, each strand poured through her fingers like sand in a timer. Bebe sat very still, her indigo gaze locked with Clara's. As if pulled by some mystical, magnetic force, Clara bowed her head and moved toward Bebe for a kiss. Bebe's eyelids fluttered and closed, and her mouth opened slightly like a rose petal to rain. Perhaps it was the loss of eye contact, perhaps it was her own fear, but at the last minute Clara turned her head and her lips grazed Bebe's cheek. She sat back quickly filled with clumsy emotions.

Bebe set her wine glass aside and stood.

"Why are you so hesitant?" she asked and settled into Clara's lap. "You must know I want you to kiss me?" Her hands cupped Clara's face. "The whole town thinks we're doing it anyway."

And she drew Clara's mouth to hers in a kiss of unmistaken intention. Her kiss was soft and velvety and held richness and depth. There was a strength in her kiss that melted Clara's bones until all of her was liquid and she could pour like water into and through Bebe. Heat and headiness overwhelmed her. She reached out and circled Bebe's waist, pulling her close, pressing her against her own burning body, wanting her to feel the effect she was having. How weak and wanting Bebe's kiss made her. Their tongues and taste mingled and fused, hands poured through hair and stroked arms and backs and shoulders until their fingertips itched with want.

Bebe broke the kiss first and gasped for air, her face flushed and moist, her eyes sparking with need.

"We need to go to bed," she said. "Right now." Abruptly, she stood to allow Clara to rise and lost her balance on shaky legs. Clara reached for her and held tight, startled that Bebe was as addled with lust as she was. Without a word, she took her hand and led her to her bedroom.

They stood by the foot of the bed and kissed uncertainly, in case anything had changed, in case one of them wanted to run, in case a bedroom meant something different, in case…in case…They melted against each other, over each other, into each other; the boundary between their bodies simply evaporated. Clara ran her hands over silken skin but felt her own flesh ripple with pleasure. She sucked on Bebe's throat, her neck, and her earlobe. Her scent flooded her. The world fell away and all that was left was this wonderful woman who touched Clara with such care and passion, as if she were crystal and might shatter at any moment. Clara sank into her. With strong, fumbling fingers she undid every tiny button, every hook and zipper and let the cloth slide from Bebe's body and pool at their feet. Her own clothes fell too, as Bebe plucked and pulled the cotton and denim from Clara's frame dropping them away like wrapping paper.

"Your skin is like vanilla," Clara whispered. Her fingers danced across Bebe's shoulders and breasts. "Like whipped cream, and sugar, and baby's breath flowers. You sparkle." She gathered Bebe in her arms and put her down onto the bed. Their heated flesh slid against each other like sand whispering down the dunes.

"You smell of old wood." Bebe bit Clara's shoulder where the muscle capped the top of her arm and then bit her rounded bicep. "Mahogany and hedgerows. Strong and dark, like trees."

Clara cupped the soft roundness of Bebe's face in her calloused palms. She kissed her brow, her eyes, cheeks, chin. The column of her throat, hot and humming under her lips, and down to the valley between her breasts where her bones trembled and flesh fluttered with the beat of her heart.

She inhaled the smell of Bebe's skin, sun-kissed and perfumed on her nape and shoulders and on into her armpit where her true scent crept through its deodorized mask. She buried her nose in the sweaty crease under Bebe's breasts and drew in a deeper, wetter smell until her head spun. Then down to the dark, tangy scents around her navel and the springy, titian vee between her legs. These scents Clara mapped in her mind forever. These scents she wanted for her own, to keep for always. Bebe's thighs were soft as butter, and behind her knees smelled of sunscreen and emollients. Her feet were dry and smelled of leather and sand. Clara traced back up Bebe's body with the tip of her tongue, exploring every crease and fold, dipping into hollows and sacred places, a long and torturous journey, until they once more lay nose-to-nose. She held Bebe's steady gaze before lowering her mouth and sucking gently on raspberry lips that kissed her back with sweet assurance.

"Think you know me now?" Bebe gently tapped Clara on her nose. "Did I pass the sanitation check?" she teased, and rolling them both over, climbed onto Clara and placed her hands on the pillow on either side of her head. She smiled down and her breasts hung tantalizingly close. Her breathing was heavy and her skin flushed.

"It's not that." Clara cradled Bebe's breasts, the nipples scratched the heart of her palms. She squeezed gently and watched a rosy flush spread up to Bebe's throat and into her cheeks. "I've been captivated by your scent since the moment I met you. But I didn't realize how it affected me."

"Until we got naked." Bebe laughed. "How come that stupid parrot knew something we didn't?"

"I knew it," Clara said. "I think I knew it all along, but I ran away." It was true. Temperance, Esme, even Ronnie, had seen it, but she had deliberately blocked it out. She had been frightened—frightened to move forward, frightened to embrace life. Frightened of this? This warmth, this simple gift of loving? What a fool she had been. She caressed Bebe's breasts, belly, and shoulders, amazed at her own stupidity, at the frozen wasteland of her existence. Amazed at how fast the thaw when it finally came. She was floating on streams of glacial water as around her the ice caps of her life crashed into nothing.

Bebe stretched her body the length of Clara until every inch touched. Then she kissed her slowly and deeply until nothing else existed. Clara's hand wormed down between them and into Bebe. Warm and wet and Night-stock scented. They plunged and reared and arched and came. Easily, quickly, choreographed, as if their bodies had waited for this dance a long, long time.

"Hush, sweetheart." Bebe held her in her arms as Clara wept.

CHAPTER FIFTEEN

Through the pre-dawn shadows Clara could make out Bebe's profile on the pillow beside her. She raised her hand and ran a fingertip along the bridge of her nose, tracing a line to her mouth. The curve of her index finger paused in the dip under Bebe's lower lip. Bebe smiled and the dip flattened slightly.

"You're beautiful," Clara whispered.

"I think you are," Bebe whispered back. "I like sleeping with you." The words drifted into embarrassed swallow. "I need some water," Bebe said, trying to cover her discomfort. Clara felt Bebe's blush through her fingertips and rose from the bed to get her a drink.

"Here." They sat side-by-side, blankets tucked up around them, and sipped from the water bottle. Outside, the wind crashed around the shack, rattling the rafters and making the walls creak and shudder.

"That wind came out of nowhere," Bebe said.

"It will blow over by daybreak." Clara reached over and took Bebe's hand. "In December and January, the storms last for days. It's wonderful out here in winter. I love it."

"I can imagine how cozy it would be." Bebe snuggled into Clara's side and drew her arm around her shoulders.

"Bebe…" Clara was unsure how to continue, but the question had been burning holes in her for so long now. "You know that fisherman you saw last week? Tom Ray?"

"Yes." Bebe nodded. "It's funny you should mention him. I was just thinking about him the other day."

"Oh? Why's that?"

"Because he had so much local knowledge about the old boat building industry. I had an idea to interview him for an article on it. My first step into freelancing."

"Ah, I see." That might be difficult, Clara thought, given that Tom is dead as a doornail.

"And as luck would have it, I bumped into him yesterday and he agreed to do it," Bebe said happily.

"What?" Clara was startled. One manifestation of Tom Ray she could manage, filing it away as a one-off ghost sighting, but two? Bebe had seen and spoken to Tom twice? Tom, who had drowned in Preston Bay forty odd years ago? It was impossible.

"He's a nice man. He loves to talk. I suppose he likes the company." Bebe sighed and snuggled in closer. Her lips brushed against the side of Clara's breast and her hand slid across her belly. "I want to make love again," she said simply.

Clara's body stirred and tuned in to Bebe's needs. She didn't know what to make of this Tom Ray anomaly. It was slipping rapidly to the back of her mind as Bebe's fingers dipped playfully into her navel. Perhaps she should talk to Esme about Bebe's visions. Bebe nibbled her neck and slid down under the covers dragging Clara with her, and Clara sank without another thought.

"Hey, you. Where have you been? I miss our chats." Jayrah's voice floated from Bebe's cell phone voice mail. It had none of the brash quality of before.

We had chats? Bebe surmised things were tougher in *Valley* now that the scapegoat had moved to greener pastures.

"Your episode has been recorded, and guess what? It's in two parts! They split Berry's suicide over two shows to milk it completely. She kicks the chair out from under herself tonight, but the viewers have to wait until Monday to see if she swings," Jayrah continued with forced brightness.

Bebe tucked the phone into her shoulder and used both hands to open the front door and bustle into the hallway. In a few minutes the cleaners would arrive to remove the soot from the carpets.

"No one knows how it will turn out." Jayrah's message went on. "Not even me. I never see Suzzee much anymore so I have no idea—"

The See Spot Go van pulled up outside and Bebe saved the call and dumped the phone in her handbag. She'd listen to Jayrah's woes later, then call back and make suitable sounds of sympathy. She was gladder than ever to be free of *Valley*.

In under two hours, the living room was spic-and-span and the curtains were in her car to be dropped off at the dry cleaners, an easy chore as she had an appointment at the hair salon over at the mall anyway. After the horrendous rose arch incident Bebe had found a hairdresser who was not only competent enough to rescue her hair but also encouraged her into a new style. Now Bebe was a regular. Today was a hair and manicure day and she looked forward to being pampered. The expensive indulgence felt right, even on her reduced budget. Her body felt sexy and vibrant; her walk was confidant, and her skin and hair glowed. She was an attractive, contented woman, and she had a new lover to thank for it. In fact, she had Clara Dearheart to thank for it. This morning Bebe had been kissed awake by Clara Dearheart, in Clara Dearheart's bed, in Clara Dearheart's house out on Three Mile Beach. And Clara Dearheart had brought her breakfast in bed, and fluffy towels for her shower, and kisses good-bye, and best of all, she was going to call later and maybe they could meet up again tonight. Bebe couldn't wipe the smile off her face.

"Darling. You're in charge of this spotlessly clean house. I expect it to look the same on my return. Understand?" She tapped his beak gently and he scuttled sideways away from her, as devious as ever. It had been an added bonus to this wonderful day to find him already ensconced in the kitchen when she'd returned that morning. Esme had dropped him off while Bebe was still out on the tiles. It was a secret blessing not to have to go to Esme's and collect him. Bebe was reluctant to explain her whereabouts last night. Let Clara deal with that little nugget of information. Esme wouldn't be long in prying it out of her niece.

Bebe drove along the rain flecked causeway road to the mall. Sunlight sparked the water on either side into a thousand points of light, and Bebe felt she was driving along a silver ribbon through a sea of diamonds. Overhead, gulls drifted on the breeze before spinning away, their mewling cries cutting the air. Bebe smiled at the day, at her reflection in the mirror, at the songs on the radio, at her memories of last night. She replayed every word, relived every detail for the umpteenth time until she glowed inside so strong it was as if the sunshine and the sparkling sea and the shining, silver road all emanated from her.

"Did Bebe stay long last night?" Esme asked before Clara's bottom even hit the chair.

"Yes, she did," Clara answered. There was no point in avoidance. It was obvious the lunch invite was for information rather than nutritional well-being. "But let it alone." She was stern. "It's too soon to say what it was, or will be, or anything like that."

Esme nodded curtly and poured tea from the china pot, a small smile hovered around her lips. "She's going to stay at Arlene's for the rest of the year."

"I know. She told me," Clara said.

"Are you pleased?"

"Yes." Clara felt petty with her curt responses. "I'm secretly *very* pleased." Her voice softened, and she looked over at Esme. "But it's early days."

"The early days are the best." Esme began handing out cups and plates.

"Has Bebe ever talked to you about people she has met around and about Preston?" Clara sipped her tea and watched Esme very carefully.

Esme frowned over at her. "Whatever do you mean?" She offered the sandwich platter. Clara selected egg and watercress and bit into it, allowing herself time to think.

"I suppose I mean…" She chewed thoughtfully, then swallowed. "I suppose I mean I think Bebe can see ghosts. In fact, I know she can. Well, at least one. Tom Ray. And I want to know why that is."

"Good grief!" Esme looked shocked. "She's said nothing to me."

"I don't think she realizes he's a ghost. She just thinks he's an odd old boy who fishes on the shore day and night."

Esme's cup clattered onto the china saucer. "This is awful, Clara. You'll have to tell her. Why on earth can she see him? Why Tom? Do you think others can, too?"

Clara shrugged. "I have no idea. I always thought it was a Dearheart thing. Why shouldn't other people see them, too? But it's weird that it's Bebe, and it's weird that she's clueless about it. I just wondered if she's mentioned speaking to anyone else…unusual."

Esme shook her head. "No. Not at all. But it does concern me a lot. We'll have to talk with her. She has to be told."

"Maybe we'd best let her sort it out for herself. The penny will eventually drop."

They sat in silence contemplating this easier option.

"Don't you think it strange?" Esme eventually spoke. "That Bebe can do what Frances always wanted to but never managed?" She shot Clara an uncomfortable sideways glance.

"I never thought about it like that." Clara looked at her large, blunt hand and the delicate cup nestling in it. "What Frances wanted couldn't be forced. She thought it was something I could teach her but withheld." A gloom welled up in her, blotting out the pleasant start to the day. An important day, at that. A day, well, night, when she had made gigantic strides out of the shadows surrounding her. Now she felt they were clawing her back under.

"What Frances couldn't accept is that it was your gift. Ronnie and I don't have it and we're Dearhearts. Truth be told, it's something I'd hate. Frances had her head full of unhealthy ideas. A lot of strange stuff has been happening at Arlene's recently. You don't think that—"

"No. No, I don't," Clara said, almost too hastily. "The house is safe. I was there when Bebe burned her hand, remember? There was no spirit activity I could pick up on. She'd simply forgotten she'd turned on the stove. It's always the simplest explanation."

"What about the rest? The smoke and the soot? Even Darling was frightened."

"We could talk about it all day. When was the last time Arlene had her chimneys swept? Even Bebe blamed some of the smoke on a neighbor's yard fire. It's impossible to have an answer for everything, but I can assure you there are no ghosts hiding in that house."

"Maybe you don't see them all. Could that be it?"

Clara shrugged and stood. This was an awkward subject and Esme was cruising too close to the truth. Until Frances, Clara would have categorically said she saw every willing spirit that passed through Dearhearts, if only for a few seconds. Until Frances. She was not even sure if Frances was still around. She'd never seen her, and that avoidance, that failure of her lover to say a single word gnawed her hollow. It was an act laden with anger and blame, and it filled Clara with unmanageable guilt.

She made a show of checking her watch.

"I have to go. Ronnie's waiting on me."

"Think about it, Clara. Really think about it. Bebe may not be aware she can see spirits, but she definitely has some sort of gift, and she has sensed something is not right in that house," Esme said in an uncanny echo of Temperance's words. Clara took a deep breath and centered herself. She refused to give in to Esme's drama. "I don't think you can afford to be so cavalier about anything concerning Bebe anymore. None of us can."

"You're determined she's being haunted."

"I'm saying Bebe is uneasy in that house. I'm ignorant about ghosts, as you well know, but I respect that Bebe shares the same gift as you, even if she is unaware of it. And if she's asking these questions then the least you can do is take it seriously."

"I'll call around later and help with that hibiscus," Clara said over her shoulder as she left. For her, the conversation was over. She was none the wiser after chatting with Esme, but agreed with her parting words. Bebe had to be told who and what she was

COOL SIDE OF THE PILLOW

agreeing to interview for a magazine article. But if Bebe did have a gift similar to the Dearhearts', then there was surely no way she could be being haunted? How can you haunt someone who can see you?

Clara swung her truck out onto Hope Street and headed to the funeral home. *Why would a spirit hang out around Bebe, flicking stove switches off and on, causing soot falls, and generally unnerving her?* Clara had never heard or seen anything like that, ever. Spirits just didn't do that. Not in the real world. They were busy people; they mostly moved on. Some, like Marcus, or Tom, or even Temperance, hung on a bit longer for whatever reason until time meant nothing to them. Marcus was waiting for his mother so he could walk home with her. Tom...well, Tom was just stuck on the shore with his fishing pole, obviously content to fish until the second coming. And Temperance? The old duck was as contrary in death as she was in life, waiting for her parrot to pop his clogs and be with her for all eternity.

Frances didn't fit in this hypothesis. She had been unhappy in life and should have departed quickly. The fact she hadn't done so upset and confused Clara. That she refused to meet or speak hurt dreadfully. Clara yearned for Frances to move on, to finally find peace. She'd wanted that for four years, and for four years Frances had avoided her.

Now Bebe Franklin had arrived in her life and Clara felt different. Something had somehow shifted. It felt as if Bebe had accomplished something four years of waiting for Francis could never do. Bebe had helped Clara reach closure, and in doing so maybe she had opened up something new.

"You look mellow," Ronnie commented when she entered the office.

"What do you mean?" She was immediately defensive.

Ronnie shrugged. "Nothing. Just you looked chill. Have you been hitting the bong?" he joked.

"No. You know I don't do that junk," she snapped.

"I take it back. All your chill has gone. Blown to bits by your crabby old self."

"Get used to it." She shoved a sheaf of invoice papers his way. "And file these under Paid."

❖

Bebe flicked through her magazine as Thelma teased the last strands of hair in place. They had been gossiping nonstop about this and that, mainly about the latest fashions and the adventures of Thelma's five-year-old at kindergarten. It had been a leisurely morning though Bebe kept peeping at her cell phone in the hope Clara might have left a message.

"...no idea what drove her to doing it. Seems a harsh way for a woman to kill herself..." The conversation from the chair next to hers finally began to register.

"It's an ugly way to go," Thelma gave her opinion to her colleague and the customer sitting next to Bebe.

They must be talking about Valley. *Berry's suicide must have gone out yesterday.* She checked her call log. Jayrah had called yesterday and not that morning. The opening episode of Berry Ripe's suicide had already aired.

"I'll never understand why she did it. It was just wrong." The conversation continued.

"Because she had been pushed into a corner by everybody," Bebe spoke up. People around here knew she worked in television. It was no big deal to explain she had written that episode. "The blackmail was just the icing on the cake..." She trailed off when she saw the blank stares. "Um. You're talking about *Valley of Our Fathers*, right?"

"No, you." Thelma jostled her shoulder in a friendly way. She removed the towel and began brushing away any stray hairs. "That Plummer girl. She killed herself a few years back. I always remember because of the flower show. She did it that day."

"Plummer? Frances Plummer?" Bebe was startled.

"That's her." Thelma nodded.

"What did she do?"

"Hung herself." Thelma stepped back quickly as Bebe jumped to her feet and struggled to open her handbag.

Oh dear God. Clara's ex hung herself and here I am playing about with suicide for a crappy TV show. What if she sees that episode? What if someone tells her and she thinks I was copying Frances's story?

"Here." She thrust several twenties at Thelma. "I just remembered another appointment."

"Wait. There's too much."

"Keep it." Bebe ran from the shop.

❖

"I'm not sure where she is." Esme was out on the back deck with her Sudoku and a cool drink. "If the funeral home is closed and she's not answering her cell phone then she's probably with Ronnie at the hospital or a client's home. Is anything wrong?" Esme said.

"Oh, Esme. Something's happened and I'm worried Clara will misunderstand and be upset with me."

"Is it about Tom Ray?"

"What? No. It's about Frances."

"Frances! You've seen Frances?"

"What? No." Bebe frowned. Esme made no sense. Bebe plowed on with her story. "I didn't know Frances had committed suicide. And I've just spent all summer more or less wrestling with the very same thing for that stupid soap. I wrote a suicide episode that went out last night and I'm worried Clara will think I've been snooping into her private life, or using her misery to make a profit, or—" Esme grabbed her hand and halted the flow of remorse.

"Bebe. Clara will think none of those things. She knows you wouldn't abuse Frances's death."

Bebe expelled a sigh of relief.

"Here, have some ginger beer." Esme poured a glass from the jug on the table. "It's homemade."

"What happened, Esme? Can I ask? The women at the hair parlor were talking about it. One said it was nearing the anniversary?"

"Four years, next Saturday." Esme looked sad as she spoke.

"Is that why you don't do the flower show? Because of the anniversary?"

"Yes. It was the night before the show and Clara was helping me set up my stand, when she…it, happened. We heard the fire engines first, and then the whole town saw the flames and smoke pouring down to the causeway."

"Flames? I thought Frances hung herself?" Bebe was confused.

"Oh, Bebe. It was far worse than that." Esme's eyes held terrible sorrow. "Frances and Clara had a house on Bayview." She pointed to the hill overlooking the town, near the satellite masts. "She drove out to Victor's gas station and filled all these containers with gas. Poor Victor, he was beside himself when the truth came out. He always blamed himself that he hadn't questioned her, or maybe stopped her. He still can't look Clara in the eye he feels so bad about it."

"Gas?" Bebe's stomach shrunk with an awful foreboding. She knew the road where Esme had pointed. She had seen the burned out shells of two houses.

"You have to remember she was unwell. In my opinion, Frances was never completely…with us. She was very much into esoteric mysticism. Frances set fire to the house while she was still in it. Then she stood on a chair, put her head in a noose, and hung herself."

"Oh my God! What an awful way to die!" Bebe was horrified.

"It's worse than that. She hadn't tied the noose right. She didn't die. She hung there and burned. And the house next door burned down too, and the lady who lived there had a heart attack and died on the road outside. It was a horrific night for a community this size. It took years for the town to get over it. And Clara never really will."

"Jean," Bebe whispered. "Jean Bury"

"Pardon?"

"Jean Bury. I met her on a walk once. A middle-aged lady in her nightgown and rubber boots. She was pointing to a burned out house, said she lived there. She said she grew roses."

Esme went pale. "Jean always won the gold for her roses. No one could beat her. You say you've seen her?"

Bebe nodded. "As clear as day. She seemed...caught in the moment."

"Poor, poor Jean."

"I've just told you I've seen a ghost and you don't bat an eyelid."

"I believe in ghosts. The Dearhearts do," Esme said.

"Well, I don't!"

"I think you'll find you do. Ghosts are everywhere, Bebe."

"That's a strange concept for a family of funeral directors to believe in." Bebe was struggling with Esme's words. She knew what she had seen, yet a rational part of her wanted to violently reject it.

"Really? Funeral directors stand on the edge between both worlds. A duty they took over from the early clergy, who, by the way, took it away from the wise women. Why should it be strange to believe in both worlds when your job is to ritualize the passing between them?"

Bebe shrugged fretfully. She hadn't expected the question and had no idea of the answer. She set it aside. There were more important issues at stake. Like Clara.

"What should I say to Clara?" She was lost. The Frances story had burdened her with an almost unbearable sadness. It was agonizing that Clara had carried this for so long.

"Whatever's in your heart, I suppose." Esme's eyes were bleak. She looked tired and depleted. "I don't want her to be alone anymore. I want her to lay Frances to rest one last time. That woman took enough while she was living, and in her dying she hurt so many innocent people. Sometimes I think it's only the pain she left behind that keeps her with us at all."

CHAPTER SIXTEEN

The hallway was oak lined and soberly austere. The late afternoon sun crawled through the tall windows, spilling long shadows across the parquet floor. Several hard backed chairs lined one wall facing two paneled doors and a hall table with an overflowing vase of white lilies. Their perfume hung sickly sweet in the sunny dust mote air.

Bebe stood just inside the main door. Her nose wrinkled. She didn't like lilies. They were pale, macabre flowers. A girl of about seven or eight sat on one of the chairs swinging her legs, idly watching the shadows grow on the parquet flooring. She was wearing a party dress with a bright yellow sash and little primroses sprinkled across the white cotton. The sun shone on her blond head with its honeybee hair clasp, and for a moment she shimmered like a beam of light. Bebe blinked and closed the door plunging the hall back into a subdued shadow. The girl looked over at her.

"Hi," Bebe said. "I'm looking for Clara Dearheart. Have you seen her?"

The girl pointed solemnly to a closed door. Bebe could make out the quiet murmur of voices on the other side.

"Oh. Is it okay if I sit here and wait?" Bebe asked.

The girl nodded, and Bebe sat beside her. Silence grew between them. Bebe began to feel uncomfortable with it while the young girl seemed barely to notice or care.

"Are you waiting for Clara, too?" Bebe asked, starting a conversation.

"Yes."

"That's a lovely dress. Are you going to a party later?"

"It's my birthday dress. I'll be eight."

"It's your party? Happy birthday." Bebe relaxed. Her nervousness at turning up at Clara's workplace dissolved slightly. She liked chatting to the shy girl beside her; it took her mind off her silly jitters. "I'm Bebe, by the way. What's your name?"

"Kaylee. Kaylee Wells."

"Well, happy birthday, Kaylee."

"Thank you."

"Is Clara going with you to the party? Is that why you're waiting here?"

Just then a door opposite clicked open and they both looked over as Clara emerged. She hesitated on seeing them. Bebe could see the room behind her was white and clinical like a hospital room. She wished she could have a tour of the Dearheart funeral home. It looked fascinating. Maybe she would ask Clara if it were possible some time.

"Hey." Clara clicked the door behind closed. She stood awkwardly for a moment.

"We were waiting for you," Kaylee said.

Clara swung her gaze to Bebe. "Oh?"

"I tried to call, but your cell phone was switched off. I hope you don't mind I came over. I've been chatting with Kaylee while I waited." Bebe became anxious. What if she'd crossed some invisible line by coming here? But she so wanted to talk to Clara face-to-face about the *Valley* gaffe before someone else mentioned it.

"It's fine to call in. It's nice to see you." Clara's smile lit up her whole face, and Bebe felt the last of her worries melt away. Clara chose to sit on the other side of Kaylee, draping her arm along the back of the girl's chair, including her in their circle.

"This is an impressive vestibule." Bebe looked around her. Then thought it was an extremely silly thing to say. She blushed a little and hated that she did.

"That's because it leads to the chapel room where we sometimes hold services. It has to look the part," Clara answered easily.

"You hold services here? I have no real idea what a funeral director does."

"We don't do the service. A priest or minister comes in for that. We merely host it in our chapel room. If you have time, I'll give you a tour."

"But Kaylee's waiting to—Where did she go?" The chair between them was empty. Bebe looked around confused. She hadn't seen the girl move.

"Don't worry. Kaylee's okay."

"She was here just a second ago. I don't understand."

"She wasn't really here. Come." Clara stood and offered a hand to Bebe.

"Is she a ghost?" Bebe asked. Her voice sounded hollow, even to her own ears.

Clara nodded and led Bebe over to the room she had just exited. They entered the clinical workroom Bebe had spied earlier.

"This is prep room one. We have two preps at Dearhearts," she said.

"Hey there, Bebe." Ronnie stood at a huge stainless steel countertop. It held twin sinks and rows of metal drawers, and it stretched along an entire wall. He wore a long green apron and was sorting out various trays and instruments that reminded Bebe of hospital theater dramas. The rest of the walls were covered with shelves holding various bottles, jars, electronic gadgetry, and yards of rubber tubing. In the center of the room sat a large ceramic table.

"That table looks so ghoulish." Bebe stared at the cold surface. It looked expensive, virginal white, and elegantly engineered for its grim job.

"Are we done in two?" Ronnie asked.

"Yeah. You can clean up in there," Clara told him. She turned her attention back to Bebe. "Let me show you the chapel next. And then Ronnie's pride and joy, the garage with all the limos."

They left Ronnie clattering his trays and went back out into the hall.

"What's in prep room two?" Bebe asked as they passed by the next door. The slight pressure of Clara's palm in the small of her back told her they would not be stopping at this door. "Kaylee?" she added in a small voice.

Clara nodded. "She's fine. Her folks believe in cremation and she was a little spooked. I talked to her about it and she wandered off into the corridor to think it over. That's where you met her."

"But where is she?"

"Moved on. Once she had settled her fears about what would happen to her body, she decided she'd better get going."

"But to where?"

Clara shrugged. "No one's ever told me. I assumed it's a private thing."

"She said it was her birthday? What happened?" Bebe felt incredibly sad.

"Leukemia. Her birthday is really three months away. She's had that party dress all year. Her parents bought it for her ages ago so she could wear it when she wanted. They gave her a massive practice party last month when the disease escalated."

"It's so sad."

"Only the part that we know." Clara took her hand and gave it a reassuring squeeze. "I've never met a sad ghost yet. I've seen impatient ones, confused ones, even angry ones, and tons of happy ones, but never sad. It just doesn't seem to compute in their world." Clara looked Bebe squarely in the eyes. "You can really see them?"

"It seems so. Well, a few, like Tom and Kaylee. And…and Jean Bury up on Bayview. Why is that? Why can I see them?"

"Jean? On Bayview?" Clara tensed.

"I go walking up there. I saw her once outside her house."

Clara paled.

"It's okay, Clara. She seemed a little confused, but more concerned for her roses than anything." Bebe slipped her arm around Clara's waist and gave her a little hug. She felt Clara relax and lean into her a little.

"That…It was a bad night," Clara said. "I don't go up there. I didn't realize Jean was still around. God love her."

"Esme told me. It sounded awful—"

"Esme told you?" Anger crept into Clara's voice.

"Hey. It's not like that. She wasn't gossiping. This is why I've been trying to call you all afternoon. I wrote an episode for *Valley* around the suicide of one of the main characters. I didn't realize you had lost Frances the same way, and I felt awful. I was looking for you everywhere and went over to Esme's. She calmed me down and told me what happened." It poured out of her as a babbled confession, and Bebe hated the way her words sounded but found it hard to stop. Clara rested fully against her now, hip to hip, shoulder to shoulder, there was no more tension in her body. Her words slowed as relief washed through her. Clara was not angry with her.

"What did you write about?" Clara asked.

"Remember Suzzee?" Bebe smiled as Clara rolled her eyes.

"Where do they get these names?"

Bebe grinned. "Well Suzzee *is* an actress after all. Pebble's parents were hippies, so that's her excuse, and Jayrah…well, Jayrah is really Jayne Rosemary." They both laughed at that. "Suzzee plays a character called Berry Ripe."

Clara snorted.

"Hey. I didn't name her. Anyway, she asked me to write a death scene timed to coincide with her contract renewal. I came up with an episode where she attempted suicide. I expected it to be my last piece, but the boss loved it and started asking for all these alterations, like hanging instead of shooting. I was so worried you'd think I poached the idea. It was so insensitive—"

"No. No." Clara shook her head. "I'd never think that of you. No one is responsible for what Frances chose to do, except Frances. I think that's part of her problem. Why she's frozen here."

"Frances is here?" A cold lump formed in Bebe's stomach.

"So I'm told, but I've never seen her. I think she's sorry but can't bear to face me." The words came out thin, and Bebe knew Clara had difficulty believing them.

"But. What?" Bebe was dumbfounded. Clara was talking about her dead girlfriend, as casually as if an old ex had just rolled back into town.

"I think if I could just meet her and tell her I forgive her, then she could pass on and be released. From her guilt." Clara was talking in earnest now.

Bebe took a step back. "And what about the weird shit happening at Aunt Arlene's house? How can you be sure it's not a ghost?"

"I know when a ghost is near. I picked up nothing at Arlene's. Believe me."

"I'll have to, because I obviously can't tell one from the other. They all look living to me. But that doesn't explain the smoke, or burning smells, or the sound of matches striking."

"That noise could be anything. It's stuck in your head as matches because you found the box Darling decimated. And the smells and smoke could be from outside the house. You suspected a bonfire in a neighboring yard once." Clara held her hand and they left the building, the visit to the chapel forgotten. "If you want, we'll go to Arlene's right now and check it out," Clara said. "But I swear to you, Bebe, I can't see any traces of ghostly behavior anywhere in that house. And I looked hard." They were in the parking lot, walking toward Clara's truck. "Hey. You've had your hair done," she said.

"That's where it all started. I heard the girls at the salon talking about Frances. They said it was nearing the anniversary." Bebe stopped abruptly, worried she'd been crass, but when she looked over, Clara's eyes were gentle and totally fixed on her.

"We need to talk about her," Clara said softly. "But not now. Not today. Let's just have coffee or something?" Her cheeks flushed bright pink and Bebe's heart squished in her chest. Every awkward word or thought she'd had in the past hour was reflected back at her. Clara was as new to this as she was, and just as emotionally clumsy. Bebe liked that they were brand new and fumbly together. Usually, she was the one out on a limb, hanging on for dear life. Now she had someone to stumble blindly onward with, hopefully into one of life's better adventures.

"I'll go for coffee if you tell me all about ghosts. Can I go up to Tom now and say, 'Hi, I know you're dead, but can we talk about it?'"

"Okay. We'll talk about ghosts." Clara slid into her cab and reached across to open the passenger door. "Is this sort of a second date?" she asked as Bebe slid in. It was meant to be a jocular question, but there was a catch in her voice and the words came out scratchy.

Bebe smiled and squeezed her hand. "I do believe it is. How brave are we?"

They pulled out onto East Avenue and headed for Main Street.

"Clara, why do only some people see them and most don't? Spirits I mean?"

"I don't know. As far as I knew only Dearhearts had the gift. I've never known anyone else who could do it."

"Gift?"

"We've always assumed it was a gift. We've had it for generations."

"Esme and Ronnie, too?"

"No. Not all the Dearhearts, just some. The ones who take over the family business. Others like Ronnie help, but he can't see them."

"But he knows?"

Clara shook her head. "I've got to tell him, and soon. Most Dearhearts know. We don't talk about it much." She frowned and concentrated carefully on her driving. "It's so weird."

"What's weird?"

"All those years together, and I never once talked to Frances about it like this, though she was fascinated by death. She guessed something was up and pestered me and my father all the time, but it never felt right to talk to her about it."

"Why was that?" Bebe asked.

"She had a sort of morbid fascination with death. Unnatural, Esme called it. And that's a big word for a Dearheart to use. Frances was into mysticism. She was into that New Age witchy look. I guess I somehow decided her fixation on death wasn't all that healthy." Clara groaned. "That was a big statement to make. Kind of superior of me, eh?"

"No. You went with your gut. How long were you together?"

"Almost three years."

"Clara, you held a family secret hundreds of years old, and that carries a lot of responsibility. You can't be expected to blab because your girlfriend wants to know all about it. You never told me, remember? I saw my ghosts independent of you." Bebe thought for a moment. "Do you think Frances saw ghosts, too?"

"No. She'd have loved to though. She was always talking about Salem and the spirit energy there. She saw arcane power as something that could be possessed and exploited in some benign way."

"Benign way? What, like shops and séances and guided tours? All that bunkum?"

Clara shrugged.

"She was comparing Preston to Salem? But what you do isn't connected to magic or witchcraft. You're a small town funeral director...okay, one who happens to see her clients."

"It's not just me. It's something the Dearhearts have always been able to do. It comes with the job. We accept it and get on with it, not try to draw attention to it. You don't do that to gifts like this."

"Where do you think it comes from?"

Clara shrugged. "No idea. And I was taught not to ask, just act on it. Maybe it's Preston, and Frances was right. Perhaps the place has a certain energy."

"Maybe it *is* Preston. No matter what happens in my life, I've always loved coming back here. Hey, maybe we're related way back when and that's why we see ghosts? Wouldn't that be truly spooky?"

"No. Wouldn't that be truly icky," Clara stated decisively and pulled into a parking space before Bean There. "Bebe." She took a deep breath. "Would you like to come over to my place again tonight?"

Bebe placed her hand on Clara's thigh and squeezed slightly. She liked the way the muscles twitched under her fingers.

"Why not come to mine? I don't want to leave Darling on his own so soon after his latest escapade, and I'm not quite up to asking Esme to parrot-sit again. Why don't you come over around eight and I'll prepare dinner?"

"But I want to help. Let me contribute."

"Okay, we'll plan a menu over coffee. Then we can grocery shop."

They entered the coffee shop, so wrapped up in each other that Bebe barely noticed the slight stir of curiosity they caused. So caught up in what might be the blueprint of their new relationship, she nearly missed the modest smiles and glances people sent their way. When she did notice she was settled into her corner booth and Clara was ordering at the counter. She smiled at one table of people she barely knew, mouthed a hello at another, and soaked up the general feelings of friendliness and welcome directed at her. She was overwhelmed by a sudden sensation of home.

CHAPTER SEVENTEEN

B ebe checked the chicken. Its baste of roasted garlic, honey, and spicy cumin sizzled and spat, browning nicely in the oven. The potatoes and onions were also starting to crisp. It was important for this to be a fine dinner. She wanted to impress Clara with her culinary skills. Bebe glanced at her watch. Clara would be arriving soon with the wine. She went to examine the dining table for the third time. It was set with the best crystal and silver and gleamed softly under the flicker of candlelight. It looked magical, except for…Bebe tweaked a white linen napkin a millimeter to the left. Perfection.

Darling glared at her from behind his cage bars and with a disgruntled squawk kicked grit out onto the floor.

"It's no use huffing at me." She lifted his nighttime blanket and draped it over his cage. "You're in there because of your bad behavior. You knew those bread rolls were special for tonight. It's your own greedy beak that got you put to bed early." She snapped the blanket closed hoping he would soon start snoozing and leave her and Clara in peace.

Bebe hesitated before the mirror over the mantle, her gaze fluttered anxiously over her appearance. She knew how easy it was to get grease on her cheek or flour in her eyebrows when she was full throttle in the kitchen. She reapplied her lipstick, tucked a loose strand of hair behind her ear, and smoothed her dress over her hips. Then she wrinkled her nose. Phew. Something was singeing.

She ran to the kitchen and checked the stove. Everything was okay. Nothing was burning. The kitchen was filled with the aroma of her delicious dinner, yet she had definitely smelled something burning. Worried now, Bebe went back to the dining room. The smell had disappeared. She felt twitchy. Had she imagined it? Based on past experiences, she very much doubted it. She wished Clara would hurry up. If it was going to be another evening of odd smells and striking matches, she wanted a witness.

The smell had definitely gone but Bebe checked the kitchen, the basement, and the living room again just to be sure. Nothing. *Perhaps I need to get my sinuses checked*—A flicker of movement out the window snapped her attention onto the garden. Bebe squinted through the glass. It was foggy outside. When did that happen? Half an hour ago the garden had been bathed in long, lazy shadows. Now the evening sunlight had vanished leaving behind a mass of gray, shapeless blobs where trees and shrubs fudged together into ugly lumps. There was definitely movement out there. Bebe could see it. Off to the left something shifted inside the murk. She concentrated on the spot. The fog swirled and swam, then shredded into wispy layers. Behind it lay the garden draped in long shadows. Tired, day-end sunshine picked out leaves and petals, bathing them in flat palettes of color. The fog hung like a veil between the house and the garden, beyond it a normal summer evening unfolded. Bebe's unease grew. This fog was unnatural. The strong breeze continued to tear at the fog breaking it into thick sinuous streaks, and through the tatters Bebe glimpsed someone over by the roses.

Someone was in the garden! The wind shifted again and the fog crested, and for an instant the rose bed came into clear view. Jean Bury stood by the roses, fussing over the blooms and picking at the leaves. Bebe stared hard. Now that she knew Jean was a ghost, she was unsure how she felt about seeing her again. She watched her for a few minutes in her fog-framed window. Jean was disheveled as ever; her raincoat was buttoned all askew. The hem of her nightdress dipped unevenly from under her coat trailing over the ugly yellow clogs she had jammed her feet into on the night of the fire. That final night now came into sharp focus for Bebe. She could envisage

Jean struggling into the first clothes she could find and rushing outside only to find her house, and the house next door, ablaze. How terrifying it must have been to see the smoke and the flames devouring everything she owned. Had she realized Frances was still inside the other house? Bebe felt an enormous pity for Jean and the horrifying events leading up to her heart attack.

She opened the kitchen door. The fog lifted. It simply danced away on the gentlest of breezes as she approached, cushioning her in a curious bubble. Bebe shivered with unease. She concentrated on Jean and walked calmly toward her, afraid to blink in case she disappeared as quickly as the last time, up on Bayview.

"Hi, Jean. How are you doing?"

Jean did not notice her. Instead, her fingers flew over the rose bushes tenderly tugging away crimped petals and black spotted leaves. She muttered to herself and threw furtive looks at the roof of the house. Bebe was unnerved. Could Jean not see her? She had seen and spoken to her before. Why not now?

"Jean?" Bebe drew closer until she could feel the distress rolling off her. "Jean, what is it? What's wrong?"

Now that she was closer she could make out Jean's words.

Over and over Jean muttered, "It's not right. It's just not right. I never liked that gal." Her eyes darted back to the roof, and Bebe, hackles rising, followed her gaze. She gasped.

The fog had not disappeared after all. It swirled along her roof in a tight, writhing knot. Except it was no longer fog, it was smoke. It was churning, ominous smoke that spewed out tatters of glowing ash that danced upward on the breeze before drifting down toward her like lazy, fat snowflakes.

"Oh my God." Bebe took a stumbling step back.

Smoke trailed from the shingles dipping down to touch her, as if sentient to her presence in the garden. It began to entomb her, clinging to her hair and skin with dry, curling fingers. Weaving into her nose and mouth, into her lungs, and drying up all the moisture. Her throat itched; her eyes stung; she was gagged by a sticky suffocation. Bebe choked. She doubled over trying to gasp in clean air and retch the malign grayness out. A smoldering ember hissed on the lawn by her feet. Another spat out of the air onto her forearm, burning her.

"She has no right." Jean's voice rose, shaking and querulous with fear and anger. "She has no right. No right."

Several more embers fizzed out of the smoke toward Bebe. She looked up and could see more skipping along the roof shingles, orange and fiery. Others leapt high in the air all silvery-blue like magical sparkles in a child's picture book. *This can't be real. It can't be happening.* A shooting ember stung her cheek; another stuck to the silk of her blouse and smoldered until she brushed it off her chest. It left a soot mark around the ragged burn hole.

"Oh my God." Bebe sprinted for the kitchen door. "Darling!"

She had to get Darling out of the house. She had to call the fire department. She had to find Clara and Esme. She needed help. This was very real and she was terrified. She also needed to keep her wits and act fast.

Bebe burst through the back door into a kitchen rapidly filling with smoke. Darling's frantic screeches drove her to the living room. Bebe ripped the blanket from his cage. Her fingers fumbled with the door lock.

"It's okay, sweetie. I'll get you out." She tried to calm him. He screeched more on seeing her and beat his wings against the bars until the whole cage shook. "Stop it, Darling. You'll hurt yourself. I'm almost there." She could hear the panic in her voice.

Inside the house there was heat with the smoke. She could feel it behind her, scorching the back of her bare arms. The smoke gathered around her. It crept through from the kitchen, cloying and malign. There were no flames, just stifling heat and heart-thumping suffocation. Darling shrieked. His cage rocked violently, making it impossibly frustrating to slide home the cage lock.

"Please keep still, sweetness. Please. Just one more second and I'll—" With a ping the clasp sprang open. Bebe grabbed the blanket and pulled Darling into it, covering him completely. He lay still in her arms.

Tears ran down Bebe's face. The smoke stung her eyes until she could barely see. There had to be a blaze somewhere close by. The heat was hurting her. She staggered to the kitchen and the closest exit, clutching Darling to her chest. She was two feet from the back door when it slammed shut in her face. Bebe reached for the metal handle and yelped; it was scalding hot. She pulled her hand away, her fingers already blistering. The electric sockets in the kitchen walls exploded, showering her in a rain of sparks. Darling squawked and struggled in her arms. Outside, Jean Bury shrieked, "Here come the sirens. Here come the sirens."

Bebe grabbed at the door handle again and, ignoring the pain, yanked hard, but the door refused to budge. She shook the handle futilely until her hand hurt too much and she had to let go. Her palm was red and blistered. It was no use. The door refused to open. Behind her, smoke thickened and the heat increased. Darling shuddered in her arms then stilled. She hugged him to her looking around in desperation. They were trapped.

❖

There was one last bottle of the Riesling Bebe liked lurking at the back of the chiller cabinet. Clara reached for it.

"You've no time! Get up to that house now!" Temperance bellowed in her ear. Clara flinched and nearly dropped the bottle.

"But this is the wine Bebe—"

"Now!"

Clara's cell phone shrilled out. Flustered, she turned her back on Temperance to answer and underscore her annoyance at another rude interruption. The call was from Esme.

"Hi, Aunt E. What's up?"

"Clara! Arlene's house is on fire. Get here at once." The line went dead.

"Shit." Clara dumped the wine bottle at her feet and ran from the shop.

"I told you. I told you so!" Temperance's words rang in her ears.

She gunned her old truck through the back streets avoiding the seafront and clogged up tourist roads. She could see a pall of smoke on the west side where Esme and Arlene lived. It rose straight into the air, twisting in on itself like an umbilical cord, rising skyward to where the wind shredded it into nothingness. It looked eerily unnatural. Clara's guts tightened with panic. She flattened the gas pedal.

Arlene's street was surprisingly calm when she screeched around the corner and skidded to a stop a few houses away from the smoke laden lawn. The house was barely visible through a thick envelope of smoke. Several residents stood on their own lawns and anxiously watched the smoke billowing before the McCall home.

"We called the fire department," a neighbor called as she ran past. "As far as we can tell the place seems empty."

Clara stood before the house undecided how to approach. Where was Bebe? Where was Esme, for that matter? They had to be nearby. Where were they? They must know she'd be out of her mind with worry. Clara squinted through the smoke. There were no flames, so where was all this smoke coming from? The wind blew from behind the house. Perhaps the fire was to the rear and the smoke was being blown to the front. An alarmed squawk from the back of the house threw Clara into motion. Darling screeched again. If he was at the back of the building then Bebe would be too. She would never leave him. Clara took a huge gulp of air and barreled through the reek and along the driveway. She ran blindly up the path at the side of the garage and emerged into a garden aglow with the flicker of flames. The rear ground floor was ablaze. Smoke poured from the windows and the wind funneled it over the roof dropping it like a theater curtain over the front and screening the drama from the rest of the world. Clara stood in a microcosm of chaos.

"Bebe! Bebe! For God's sake, where are you!" she screamed. The heat was intense, pushing her back. Around her blackened foliage curled and shrank on the stem. Flower heads drooped, and glowing embers skittered across the lawn before burning out. Eventually, one would catch and the garden would begin to burn.

"Bebe! Bebe!" Clara pushed forward, raising her hands to guard her face. Her head was thumping so hard she could barely think. Her heart was cramping in her chest. She couldn't go through this agony again; she'd go mad. "Please, Bebe. Please, please."

Never again. Never again. Clara took a gulp of acrid air and eyed the back door. Smoke seeped out of the cat flap. Through the glass panel the kitchen was dark and smoke filled. The flames had not reached it yet. The door swung open slowly, as if inviting her to enter. Clara knew it was a stupid, deadly thing to do. But she'd been here before, four years ago, standing outside a burning building as her soul turned to ash inside her living flesh. If this was her curse then she could not bear for an innocent like Bebe to share it with her. For all she knew Bebe was lying unconscious inside, overcome with smoke just inside that door. And where the hell was Esme? Please, God, she wasn't in there, too. Surely Esme would have more sense?

The door swung open wider. Smoke did not billow out. In fact, it looked curiously calm inside, like an oasis in a firestorm. Clara took a careful step forward. She heard Darling screech, but from where? She felt disorientated, adrift from reality. Only her anxiety anchored her in the moment. She took another step toward the heat. A figure moved from inside the shadows of the kitchen.

"Bebe!" Clara ran to the open door. *Bebe?* Choking smoke burst from the kitchen and enveloped her. She spluttered, covering her nose and mouth. Her eyes streamed, and she staggered forward another step. The smoke billowed and blew, swirling around her with grasping fingers, then it disintegrated forming a window, a hole of clear air framed by the doorway, and Clara found herself face-to-face with Frances.

❖

"Bebe! Over here. This way!" Esme yelled from the living room. She waved for Bebe to follow her. Bebe held Darling awkwardly in her arms, keeping her burned hand away from the blanket wrapped around him. The living room was clear, but immediately filled up with smoke as she entered. It seemed to swarm her body and out into the space around her. She spun on her heel. The kitchen was now clear? The smoke and embers were following her as she moved through the house. What the hell was happening? Heat scorched her face and arms. She turned away and quickly ran in the direction Esme had taken.

"Esme. Wait. Where are you going?" They were moving deeper into the house. Shouldn't they be heading for the nearest exit?

"Through the utility to the garage. Hurry, Bebe." Esme's call came from farther up the hall. The smoke dampened her voice making it sound farther away. Bebe's eyes streamed with tears. She could barely make out Esme's blurred outline and was desperate not to lose sight of her. Her throat ached and the skin on the back of her arms and on her calves stung with heat. The searing pain drove her forward after Esme and into the folds of smoke. Darling lay mute in her arms. They were both suffocating slowly. She was in hell, not the fiery brimstone of Bible-thumping preachers, but a slow, broiling hell. She was stewing in her skin, her mind addled with confusion.

"Bebe! Here it is!" Esme called and Bebe focused on the direction of the shout. "Here's the door. Follow my voice." If she did not concentrate, she would die, and so would Darling, and possibly even Esme who had braved the fire to find her. She made out Esme's tall figure, a wavy, smoke-filled shadow hovering by the utility door, and stumbled toward her. Behind her, she heard the crackling of flames. The fire was following her out into the hall. It would hound her every step until she was finally cornered.

"Esme. Help." She thrust Darling, blanket and all, into Esme's arms. He had begun to struggle weakly and her hands hurt too much to hold him.

"Follow me, child." Esme led her into the soothing air of the utility room. Bebe collapsed against the dryer, her knees buckling. She sobbed in huge breaths.

"No time." Esme was plucking at her shoulder, trying to haul her toward another door, the one that led to the garage. "Keep moving," Already the smoke was seeping under the utility door filling up the small room.

They fell through into the garage.

"This is the way out." Esme pushed ahead to an outside door that led out onto the path at the side of the house. Bebe staggered after her, unbelieving they were so close to freedom. Any minute now she expected the door to slam shut and lock them in. The house had turned against her. It was haunted and evil, and she didn't want to die in this burning claustrophobic box.

They burst out into a smoke-filled night filled with cold stars and the crackle of flames. With a loud squawk, Darling shook himself free and flew from Esme's arms toward the trees in the back garden.

"No." Bebe cried. Esme charged after him. "We need to go to the front of the house, Esme," Bebe called after her, but Esme had rounded the corner and disappeared. Bebe reluctantly followed. They could always escape into a neighbor's yard, but she was abhorrent to stay so close to the burning house. Bebe was exhausted and anxious. Every bone in her body wanted to run away. She tried to rationalize that Darling would be fine. He could fly from danger, but she could not leave Esme alone.

Bebe rounded the corner and halted.

"Clara!"

Clara stood stupefied before the open kitchen door. Smoke poured out but diverted around her, leaving her standing in an oasis of clear air. Burning embers fluttered crazily above her. In the last seconds of descent, they blew away and fell sizzling at her feet, peppering the ground all around her.

"Clara!" Surely she could not be considering entering the building? "Clara! No!"

❖

The smoke billowed toward Clara, wrapping around her and Frances, encapsulating them both in their own little bubble.

Frances. Clara could hear the fire crackle and feel its heat on her face and through her shirt, though it did not discomfort her. Reality fell away. She could be with Frances; the offer was there, reaching out to her. She understood that now. Wasn't this what she had wanted? Hadn't she pined away four years for this moment, to talk to Frances once again? To be with her?

Clara hesitated, the fog in her head cleared for one lucid moment. She did *not* want this. She did not want to burn, to die. She wanted to talk to Frances, to understand, to say good-bye. She wanted closure.

Frances receded further into the kitchen beckoning Clara to follow. Wisps of smoke trailed across her form, partially obscuring it. She was fading into the smoke, disappearing. Clara couldn't lose sight of her. This was her only chance, but her legs would not move. Her feet felt cemented to the ground, rooted to the singeing earth. Her body refused to step into the kitchen.

Frances beckoned, her mouth moved. Her words were lost in the roaring chaos, but Clara read her lips. "We are the same now. We are the same."

No, we're not. The thought was crystal clear in Clara's mind.

"No, we're not," she yelled into the billowing smoke. "You're dead, Frances. You died." *Surrender to it and go home.*

"I know all your secrets." These words she could hear, tight and peevish as in Frances's most disgruntled moods. And somehow, maybe because of the tone, Clara knew that meant Bebe, too. But Bebe was not her secret. Bebe was her future and Frances resented that.

"You need to rest, Frances. You need to let go." Clara raised a hesitant hand toward her; a spark caught the back of her hand and burned. The smoke scratched her lungs. The encapsulating bubble they both stood in was stretched thin and the fire was encroaching into this moment Frances had manufactured. Frances took one more step back as if daring Clara to follow, to keep the bubble intact.

"No." Clara stepped back too, and the bubble burst. The inward wave of heat almost blasted Clara off her feet leaving her dazed and unfocussed. The air around her roared and hissed. Her skin was scorching, and then, out of the mind-numbing chaos came the glorious scent of Night-scented stock. It filled her head and cleared her thoughts. She had to run. She had seconds left to get clear, but blinded by smoke and ash, she had no idea where to turn.

"Clara! Clara! No!"

Bebe! She stumbled toward Bebe.

❖

The kitchen door slammed shut, screeching on its baking hinges. From above, a roaring wail preceded an avalanche of sparks and smoking shingles.

"Clara! Run!" Bebe screamed. Clara leapt aside and ran toward her, the burning debris crashing at her heels. She grabbed Bebe by her arms, her eyes wild and haunted. "We have to get out of here." Together, they ran back onto the lawn, standing a safe distance from the inferno and watched aghast as the house gave itself over to the flames. The chimney spat out sparks that cracked and popped in the night sky, and smoke poured up into the night sky.

"Oh my God!" Bebe pointed. "Someone's in there. Who is it? Is it Esme? Where's Esme?" She strained to leave Clara's grasp.

Clara tightened her hold. "It's not Esme."

The large picture windows exploded in the heat, and within they watched a blackened, burning figure crash through the flames.

"It's Frances, isn't it?" Bebe asked quietly. The sag of Clara's body was her answer. The figure spun and wove through the blaze with unbearable fluidity. Bebe turned her gaze away, unable to witness any more of this agony, when the repeated patterns of movement began to register. The burning figure was not writhing in pain, it was spinning and leaping and dancing. Wide-eyed, Bebe watched.

"Is she dancing?"

"Yes. She's celebrating, I suppose."

"Celebrating? Celebrating what?"

"Death. Fire. The great beyond. God only knows. But she's found the secret she spent most of her adult life looking for. The afterlife." Clara's voice was flat.

"What's the point of an afterlife if you don't live your before life to the full?" Tom Ray stood beside Bebe. She jumped at his booming voice. He stood in his yellow oilskins, slick with seawater and slightly steaming in the heat pouring off the house. He grinned down at her; his teeth gleamed through his bushy, salt encrusted beard. "You can't put the cart before the horse."

Bebe looked behind him, the back lawn had filled with people, hundreds of people. They stood in wavy iridescent rows, pulsing a beautiful pearlescent light into the night garden. They stood on smoldering grass, teetering around the wilting flower borders so as not to step on the drooping flowers. They stood silently, and all were transfixed on the burning building.

"Who are all these people?" Bebe whispered to Clara.

Clara pulled her gaze away from Frances's death dance and glanced behind her. She scoured the crowd for a moment before turning back to the flames.

"The dead. They're the dead of Preston."

"They're all ghosts?" Bebe squeaked. Marcus waved at her from several tiers back and beamed his big, friendly grin. Nervously, she waggled her fingers in a little wave back. She scanned the crowd and quickly found Jean Bury still muttering and plucking at roses barely paying attention to the drama around her. "Why are they here?"

"We've come to take her home," Tom Ray boomed out. "Frances needs to go. She's been here long enough. There's nothing for her here. Nothing to wait for, and nothing to do, and nothing for her to learn. She needs to move on." His voice was firm and brooked no argument. Bebe had none. If Frances was behind the house haunting, then she was malicious and dangerous and certainly did not belong among the living. Bebe would be glad for her to move on and learn something, somewhere else.

The house shuddered then groaned like a galleon. The chimney stack crumbled in on the roof, spraying the air with multitudes of bright orange sparks. Smoke poured from every upstairs window. Flames danced in all the downstairs rooms.

"The roof is going to go." Clara grabbed her hand and dragged Bebe further back. With a majestic sigh, the remaining shingles slid off the pitched roof and thundered into the yard below. The flames inside shot upward to the night sky where the harbor breezes fed them with fresh fuel. They licked through the upper floors and finally spread through the open roof. Sirens blared over the roar of flames. Yells and cries from the other side of the house began to siphon through. The thunderous hiss of water hoses began. Around them, the ghostly light receded.

"We need to get out of here." Clara bundled Bebe toward the neighboring fence. Shrubs and patches of lawn began to catch fire. The air around them was a flurry of burning embers that caught at their clothes. Soon they too would be alight.

"Quickly." Clara slapped away an ember from Bebe's hair.

"Where's Esme?" Bebe cried. She turned back to the garden, but it was empty and bleak. The ghosts had gone. Only Clara and Bebe stood by the fence. Clara leaped over and reached for Bebe. "We need to find Esme," Bebe cried, panicked.

"Esme?" Clara grabbed at her. "Esme was here?"

"Yes. She helped me get out of the house, then she ran after Darling when he flew off."

"Well, she's probably around the front of the house. Come on, jump."

Bebe took one last look at the burning shell of Aunt Arlene's house. There was no figure spinning through the fire. The windows were a blank wall of flames. There was nothing magical or supernatural about the blaze or the garden anymore. It was a burning shambles and they were lucky to be able to scrabble away from it relatively unhurt.

With a subdued rumble the back wall of the house trembled, then sank gracefully to the ground damping most of the blaze with debris. Bebe scrambled the last few feet over the fence and into the neighbor's yard. It was as if she'd crossed a border into another country, another hemisphere. Her lungs involuntarily expanded with cleaner air. Her tears finally began to rinse her eyes rather than blind her. Her seared skin began to cool in the breeze that blew in from the bay. Clara clung to her, helping her move slowly to the street and the plethora of emergency vehicles and flashing lights and astounded bystanders. They had survived.

Ambulance personnel swarmed them, bundling them gently into the waiting vehicles.

"Where's Esme?" Bebe kept repeating as kind hands held her steady and pressed a mask over her nose and mouth. "Where's Esme?" But no one had any answers.

CHAPTER EIGHTEEN

E sme was at home.

Clara and Bebe were admitted to the hospital for an overnight stay, and Clara became concerned when Esme failed to show up. Frank Doyle went over to her house and found her. She was in her favorite chair with a cold cup of Earl Grey at her elbow and the paper opened on her lap at the Sudoku. The coroner put her time of death at around six p.m. She had died from heart failure. He proposed she had felt no pain and had slipped away while napping.

The following day Bebe and Clara left the hospital. A neighbor found them at Esme's, both shell-shocked and going through the motions of locking up her house. He had Darling with him. He had found him in his garden.

"He was a great bird. A real entertainer. I remember him from when I used to visit Temperance," he said sadly, handing over the shoebox.

Bebe cried three days solid. Clara for two, then she had to go back to work.

❖

"You know this means Aunt Arlene will never let me cross her doorstep again." Bebe pressed the sand-speckled earth firmly around the newly planted Goldenrod. She shuffled along the border a few inches on her knees and began to dig a hole for the next plant.

"An electrical malfunction. That's what the fire report said. She can hardly blame you for that."

"Well, they could hardly say malign spiritual activity. Even if they knew what it was." Bebe buried her trowel deep in the soil with a satisfying grunt.

"No, hardly. And remember Arlene was insured to the hilt when she knew you were coming. Let her moan, but she'll be relieved you weren't hurt."

"That's easy for you to say, but it's another nail in my reputation. I'll always be the family klutz."

"Yes, you will, dear."

"This soil is terrible. It needs a ton of mulch. I might as well dig a hole in the beach."

"That's why we only grow seascape plants. They know how to adapt."

Bebe sat back on her heels and gazed out over the little picket fence down to the shoreline. Breakers rolled in, curled and cocky on the strong breeze blowing shoreward. The breeze continued, blowing right up to the sand dunes, rattling the grass like maracas and cooling the sweat on her brow. Above, the gulls wheeled and called out mournfully. It was an absolutely perfect day.

"How long can you stay?" she asked.

Esme hunkered down beside her. "As long as I want. But I'll probably wait until I'm certain Arlene's okay before I go wandering off." She smiled and raised her face to the salty breeze. "Such a beautiful day."

"Arlene was in a terrible state when I called her. She'll miss you dreadfully."

"She will, but after a bit the pain will lessen and she'll realize she has to let me go. And I will go. To somewhere wonderful."

"But I'll miss you, too. And Clara will want you to stay forever. I know she will."

Esme shook her head. "That's not what it's all about, and you know it. Once we truly say good-bye in our hearts, we free the dead. I need to move on, Bebe. I want to see the great unknown. I can sense the excitement and wonder of it calling to me."

"Some spirits stay for a while. Not all of them rush pell-mell for the door," Bebe said sulkily. "Look at Marcus and Tom Ray."

"Look at Frances," Esme said gently. "Frances always avoided Clara. She knew Clara wanted closure and that would mean she'd have to pass on. For years, she was frozen here, afraid to take the next step despite her greatest wish being to master death. She had to be frog marched home in the end."

"Why was she so scared?"

Esme shrugged. "Guilt. Madness. She did a lot of damage. Maybe she was afraid there was a place up ahead where she'd have to answer for it. But there was no place here, among the living, for a spirit like hers."

"Why do you think she hated me so much?" Bebe asked. "She haunted me in a house that wasn't even her own. That's just rude."

"I think she would have hated anyone who helped Clara heal. If Clara fell in love again then she would eventually let Frances go in her heart, and Frances was too scared to ever let that happen. In her own way she haunted Clara, too."

A car horn sounded on the track at the rear of the dunes behind the beach shacks.

"Clara's back." Bebe leapt to her feet and brushed the sand from her skirt. By the time she'd straightened Esme stood several yards away on the top of a sand dune.

"Wait up." Bebe scrambled after her. She'd never get used to Esme's teleporting all over the place. She reached her, all hot and flustered after a ragged climb, and together they watched Clara's old truck trundle the last stretch to the parking space closest to her shack. Through the windshield Bebe could make out her disgruntled face and smiled, no doubt in her mind as to the cause of it. Glowing in the passenger seat next to Clara, and talking nine to the dozen, sat Temperance with her precious Darling perched on her shoulder. He seemed to be repeating most of everything she said directly into Clara's ear.

"I wonder what instructions she's getting?" Bebe said, the laughter in her voice barely subdued.

"I'm sure it's all highly educational." Esme chuckled.

Clara slid out of the cab and slammed the door. She lifted a hand to shield her eyes against the sun's glare and gazed up to the dunes to where Bebe and Esme stood, joined almost immediately by Temperance and Darling.

"She drives like a lunatic," Temperance grumbled.

"Hello, my handsome." Bebe pursed her lips and blew a kiss at Darling. He dipped his entire body, as if to avoid it.

"Where have you been?" Esme asked Temperance.

"Felt like the Santa Pod drag races," Temperance said. "We went to get surprise candy for this one." She nodded at Bebe. "Something about a two month anniversary."

"Well, it's hardly a surprise now," Esme said with a look of reproof. "Perhaps we'd better go if it's a special occasion." She raised her eyebrows and linked arms with Temperance, and they were gone in the twinkling of an eye.

Bebe watched Clara trudge up the dune to join her. She had an arm behind her back, no doubt hiding the not such a surprise box of candy.

"Hey." Bebe greeted her with a hug and a warm kiss. "How was work?"

"Good. Ronnie says hi. He says do you want to go to dinner with him and Sandy at Petty's tomorrow night?"

"But it's our special two month anniversary," Bebe said in mock horror at such a suggestion.

"How'd you—Temperance told you, right?" Clara whipped out the gift-wrapped candy she had been hiding behind her back. "Here. All your favorites. But I suppose she told you that, too." She grinned.

"Actually, I remembered all on my own. But my gift isn't ready yet. In fact, you can help me finish it off. I got Goldenrods for the garden. Esme recommended them."

They stood for a moment on the top of the dunes, arms wrapped around each other's waist looking out across the bright sunlit bay. Waves clambered onto the beach rushing the tidewater up the compact, shiny sand. Farther down a man cast an expert line into the surf. He was big and bulky and dressed in ancient yellow oilskins.

The sea gulls hovered and the breeze blew fresh and warm and full of brine.

"The sky is the color of your eyes," Clara murmured.

"The waves are the color of yours."

"Then we belong here on the beach."

"We do. This is home. Our home. Let's make it ours forever."

The End

About the Author

Gill McKnight is Irish and moves between Ireland, England, and Greece in a non-stop circuit of work, rest, and play. She loves messing about in boats and has secret fantasies about lavender farming.

With a BA in Art and Design and a Masters in Art History, it says much about her artistic skill that she now works in IT.

About the Author

Books Available From Bold Strokes Books

Harmony by Karis Walsh. When Brook Stanton meets a beautiful musician who threatens the security of her conventional, predetermined future, will she take a chance on finding the harmony only love creates? (978-1-60282-237-5)

nightrise by Nell Stark and Trinity Tam. In the third book in the everafter series, when Valentine Darrow loses her soul, Alexa must cross continents to find a way to save her. (978-1-60282-238-2)

Crush by Lea Santos. Winemaker Beck Montalvo loves a good challenge, but could wildly anti-alcohol, ex-cop Tierney Diaz prove to be the first obstacle Beck can't overcome? (978-1-60282-239-9)

Men of the Mean Streets: Gay Noir edited by Greg Herren and J.M. Redmann. Dark tales of amorality and criminality by some of the top authors of gay mysteries. (978-1-60282-240-5)

Women of the Mean Streets: Lesbian Noir edited by J.M. Redmann and Greg Herren. Murder, mayhem, sex, and danger—these are the stories of the women who dare to tackle the mean streets. (978-1-60282-241-2)

Cool Side of the Pillow by Gill McKnight. Bebe Franklin falls for funeral director Clara Dearheart, but how can she compete with the ghost of Clara's lover—and a love that transcends death and knows no rest? (978-1-60282-633-5)

Firestorm by Radclyffe. Firefighter paramedic Mallory "Ice" James isn't happy when the undisciplined Jac Russo joins her command, but lust isn't something either can control—and they soon discover ice burns as fiercely as flame. (978-1-60282-232-0)

The Best Defense by Carsen Taite. When socialite Aimee Howard hires former homicide detective Skye Keaton to find her missing niece, she vows not to mix business with pleasure, but she soon finds Skye hard to resist. (978-1-60282-233-7)

After the Fall by Robin Summers. When the plague destroys most of humanity, Taylor Stone thinks there's nothing left to live for, until she meets Kate, a woman who makes her realize love is still alive and makes her dream of a future she thought was no longer possible. (978-1-60282-234-4)

Accidents Never Happen by David-Matthew Barnes. From the moment Albert and Joey meet by chance beneath a train track on a street in Chicago, a domino effect is triggered, setting off a chain reaction of murder and tragedy. (978-1-60282-235-1)

In Plain View by Shane Allison. Best-selling gay erotica authors create the stories of sex and desire modern readers crave. (978-1-60282-236-8)

Wild by Meghan O'Brien. Shapeshifter Selene Rhodes dreads the full moon and the loss of control it brings, but when she rescues forensic pathologist Eve Thomas from a vicious attack by a masked man, she discovers she isn't the scariest monster in San Francisco. (978-1-60282-227-6)

Reluctant Hope by Erin Dutton. Cancer survivor Addison Hunt knows she can't offer any guarantees, in love or in life, and after experiencing a loss of her own, Brooke Donahue isn't willing to risk her heart. (978-1-60282-228-3)

Conquest by Ronica Black. When Mary Brunelle stumbles into the arms of Jude Jaeger, a gorgeous dominatrix at a private nightclub, she is smitten, but she soon finds out Jude is her professor, and Professor Jaeger doesn't date her students…or her conquests. (978-1-60282-229-0)

The Affair of the Porcelain Dog by Jess Faraday. What darkness stalks the London streets at night? Ira Adler, present plaything of crime lord Cain Goddard, will soon find out. (978-1-60282-230-6)

365 Days by K.E. Payne. Life sucks when you're seventeen years old and confused about your sexuality, and the girl of your dreams doesn't even know you exist. Then in walks sexy new emo girl, Hannah Harrison. Clemmie Atkins has exactly 365 days to discover herself, and she's going to have a blast doing it! (978-1-60282-540-6)

Darkness Embraced by Winter Pennington. Surrounded by harsh vampire politics and secret ambitions, Epiphany learns that an old enemy is plotting treason against the woman she once loved, and to save all she holds dear, she must embrace and form an alliance with the dark. (978-1-60282-221-4)

78 Keys by Kristin Marra. When the cosmic powers choose Devorah Rosten to be their next gladiator, she must use her unique skills to try to save her lover, herself, and even humankind. (978-1-60282-222-1)

Playing Passion's Game by Lesley Davis. Trent Williams's only passion in life is gaming—until Juliet Sullivan makes her realize that love can be a whole different game to play. (978-1-60282-223-8)

Retirement Plan by Martha Miller. A modern morality tale of justice, retribution, and women who refuse to be politely invisible. (978-1-60282-224-5)

Who Dat Whodunnit by Greg Herren. Popular New Orleans detective Scotty Bradley investigates the murder of a dethroned beauty queen to clear the name of his pro football–playing cousin. (978-1-60282-225-2)

The Company He Keeps by Dale Chase. A riotously erotic collection of stories set in the sexually repressed and therefore sexually rampant Victorian era. (978-1-60282-226-9)

Cursebusters! by Julie Smith. Budding-psychic Reeno is the most accomplished teenage burglar in California, but one tiny screw-up and poof!—she's sentenced to Bad Girl School. And that isn't even her worst problem. Her sister Haley's dying of an illness no one can diagnose, and now she can't even help. (978-1-60282-559-8)

True Confessions by PJ Trebelhorn. Lynn Patrick finally has a chance with the only woman she's ever loved, her lifelong friend Jessica Greenfield, but Jessie is still tormented by an abusive past. (978-1-60282-216-0)

Ghosts of Winter by Rebecca S. Buck. Can Ros Wynne, who has lost everything she thought defined her, find her true life—and her true love—surrounded by the lingering history of the once-grand Winter Manor? (978-1-60282-219-1)